The Girl of Tokens and Tears

Book 2
The Half Shell Series

Susan Ward

ISBN-10: 1497494893
ISBN-13: 978-1497494893

Dedication

For my beautiful daughter Shelby, a.k.a. Shell-bell, who believes in love, the impossible, enchantment, and magic the way all young college girls still should. I'm so proud of you. I should say it more. I love you, baby girl!

PROLOGUE

New York City, Spring Break 1989

You can't hold the minutes back, no matter how hard you try to. The minutes only go faster when you do not want to let them go. I want to stay here in this perfect quiet with Alan, but Sunday morning is here and I can't do a damn thing about it.

I roll over in Alan's arms. I look at the clock. 9 a.m. Jack and I settled on 10 a.m. after heated negotiations for the ritual of packing up Lena's things and finally saying goodbye to Mom. I have a little time. Not much. I really should get moving. I can shower after the packing. It will save me a little time now, but not enough. No amount of time will ever be enough, and I still don't know what I'm going to do after saying goodbye to Lena.

I turn my face into my pillow to hide my tears. I'm going to lose him. Alan won't want to be with me if I go back to Santa Barbara. Oh, he'll try. He'll do all those be-kind type of things. There will be the phone calls and maybe a letter or a present. But that won't last long because the real world exists whether we want it to or not, and the real world made us over from the start.

The bed shifts under his weight as Alan turns me slowly in his arms so I can face him. My head is nestled on his arm. His eyes are black and searching.

I gaze at his beautiful face. It is emotionless, compassionately so, and I hate that he can give nothing away if he wants to. His eyes stare into mine, hardly blinking, calm and smiling, merely because he wants them to. Reaching up, I caress his cheek and run the tip of my fingers across the perfect structure of his jaw. I want to remember each line on his face exactly how he looks at this moment.

Time moves in, hovers and slips away. I can't stop it.

I rummage on the floor for Alan's shirt and pull it over my head. I climb from the bed. "I've got to go, Alan."

I start to gather my clothes and carelessly shove them into my duffel, carefully avoiding Alan's eyes. I can feel him watching and I wish he'd just say something, because the faster I get through this the sooner the pain will go away.

"Do you want me to go with you?" he asks.

I shake my head. "No. I'm meeting Jack at the apartment. We're packing up my mother's things today."

Alan sits up. A torturous and heavy pause in the room hits me like a punch. "And then?"

"I catch a plane and go home to Santa Barbara."

More heavy silence. The lump in my throat is strangling and I can't look at him because if I do I don't know what I will do.

"You can't be serious, Chrissie. You're not leaving."

The room is filled with Alan's panic and his need. It moves across my flesh like a chilled nightwalker.

"I have to go, Alan. I'm not ready to be everything you want me to be."

"I don't want you to be anything other than you are," he whispers, his voice raw. He crosses the room and stops my hands in their frantic efforts of packing. "You're not leaving, Chrissie." His thumb traces my lower lip. "I love you."

"I love you, too," I whisper, almost unable to push the words out of me. "But I have to go home."

I step away from him and gather my clothes to wear. I lift his shirt to my face and breathe it in deeply. "Can I keep this shirt?"

"Why?"

"I love the smell of you. I want to smell you until I can't anymore. In a perfect movie, lovers would never end, they would slowly fade away. I want to smell you until I can't smell you anymore."

He closes his eyes. Oh shit, that was a really shitty thing to say, but I didn't mean it and I wish I hadn't said it.

"You can keep the fucking shirt, Chrissie."

My scalp prickles as every nerve in my body is suddenly blasted by a chill. The earth falls away beneath me. Oh no, this is not how I want this to go between us. What have I done? I don't want us to part angry.

Alan pulls on his jeans and crosses the room to light a cigarette. Finally, he runs a hand through his hair and doesn't look at me. "I'm sorry. You may have the shirt, Chrissie. My reaction to the shirt thing has nothing to do with you. It is an enormous irritant. The shirt thing. But I shouldn't be rude to you. Sorry."

My eyes open to their roundest and it takes everything I have not to cry. That was unkind, Alan. Why do you have to be such a shit at times? A shit who lets me know that girls taking souvenirs after climbing from your bed is a frequent event; a shit who on purpose reduces me to meaningless, when my words were only an accident; a shit because…

"You can stay, Chrissie. You can stay with me in New York. We can get married. Whatever you want. I'll quit now before the tour starts. I don't want you to leave."

I have to get out of the room quickly. Any more and I'm going to crumble and stay. "I can't stay, Alan. And you don't really want to marry me."

That spikes his anger. "Don't tell me what I want."

Oh jeez, another stupid blunder. I'm going to ruin us if I don't get out of here quickly. I sink my teeth into my lower lip and continue to dress. The words clog in my throat and they are too painful to speak. I hear them in my head: Oh Alan, I've got my own shit to fix!

"I can't stay," I repeat.

"If you leave we are over."

Oh God, I see it and I don't want to. Alan loves me, but right now Alan loving me is more a thing about him than me. He doesn't want me to leave because he's afraid to be alone. That's the fear and desperation I see in his eyes and it is the wrong reason to stay.

We both have so much messed-up shit we need to work through. It would be wrong for us both if I stayed. But I don't remember me before Alan and I don't know if I really want to.

I reach for my purse. He flinches as though I hit him.

"At least let me take you home," he says in despair.

"No. I think I want to walk today. Can you have Colin deliver my things to the apartment?"

"You can't walk home, Chrissie. There are at least two dozen photographers at the curb waiting to pounce on you. Don't be unreasonable about this."

How could I have forgotten about the tabloids?

"Then I'll go with Colin alone. Can you call him for me? I want to go to the garage alone."

I rush quickly from the bedroom and head for the foyer. I listen. I'm so relieved that Alan doesn't follow me. I press the elevator button and the doors open. I couldn't leave if he followed me, but that he didn't really hurts me.

I lean back into the icy metal wall and stare at the square mirror images of myself. Oh please, doors, close! Close quickly! Then I realize I haven't pushed the garage button. I hit it and I'm numb. The metal moves, taking me away.

Oh God—I've left him. Alan Manzone asked me to marry him and I've walked away. The only guy I've ever loved. The only guy who will ever understand me. The second the door slammed closed I knew it with certainty: Alan is the love of my life. Crippling pain slices through me and I'm not at all sure I've made the right decision.

The love of my life…and I walked away. What have I done? The pain is indescribable, but I can't surrender to my grief. I've got to pack up my mother's things with Jack, catch a plane, and somehow return to Santa Barbara and fix my perfectly fucked-up life.

Deep down I know I'm doing the right thing. The right thing for Alan. The right thing for me. It just doesn't feel that way today. Alan is right: I never know what I want, but I always know how I feel.

~~~

Everything seems longer and slower and harder. Usually any return home feels faster and easier because it's familiar. There is nothing familiar today. It is just long and slow and hard.

I have survived the first day without Alan and the trip to the airport with Jack. Internally I'm still messy, but a different kind of messy. Parts of me have been quieted, new parts of me stirred awake, parts of me I leave behind, and parts of me I take.

I repeat that last part in my head. I want to put it in my journal once we are aboard the plane. There should be something in my journal about Alan.

We're ushered into the VIP wait lounge in the airport terminal, and for today that is more about me than Jack. The tabloids have been our crushing shadow all day. I don't care. They don't know what the last three weeks have been about, and they never will. Let them write what they want. No one other than Alan and I will ever know or understand it.

It is too honest. Too human. Too real. I love Alan and he loves me. That's it. End of story. And I leave New York for the simple reason that that is what girls like me do. We say goodbye. We board the plane. We go home and fix our own shit.

Jack hasn't said a word since we finished clearing out Mom's personal things from the apartment. It never occurred to me until I came to New York that Mom's
~~~

things were exactly where she left them and Sammy's room remains exactly the same as it was that day. Jack has lockboxes, too. I'm like him that way: keeping things in little boxes, hurting privately and slow to share my pain.

Jack's silence today is more about him than about me, and I'm OK with that. I understand it because I said goodbye to Alan today.

More airport security comes when it is time for us to board the plane, and by how everyone on the plane stares at us I can tell we are the last ones on the plane even though our seats are first class.

I laugh. No proletarian seats today.

We're in the air before Jack speaks.

"It's going to be OK, Chrissie. It will all blow over. It always does."

But I don't want it to blow over. I'm in love with Alan.

I smile. "Why did Rene leave yesterday?"

I was so consumed with Alan I didn't stop yesterday to wonder why Rene left me.

"The school is graduating you early, Chrissie. They remarked that they would prefer you clear out your things on Sunday so as not to disturb the returning students. Rene and Patty are packing up your things from your dorm room today."

Oh shit.

"Are the Thompsons angry we've been kicked out of school? I know how Rene's mom feels about never having the crap be public."

Jack gives me a small smile. "They didn't kick out Rene. She left in solidarity and the Thompsons are cool with it."

It's awful, but I start to laugh anyway. I can't help it. I was kicked out of school before Rene. What were the odds of that? I laugh harder and Jack joins me, and suddenly we are laughing in a crazed way that doesn't match any of this.

When the laughter quiets, it is a comfortable thing. A comfortable thing, for the first time in a very long time, between Jack and me.

"I think tomorrow we should go buy you a new car," Jack says somewhere over Colorado. "A Volvo. The safest car on the road, but not flashy. Hopefully, it won't be something anyone wants to steal."

OK, what's up with that? I expected to be dragged to an in-care lockdown therapy center. What's with the car shopping, Jack? Things might be better between us, but it doesn't make Jack's parenting any less confusing.

"Why are we buying me a Volvo?"

"You're out of school early, Chrissie. You were planning a road trip across country this summer with Rene. Leave early. Get lost for a while. Let it all go. Sometimes it's the only way you can find yourself."

I smile and think of Alan. Jack is right, but I also think I might have already found myself, and that returning to Santa Barbara is a very big mistake.

When Jack falls asleep, I pull out my journal and make my Alan entry. I stare at the newspaper photo I have tucked there. I love this photo of Alan and me. Us on the terrace, curled around each other, waiting for the sunrise. How did they get it? Telephoto lens? I wonder if you can ever get a real photo from a newspaper. It just seems to capture us, and everything that was us, through these unexpected weeks. I start to cry. The caption is cruel and wrong—those fuckers in the press never get anything right—but the photo is totally us.

I wish I could see the future. I wish I knew with complete certainty if my decision was right. I wish I were older, looking back after having gotten through this.

What if I'd stayed?

I turn to stare out the window. I can't see the earth and I can't see the sun and I can't see the journey ahead of me.

Chrissie's Journal

It's funny how something can consume your life and then just disappear. After spring break in New York, I never burned myself again. I try to make sense of it all, but I can't. If anything should have fueled my self-burning addiction, it should have been leaving Alan and realizing I've lost him for good.

I read the self-help books that Rene's mother gave to me when I returned to Santa Barbara. They all confirm the same thing: that my illness is not something that should just end. It would require long-term counseling to resolve my issues that created such a destructive disorder. But I skipped the counseling and just went across country with Rene in the Volvo my dad purchased for us, started UC Berkeley in the fall as planned, and when I arrived at school it was gone, and the impulse to burn my flesh hasn't come again.

I think of Alan every day and yet the impulse, the whispering sadness, the need to hurt myself stays away.

I'm grateful that the burning thing is over, but I still can't help wondering why it ended. Maybe it's as simple as having the fragments of memory form into a clear picture of that horrid night Sammy OD'd, so that I can now deal honestly with my brother's death. Maybe it's as simple as having confronted Jack and starting the process of working through my issues with my father. Maybe it's as simple as Alan asking me never to do it again for him. I don't think I'll ever know for sure how I got beyond the obsession to burn myself, but I did, and it ended.

If the authors of the self-help books were to ask me, I would probably tell them it ended because of Alan. He asked me not to burn myself and it's as simple as that.

The answers are always simple if you let them be.

CHAPTER ONE

UC Berkeley, Fall Semester 1989

I hurry across campus, up the unavoidable hills I'm really starting to hate after only two months at Cal, and I wish I had time to stop to remove my sweater.

I'm starting to believe that UC Berkeley isn't going to be any better for me than high school had been. In fact, I feel pretty much the same here: lost, a little sad, and as if I don't fit in anywhere. I never expected to miss Eliza and her mob of pretty mean-girls from high school, but as I cut my way through the herd of students all going somewhere, I find that I do.

I never did fit in with the popular-girl clique, but having them antagonizing me and my suffering in return somehow made me connected with them. And by extension, connected to the high school experience. I don't feel connected to anything here.

Here I just walk to class alone since I'm in the Music College and Rene is in the Science College, and for the most part, no one ever interferes with me beyond a sudden fixed stare.

I shake my head, realizing that in the two months I've been here I haven't done myself any favors. I can't seem to find a comfortable routine, I haven't made any new friends, and how much I still hurt over Alan makes me do stupid things.

In my freshman composition class the first assignment was to write a fifteen hundred word essay introducing myself. I stared at the prompt and thought *really,* convinced that this exercise had been created by my professor just to add to the emotional heap already burying me.

After procrastinating over the assignment for days, I opted for concise, since there's pretty much nothing left to share after those months of horrible tabloid press following my weeks with Alan: *My father, Jack, is a music icon from the 60s who is still on an FBI watch list. My mother, a celebrated violinist, died of cancer when I was seven. I was practically raised by an illegal Nicaraguan refugee. At the age of eight, I watched my brother die in his bedroom of a heroin overdose. I hid in bathrooms from thirteen until eighteen burning my body with the infinity clasp of a Tiffany bracelet. I'm a technically proficient cellist who bombed an audition at Juilliard, deliberately. During my senior year spring break I had a three-week whirlwind affair with a deeply troubled yet brilliant British rock superstar. Oh, and UC Berkeley is just my fallback plan and I don't really know why I'm here.*

One-hundred twenty-seven words. Concise: that's what my professor wrote above the numerical grade equaling 'F'. When I asked him why he failed me, he didn't even respond to me verbally. Beneath the 'F' he rapidly scribbled: *Sorry, Miss Parker, at Cal we start with following the prompt. Maybe by next Friday you can submit fifteen hundred words on why you're here.*

Why am I here?

Of all the prompts he could have given me, that's the one I can't answer even after two months in college. Somehow, I managed to turn out something. Fifteen hundred words as required, thankfully canceling my prior 'F' grade with a low 'C', but it didn't help clarify a single thing for me.

Why am I here?

As I pull back the heavy door to the lecture room, that familiar question turns into another familiar question: why am I always late?

There is absolutely no way to make a subtle entrance to a lecture hall wearing flip-flops. I cringe as I hear the slap, slap, slap against the floor, and for some reason I always manage to arrive during a moment of quiet and there's never a seat in the back of the room left for me. Nope, there's only one in the front, that's it, within range of Professor Lambert.

Slap, slap, slap. Stare, stare, stare. Glare from Professor Lambert. I sink into my seat. I set my tote on the floor beside me and tuck a stray lock of golden-blond hair behind my ear.

The stare doesn't lift. The silence doesn't break. Professor Lambert doesn't like me. I look up and smile at him.

"Good of you to join us, Miss Parker," he says. "May I continue?"

I smile. I attended high school at a private Catholic boarding school. Like I'm going to fall for that one and answer a sarcastically put rhetorical question. And that's what it is. If I were stupid enough to answer, the whole thing would just go downhill from here.

I focus on pulling my spiral notebook from my pack. I grab a pen, open to a fresh page, scribble the date, and begin to make little geometric shapes. I tune out the voices in the classroom and focus on the little city I'm inexpertly drawing on the paper where my notes for this class should be.

I wonder where Alan is today…

"Miss Parker!" a voice above me snaps loudly.

I look up to find Professor Lambert hovering over me and all the seats around me vacant. *Oh God, what did I miss?*

"May I continue, Miss Parker?"

Two 'may I continues' in a single day. A new record. I nod and quickly drop my eyes.

"Well?" Harsh. Imperative.

I look back up. Like a flight attendant he holds out his arms, pointing at each side of the room. "There are two lines, Miss Parker. You'd know that if you paid attention in class. A little boy line. A little girl line. Please join the appropriate line."

My cheeks burning, I snap my notebook closed and hurry across the room. Slap, slap, slap. Damn flip-flops in a silent room again. I take my place at the end of the line.

"There are five solos in the ensemble," Professor Lambert continues as he slowly walks the room. "They will be handed out based on class participation and exercises, so make sure you've all signed up for a lab with Jared and attend. And of course, ability."

He sinks into a seat in the middle of the lecture hall. "Based on the selection you will sing today—and I do hope you've all come to class prepared—I will assign you to groups of four. These will be your permanent group assignment until the end of the semester. No changes will be made. And you will endeavor to master the extremely difficult contrapuntal harmony I will assign, due at the semester end."

The girl beside me gives me a gentle nudge. "Why does Lambert have such a hard-on for you?" she whispers.

I shrug. If the girl doesn't know the answer to that, then it means she doesn't know who I am and doesn't read the papers. Far be it from me to fill her in.

"I'm Teri," she says.

"Chrissie."

"Why don't you ever talk to anyone?" she inquires in an overly bright way that tells me this girl is both chatty and friendly. "I never see you talk to anyone."

I shrug again, and this time Teri frowns. "I'm nervous as hell about this. Lambert can be so rude. What did you prepare?"

Prepare? Oh crap, I must learn to read the syllabus more carefully. I stare at the sheet music Teri is holding: a choral selection. This project requires a choral selection.

I shake my head.

Teri's brows jerk upward. "You mean you didn't prepare anything?"

I shake my head, praying Teri will let up on this. Hasn't she figured out if I answer her verbally, Lambert will take it as an excuse to pounce on me again?

"Do you want to grab something to eat after class?" she continues.

I shake my head.

"Why not?"

I let out a ragged exhale of breath. "I can't. OK?"

I do an exaggerated shift of my eyes to Professor Lambert and give Teri a heavy, meaningful stare. I can tell by her expression she doesn't get the warning I'm trying to silently convey, and she sinks against the wall slightly pouty.

Now I feel bad.

"It's not you, OK?" I whisper.

Teri shrugs.

"I'm almost failing this class. I can't give Lambert another reason to fail me."

Teri nods, still awash with sulkiness, and I give up.

I move along the wall, leaning and waiting for my turn to sing. There are penalties for not paying attention in class. If I'd listened the last two months I would have known I'd be required to have something prepared for today. And if I'd paid attention earlier, I could have gotten in line first and been out the door like the other students already finished performing. Now I have to listen to all of my classmates sing.

At the front of the line I smile at Jared, Professor Lambert's graduate teaching assistant, waiting on the piano bench for the next victim. Jared has been sort of nice to me this semester and probably would be much nicer if Lambert's dislike of me wasn't so obvious.

Jared looks at the sheet Teri holds out, opens the music book and then hits the metronome, allowing Teri a few ticks before he begins to play. I listen patiently, chiding myself to smile at her, even though her singing is only average and not very good. She's a nice girl, though, she did try to befriend me, and I'm sure I came off snotty and weird.

She waits, looking very nervous now that the performance has ended. I nod to assure Teri it went well as we wait for Professor Lambert's critique.

Lambert looks over his glasses at her, pauses, and then announces, "Well done."

Teri beams and rushes off toward her chair as I approach the piano. Jared looks at me expectantly, raising a brow. "Did you forget your music?" he asks, a hint of dread in his voice as if he's already anticipating how badly this will go for me.

I nod.

"Is there a problem, Miss Parker? Why does that not surprise me?" Professor Lambert asks, heavily exasperated.

The classroom is nearly empty, there's just Lambert, Jared, and Teri in the large hall, but my cheeks color hotly with the same burning intensity they would if it were a full class here.

Jared starts to rummage through loose sheets. "I'm assuming you can read music."

I nod. Of course, I wouldn't be stupid enough to enter a music program and not be able to read music. I'm a complete failure at the college thing, but I'm not stupid.

I take the sheet to the music stand, and I'm relieved to discover Jared picked a simple choral piece not from the book. Jared hits the metronome, but there's something in that tick, tick, tick that just isn't working for me. I look out at Lambert. "Must I have the metronome? It's distracting."

Lambert makes an exaggerated wave of his arm. "Stop the metronome, Jared. We don't want Miss Parker distracted here!"

He says that with just the right amount of criticism and, as I wait for Jared to stop the ticking and prepare to play, I admit that at least that one was fair. I have been, if nothing else, distracted my first semester here. It's not easy to carry on with your life in focus when you're trying to recover from a broken heart.

I shake my head, trying to push Alan from my thoughts. He didn't mean to break my heart. I broke it for him. I'm the one who walked away. It doesn't matter that a part of me didn't believe that we would really be over, even though he said we would be. It doesn't matter that a part of me never expected him to marry someone else so quickly. None of that matters now. Alan is married, and I'm at Berkeley.

I struggle through the selection, not from a lack of ability to wing it, but because the rising emotion inside me caused by the thought of Alan just won't calm.

When I finish I'm grateful it's over and I lean clutching the music stand. At least it wasn't awful. It was in tune, the pitch was good, and the timing was perfect. It definitely wasn't glaringly more terrible than any of the other performances I've heard today.

I wait in the silent hall as Lambert jots down more notes on his paperwork. "You need to sing more from your diaphragm," he says finally. "Make sure you do breathing exercises during your lab with Jared."

That's it? Not bad, not good, just something I already know. When I'm tense I never sing well from my diaphragm.

I hurry back to my seat and start to collect my belongings. Teri rushes across the room to my chair. "Crap, you were really good," she exclaims enthusiastically. "Where did you study voice?"

That question confirms she doesn't know anything about my personal history. I continue to collect my things, pulling out my midterm paper from my backpack. "I've never studied voice. I'm a cellist. I wouldn't be in this class if I didn't need it to fill out my graduation requirements."

Teri's eyes widen. "But you're good. Really good. You have an awesome voice. Do you want to go grab something to eat?"

"I can't," I say, a little more friendly. "I want to talk to Professor Lambert."

"I can wait," she assures, eager and hopeful.

"I'm meeting someone after class, but maybe tomorrow. OK?" I take out a pen and hold out my hand for her notebook. "I can give you my number. Maybe we can have coffee, study, or something?"

Teri smiles. "OK. Tomorrow. Cool."

I wait until Teri and Jared are gone from the hall. I approach Professor Lambert's desk. He doesn't look up and I wait quietly, patiently, for him to acknowledge me.

With irritatingly slow movements of his pen, he finishes whatever it is he's writing, and then leans back in his chair, causing it to squeak as he stares up at me. "Is there something you wanted, Miss Parker?"

I swallow hard, hugging my books more closely to me as I meet his cold stare. I lay my midterm on his desk. "Yes. I want to know why you failed my paper."

He lifts the paper. He gives it a short scan. "Were my comments not specific enough?"

I flush. "Yes, they were very clear. I followed the prompt. Why did you give me an F?"

"Did you understand the assignment?"

I feel a rush of cold across my skin followed by heat. "I think so. You wanted a paper on contemporary music influences that will have lasting impact on music theory and composition. Ten thousand words. Provide two examples. Explain how their influence will change music. The examples you provided were Bach and Bob Dylan."

I watch the smile slowly claim his lips. Its affect is the opposite.

"Yes. You did understand," he says in a tired, exasperated way. "You provided me ten thousand words on a little-known band from Seattle and the British hard rock band Blackpoll." A long pause. The silence in the room is suddenly smothering. At last, he says, "Interesting choice. You would have at least gotten a C if you had taken the predictable way out and written about your father."

That was said in a way that was just plain mean and insulting. I fight back tears. "I thought the purpose of this assignment was to defend my premise. Not to have you like it."

Lambert looks down. "It would have been encouraging if you had taken this assignment seriously."

I don't know what to say to that. I thought I did. "Can

I submit another paper?"

"There are no do-overs, Miss Parker. You're in college now."

I stare at him. Finally he looks up. I fight to meet his gaze. "Why do you dislike me so much?" I say in an embarrassingly thin voice.

His gaze falls away. He slouches over his desk and starts writing again. "It's not you. It's the idea of you," he says with harsh indifference.

My cheeks burn. "What does that mean?"

He leans back in his chair again. "Every year I see a dozen incoming freshmen exactly like you. Rich, privileged, taking up seats they don't really want that could go to students who have worked hard and want to be here. You're at University California, Berkeley and you act like it is an inconvenience to be here! You take up space and by the end of the year"—his eyes widen harshly beneath his thick brows—"you will be gone."

The emotion shoots through my veins all at once. My insides are shaking. "I'm here to get a degree in music. I want to teach music to children in the inner cities."

"How Berkeley politically correct of you. I'd feel better if I believed you." I watch as he fixes his focus back on his work. "I've seen the newspapers," he continues, not bothering even to look at me. "Your father is a great man. He stands for something. What a disappointment you must be to him."

I can't believe he just said that. I can no longer prevent the shaking from being visible on my body. Even if I could think of a suitable comeback, I could never have gotten the words out of me. My throat is clogged with tears.

I head toward the door.

"Prove me wrong, Miss Parker. Figure out why you're here, and then make the most of it," Professor Lambert calls out and I continue out of the classroom.

I let the heavy wood door slam behind me. Running down the hall, I crash into a janitor, who steadies me with quick hands and sets me safely back onto my feet again. Without a word to him, I race out of the building.

I find vacant my favorite spot with a view of the Berkeley Campanile and the giant concrete slabs with sculptures of bears atop them in a grassy and shaded area of the campus. I sink down, curl into a ball hugging my knees, and fight to stop the tears.

I can't believe I chose this over marrying Alan…

"Here, you look like you could use this," says a quiet, male voice above me.

I look up only far enough to see the carry-size pack of tissue held out to me in long, tan fingers. I take one and anxiously dab at my tears. On the concrete walkway below there's a pair of some kind of work shoe and dark blue pant legs that look like they belong to a jumpsuit or something. Oh God, it's the janitor I barreled into. How humiliating is this? To be the girl alone on a concrete slab, crying, and being consoled by the janitor.

I don't look up, praying he'll go away.

"Can I sit on your bench?" he asks politely.

"It's not my bench and it's a free country."

I cringe. That sounded childish and snooty. No wonder I haven't made a single friend here.

"I'm sorry," I add.

"No problem. You're upset. I get it. I just want to eat my lunch. No harm, no foul."

He makes a small laugh over his own comments. I avoid looking straight at him, inhale another sniffle, and touch my nose with the tissue.

"Thank you. You've been very nice," I whisper.

He settles near me, copying my posture: feet on the bench, his legs bent, and facing me.

"You know, Lambert will only bully you if you let him," he advises kindly. "And he only bullies the students he thinks have potential."

How would you know? You're the janitor, I say to myself. "Thanks. I'll try to remember that. He doesn't hate me. I have potential."

He laughs and, from a pack on the ground, he takes a brown lunch bag and sets it beside him. So he really did just come out here to eat his lunch. The janitor suddenly popping up here has nothing to do with the sorry sight I must have been running out of Lambert's classroom. A small measure of calm returns to me.

"Rough year?" He's carefully unwrapping some kind of minimart precooked burrito thing.

Jeez, is he going to eat that cold?

He holds it out to me. "Do you want a bite? It isn't as terrible as it looks."

I start to laugh, even though I really don't want to. "Thanks, but no thanks!"

"Come on. What's not to love? Week-old beans. Week-old rice and I'm not even sure what the sauce is. Be bold. Be brave. Eat a minimart burrito from yesterday."

OK, that was funny. I look at him then, locking onto his green eyes. There's a really sweet, teasing glint in them. His eyes are large, brightly colored, and filled with a smile. Shoulder-length blond-streaked brown hair peeks out from beneath an army green bandana, and the face of the janitor is tanned, really good looking…and really familiar.

Why does it feel like I know him?

"Are you homesick? Is that why you mope around campus all day?"

I lift my chin. "I don't mope. And how would you know what I do all day?"

He takes the keys hanging from his belt and shakes them. "There's not much to do when you push a broom in the music department except listen and watch everything." He takes a bite of his burrito. "You have Lambert's class from 10 until 11. You sit on this bench until noon. You have a practice room from 1 until 2. You sit on this bench until 3. You have your lab with Jared the TA—who's hot for you, would really like to date you, and is afraid to ask—that's at 3:30. And then sometimes you do another hour in a practice room, but most of the time you disappear from campus. You're back at 7 for symphony. That's your Tuesday/Thursday schedule."

My eyes widen and I tense. Jeez, maybe he's not just the janitor. Maybe he's a stalker or something.

"How do you know all that?" I ask anxiously.

"I push a broom, remember?" he replies casually.

I start to gather my things.

"Hey," he says, putting his hand on my arm. "You

don't have to run for security, Chrissie. I would never hurt a hometown girl. The rest of the girls I stalk are in big trouble, but you're pretty much safe from me. We've got that whole SB thing going on. We're hometown bonded."

His boyish eyes start to twinkle above an endearing smile. I stare at him. Chrissie—he knows my name. SB thing? He's from Santa Barbara, too. I study him more closely and I just can't place the face. I know the face, but I'm not connecting the dots, and I'm not tapping into that instinct thing telling me if I used to like him or if I should run.

He frowns. "Now I'm hurt."

Crap, he can see I'm not remembering him.

He tosses his unfinished burrito into the bag. "Do you forget every really, really cool guy who does you a really, really big favor?"

I feel my heart drop to my knees. *Really, really cool guy…* Oh crap! This day just keeps getting worse. Neil Stanton. Yep, I definitely remember him. The jerk from that night Rene and I went clubbing at Peppers before leaving for spring break in Manhattan. The guy who thought he needed to give me life advice after making a fool out of me. In my memory I can hear him say *Didn't Daddy teach you anything about how the world works?*

I do my best imitation Rene rich-girl-put-down face. "Sorry! It's just that Daddy taught me not to speak to the janitor."

He rolls his eyes and shakes his head. "And here I was just trying to be nice to you. Why is it girls only remember the parts of everything you don't want them to? Never the nice parts. Just the parts you want them to forget."

He crunches up his lunch bag and sinks it into the trashcan five feet away. "And I'm not a janitor. I'm a facilities technician one."

OK, the way he said that was kind of cute and our evening at Peppers was fun…well, right up to the point of his parting lecture. He's incredibly good-looking. I struggle not to let down my guard just yet. I'm not sure why he's here or why he would want to meet up with me again.

I arch a brow. "Do you push a broom? Do you mop floors? Do you empty trashcans?"

"Yep."

"Then you're a janitor," I counter, but I can feel myself smiling against my will.

He shrugs. "That's what my dad calls me, too. Hey, do you want to go grab something to eat? That burrito just didn't do it for me. Or did Daddy teach you not to have coffee with the janitor?"

Have I really just been asked out by Neil Stanton, former musician turned janitor? Does this count as being asked out? I stare at him, not really sure what this is.

"I can't."

"Sure you can. You can miss your practice room one time and you don't have your lab with Jared until 3:30."

Well, he's right about that. Missing my practice time won't hurt me. I don't really practice in the rooms and I never study. I book the practice rooms just for someplace to go, someplace easier to be all alone on campus.

I gather my things and fall in beside him. We walk in silence toward the food court area. Staring at the ground, I try to figure out why I've decided to join him.

Neil shoves his hands into his loose pockets. "So what's he like? It must have been incredible hanging out with him."

Him? I tense. I don't need the 'him' explained to me. I hate being reminded of all the junk that was in the press last spring.

I shrug. "Alan Manzone is a nice guy."

Neil frowns. "That's it? You spent three weeks with the greatest guitarist of our generation, a musical genius, and that's the best you can do? Nice guy?"

I feel my temper flash. "Listen, there are two things I never talk about. Alan Manzone and my father. If you can't get that, then we are done being friends."

He pauses mid-step and gives me a quizzical stare. "Crap, you do presume a lot, don't you?"

I flush. "Meaning?"

He shrugs. "I'm not sure I want to be your friend." He continues to walk.

I stare after him. God, Neil is still as irritating and unpredictable as he was the first night I met him. I shake my head in frustration. Why am I following him? I do double-time steps to catch up to him.

"So what are you doing here, working as a janitor?" I ask, struggling to keep pace with him. "Last April you were living in Seattle, had a band, and were just taking off on a six-month tour."

He looks at me and smiles. "So it's OK for you to ask about my personal shit, but I ask you one question and you fly off the handle."

The flush moves down my face and covers my neck. "I didn't fly off the handle. I was just making clear the boundaries."

"Ah, boundaries." Neil shakes his head. "Why do girls always think it's necessary to establish boundaries? We're just having coffee. We're just talking here. I don't know if we'll do it again. I don't know if I even like you, but you've jumped into setting boundaries."

The way he says that makes me sound ridiculous. And yet, there's something kind of sweet and good-natured in how he says it which keeps me from being totally pissed off.

"Maybe we find it necessary because guys get everything wrong all the time," I counter, shaking my head in frustration.

Neil stops walking again. "So I've already failed and we're just having a conversation."

"Something like that."

He rolls his eyes. "Remind me never to ask you on a date."

The burn on my face has just turned up to surface-heat-of-the-sun level. "Trust me, that is never going to happen."

His smile is pleasant this time. "Good. We're on the same page. Détente. Can we get coffee now, please?"

He pulls back the door to a small, independent coffee shop. It's dark with a hippie-style feel to it and only sells vegan drinks and snacks.

"Why isn't there a McDonald's in the food court? What's with the weird 60s vibe and vegetarian shit?" Neil asks.

I study the muffins in the cooler case. "Really? You're asking me that? You work here and you don't know the answer to that?"

The counter girl stops in front of him. Neil points at an apple muffin and orders a large black coffee. "Do you know what you want yet?" he asks.

I shake my head.

"Do you want coffee?"

I nod. He orders my coffee. I point at the vegan chocolate cookie in the case. "I think I'll have that."

We stand side by side at the cash register waiting for our order. Why is it taking so long? All we ordered were two coffees, a muffin and a cookie. I rummage through my pack for my wallet.

"No, Chrissie, I can pay for a cookie and a coffee," he says, clearly irritated with me.

I lift my brows. "I didn't want you to think this is a date or anything."

He rolls his eyes. "No chance of that."

We settle at one of the tables in front of the shop.

After adding vegan creamer and raw sugar to my coffee, I look up at him. "Really, how did you end up here?"

He leans back in his chair. "Got tired of the Seattle thing. Got tired of the road. Four months out, broke and it just wasn't happening. My uncle got me this job and I figured, why not? Just get away from it all, clear my head, get straight on what I want to do again. Shit was getting crazy on the road. We were forgetting why we were out there. I wanted to get back to writing music again." He lifts his keys from his belt and rattles them. "And they've got everything here I need. Recording studios, rehearsal rooms, talent. And I've got the keys to everything."

I break off a small piece of my cookie. "So you're going to push a broom and wait for musical inspiration to flow through you? Is that what you're telling me?"

"Pretty much."

"Good luck with that." I take a sip of my coffee.

He points at me and shakes his head. "You know you don't have to be so negative. That's half your problem. Haven't you noticed that everyone is freakishly happy here?"

I laugh. "No, I haven't noticed that one."

"Well, they are. Even worse than in Santa Barbara. I used to think it was something they put in the water at home, but they are just like that here. But Berkeley is OK. It's a good place to chill, Chrissie. A good place to get it together."

I fix my eyes on the last bite of my cookie. Get it together. God, is it so obvious that I'm not together? Somehow I don't think that I'll ever get it together.

Neil picks up our trash from the table and tosses it into the can. "I can tell you one thing, after pushing a broom behind people, you never leave a mess anywhere."

I laugh and grab my pack. We walk back toward the music department and neither of us talks. Neil lumbers beside me, hands in his pockets, a kind of cute half-smile on his face.

He stays with me all the way to the door of my lab.

"I'd give you my number," he says unexpectedly, "but I don't have a phone. Don't want to commit to anything since I don't know how long I'll be here."

He says that in a way that tells me he remembers me offering him my number last April, and that he blew me off without taking it. It was a very well done brush-off.

I lift my chin, smiling. "I'd give you my number, but it won't do you any good since you don't have a phone."

He pulls open the door. "I've got an idea. You need to reach me on Tuesdays and Thursdays, just step into the hall and shout 'Neil.' I promise I'll answer if I'm here."

I laugh. "OK. It's a deal. I don't have to tell you how to reach me. You seem to know my schedule pretty well."

"Yep." His expression turns from smiling into something serious. "It's Thursday. You have rehearsal until 9 p.m. I'm going to meet you at nine and walk you home from symphony practice. You shouldn't walk this campus alone at night. Don't you read the security bulletins? You need to take the alerts seriously. Pushing a broom I hear lots of things. Make some friends, Chrissie. Talk to people. Don't expect me to walk you home every Tuesday and Thursday."

I flush and nod. That was a really sweet thing to say, but then, Neil was kind of sweet at times that night at Peppers. And it is *so* embarrassing that he's noticed I don't have any friends.

"See ya at nine, homegirl," he says laughingly.

"See ya at nine, homeboy."

~~~

At nine, I find Neil waiting on the steps of the symphony
~~~

rehearsal building smoking a cigarette. He stomps it out and crosses to me, taking the cello case from my hand.

So he did show up to walk me home. I'm surprised and a little confused that he did. Why is he suddenly acting like my big brother?

"You've got to tell me which way you live," he says.

I smile at him, more friendly this time, since it is nice having him waiting here. "So I guess you're not a stalker since you don't know where I live."

He lifts his brows. "Maybe I'm a stalker and I just want to find out where you live."

I shake my head and sink my chilled hands into my pockets.

"Cello?" he asks.

"Yep. Why do you say it that way? Cello. Like it's strange."

He shrugs. "I don't know. I just thought you'd be like your old man. Guitar. Or piano. Isn't that what girls like you play? Piano?"

I arch a brow. "Girls like me?"

"God, I didn't mean anything bad. Rich. Fancy. Pretty. Cello doesn't seem like a pretty-girl thing."

Leave it to Neil to combine an insult and a compliment. God, he's a strange guy. Strange, and yet really likeable simultaneously somehow.

"I like the cello," I say.

"Well, you don't have to get defensive about it. I like the cello, too."

I'm angry again because for some reason, this conversation reminds me that Alan said my talent would never make me more than third chair in a third-rate orchestra.

"I'm second chair in a first-rate orchestra," I announce.

He frowns and his eyes narrow. "OK. Did I suggest that you weren't good? I said the cello surprised me."

My face covers in a burn. "Can we not talk about the cello, please?"

I turn off onto a dark path that cuts through campus.

He stares at me. "Easy for you to say. You're not lugging it. Are we turning?"

"Yes. It's shorter. We're going to cut through here."

"You do this at night, alone?" He sounds surprised. A touch concerned.

I frown. "Of course. How do you think I get home?"

Neil shakes his head. "God, you have no common sense at all, do you?"

"Obviously not. I'm with you."

I make a face at him and he tosses me a heavily exasperated look.

It's a long walk back to the condo. I live off-campus, on a hill in an upscale, high-rise condo complex. I have a car in Berkeley, but I rarely take it since, even with my overpriced parking permit, the traffic is awful and it's a hassle to find a vacant space in any of the campus lots. It's faster just to walk everywhere.

It takes thirty minutes to get from the rehearsal building to my front door. Neil hands me my cello.

He stands there on the steps, silent, staring at me as if he's waiting for something.

"Do you want to come up?" I ask.

Neil shakes his head. "No, that's OK. I better cut out. I left my car on campus. I would have taken it if I'd known it was so far."

He takes a step back from me.

I smile. "Thanks, Neil. You've been a really OK guy today."

He shrugs. "You're the only person here I know from home." He smiles. "Remember, Berkeley is only as bad as we make it."

I laugh. I sense that Neil feels the same way about Berkeley as I do. "It is kind of different here, isn't it?"

"It's what you make it. That's Berkeley."

I start to laugh. Neil's stares at me and I can see that he doesn't understand why I find that one so funny.

He frowns. "Am I missing the joke here?"

I shake my head and try to stop my laughter. "It's just, you've got to know my dad. I swear to God, he said the exact same thing to me. 'It's what you make it. That's Berkeley.'"

Neil starts to laugh. "See you, Chrissie."

As he walks down the sidewalk I can hear him whistling one of my dad's biggest hits from the 60s.

~~~

Inside the condo I find Rene huddled over the kitchen table, books, notepads, colored highlighters, Post-it notes, and paperclips scattered everywhere.

I set down my cello case and drop my carry tote on the counter. "You'll never guess who I had lunch with and who walked me home from symphony tonight."
~~~

Rene shakes her head in aggravation, jerking on the ends of her dark brown hair, tightening the ponytail atop her head.

"I don't have time to guess, Chrissie."

I reach into the refrigerator for a Diet Coke. "Neil Stanton, from Santa Barbara. He's working as a janitor in the music department, if you can believe that."

Rene frowns. "Neil who?"

How could Rene not remember him? "That guy. That guy from that night at Peppers before we left for New York on spring break. The guy who did me a really, really big favor."

Rene looks at me, eyes narrowing as though trying to remember.

I lift a brow. "You screwed his friend in my dad's car. Josh something. That was his name, I think."

Comprehension floods the pretty lines of her face. Then she scrunches up her nose. "Josh! What an asshole. He never called. Why would you have coffee with Neil? Wasn't he a jerk to you that night?"

"Well, not completely. He was kind of nice at times." I sink down at the table across from her. "I've had a weird day. Lambert was all up in my face again and then Neil asked me to go for coffee and I just sort of went."

Rene grabs her pink highlighter. "Chrissie, can we talk later? I'm buried here. Organic Chemistry is kicking my ass and I have a test tomorrow."

"Fine. I always listen to you talk about your guys. Your dates."

"You're studying music. You already have a PhD in that. I'm studying molecular cell biology. Trust me,

Chrissie. You don't get into medical school with courses like 'The History of the Vietnam War Through Music.'"

I roll my eyes. She can be so rude at times. "It's through film, not music, and I actually like that class."

"Whatever!"

I grab my Diet Coke and head for my bedroom. Rene obsessed with her books and grades—I'll never get used to that change in her.

I sink onto my bed and turn on the TV, then adjust the volume low. My thoughts drift back to my summer road-trip across country with Rene.

It was a weird trip, but Jack was right, it was good for me. I think it was keeping busy, always having something new to see, that got me through everything that I needed to work through after my breakup with Alan.

Spring break in New York was some kind of strange pivot point for both Rene and me. Afterward, I was different. Rene was different. And our friendship was different. In May, when we left Santa Barbara for the East Coast, Rene was tamer and more serious about life. I wonder if that had anything to do with her father remarrying and her finally accepting that he isn't ever coming back to her and her mother. And I was less introverted. I know that has everything to do with me being with Alan. We each left New York with good shit and bad. It made us both just sort of ready to have a really chill trip, enjoying that best friend thing.

Of course, that doesn't mean we didn't do a dumb thing or two. I laugh as some of Rene's antics dance in my memory. In every state Rene left behind a guy. And me…I shake my head…I had my first, and what I hope will be my only, one-night stand in August.

It just seemed like the right thing at the time. We were in New Orleans in a club, and the lead singer of the band was hot, and it just happened. It wasn't good, it wasn't bad. It was just sort of blank. It doesn't belong in either section of my journal: good experience or regret.

Rene said it was just one of those things girls do after a painful breakup, but I don't know. I think I just wanted to know what it would be like to have sex with someone other than Alan. It was weird. Not bad, just weird.

Rene had a readymade answer for that during my morning after of indifference over the entire experience: *That's the curse of having your first time be with a guy who cared about you, Chrissie. Once you've gone to bed with a guy who cares, it pretty much ruins every other type of sex.*

Cared, past tense. Rene didn't mean it that way, but it still hurt. I don't like to admit it, but even after seven months I'm still emotionally, if not physically, involved with Alan. After the one-night stand I called it quits on guys. I'm just not there yet, in the past tense emotionally with Alan, ready to start something with someone new, and since Berkeley I haven't even tried the guy thing. Shit, I hardly go out.

I shake my head. It makes it so much stranger and confusing that I just went off with Neil today. I wonder why I did that. We didn't exactly end as friends after our one night in Santa Barbara last spring and he's definitely not my type. Still, I did have fun with him today, even though we traded verbal insults most of the time. He's really cute.

I toss the TV remote away, climb from the bed, and begin to undress for the night.

Maybe I went to coffee with Neil because he isn't my type and I'm not emotionally done with Alan, even if Alan *is* emotionally done with me. I knew when I left New York we were over. Still, I wasn't prepared to open a newspaper in August to learn that Alan had married Nia. Nope, I didn't expected that one or that our ending would be such a clean break. Seven months. Not one call from Alan. No letter. Not even a token gift sent. Just over.

I rummage through my drawers and lift out Alan's t-shirt, the one I took the last day we were together. For some reason, I want to wear it tonight. I pull it over my head, shut off the TV, and climb into bed.

So much has changed and it's only been half a year since spring break. Neil Stanton became a janitor. Alan Manzone married Nia. Rene studies more nights than she parties. And I'm lost and alone at Berkeley.

It seems life pushes us all onto roads we never expect.

CHAPTER TWO

I collapse back onto my bed. It's finally Friday. I've made it through another week here. God, how pathetic is that? I make a mental note of each week of class I've survived at Cal.

I roll over and check the clock on my nightstand. Where's Rene? It's after five p.m., her classes ended at one today, and she's always here at the condo when I get home from my theater class. I go to the kitchen to see if she left a note. Nothing.

I grab the wine from the fridge. I stare at the bottle, then roll my eyes. Rene and her little fancy frou-frou ways. She thinks drinking only white wine makes her look more sophisticated. We drink one day a week because her biology program is really intense, for all that I give her crap over her turbo-focused, nonstop studying. We only drink on Fridays, and she calls it California Chardonnay Friday. She can be so pretentious at times.

Well, I guess I'm going to have Chardonnay Friday alone tonight. I pour myself a glass and go into the living room, settling on the couch. I grab the TV remote and start clicking through channels. Nothing. Nothing. Nothing. I stop. An entertainment news magazine show. That'll work.

I reach for my wine and the phone rings. Good. Maybe it's Rene. She can tell me what's up with the disappearing act, and why she ditched me on a Friday night.

"Hello," I say into the receiver.

"How's everything going with you, Chrissie?"

Jack. I smile. "Great, Daddy. Just finished my midterms and I'm just chilling out tonight."

"Well, see that you don't have too much fun. You still have a lot of school left before the end of the semester. Pace yourself."

I roll my eyes. Jack definitely worries a lot more about me since New York than he did before Alan.

I take a sip from my glass of wine. "I won't have too much fun. I told you I'm staying in tonight. What are you up to?"

"Doing a little work. I'm driving up next weekend. I have a thing in the city. I thought I'd stop by and see my girl. How does that sound to you?"

"Sounds great," I say.

"I'll cook dinner for you, unless you want to go out."

Out with Jack. It's always such a hassle going out with him. It's not his fault. He doesn't do anything. It pisses me off, and that makes me angry because it's not his fault.

"You could make enchiladas and show me how," I say. "I miss Maria's cooking."

"Then I'll make enchiladas and show you how." I can hear the smile in his voice.

"Good, then it's settled," I say.

"I'll have Maria call you with a shopping list and, this time, no substitutions. If you can't find it, ask."

I roll my eyes and make a face at the phone.

"I've got to run, Chrissie. But I'm looking forward to seeing you next Saturday. It's a one-hour flight. You could come home once in a while."

"I'm just trying to get settled into a routine here. I'll be home all winter break."

"Really? I expected you to have something going on over the break."

"Nope. I'm spending it in Santa Barbara."

A pause. There's going to be a click soon.

Quickly, I say, "Daddy?"

"Yes?"

"I love you."

Another pause. Short. "I love you too, baby girl."

I stare at the receiver for a long time before I hang it up. I wasn't the only one who came back from New York different. Jack did, too.

I go to the kitchen for more wine. The phone rings again. Jeez, it's like Grand Central Station tonight. I never get two calls in the same night. It's probably just Rene, calling to tell me why she blew me off tonight.

I race to the couch, climbing over the back. I reach for the cordless phone and sink down on the seat.

"Hello," I say into the receiver, trying to wipe the wine I spilled off the seat cushion.

"Hey, Chrissie. What you doing tonight?" The voice is overly animated, overly chirpy.

I frown. The voice is familiar, but I don't know who the girl is.

"Just watching TV," I answer carefully. "What's up with you?"

"I'm sorry I didn't call earlier. We were going to have coffee today, but things got crazy and I forgot."

Oh, yeah. Teri from Lambert's class. I'd forgotten I'd given her my phone number.

"It's OK," I say, and it really is OK. I don't know if I want *her* to be the first friend I make at Berkeley. She's sweet, but there's something about her that is a little pushy and irritating. "You got plans for tonight?"

"That's why I'm calling."

She sounds excited.

"Yeah. What you got going on?" I ask.

I take a sip of my wine.

"We're all going into the city to this club we know down on the waterfront. Live music. Hot guys. You should come with us. Like, everyone is going to be at The Palms tonight."

"Sounds fun," I say, noncommittal. "What time are you guys heading out?"

"We're all meeting in my dorm room at Sterns Hall around nine," she says. "It's a lot of fun. Come, Chrissie."

"I don't know. I'm waiting for my roommate. We're supposed to do something, but if I can come, I'll meet you at Sterns around nine."

"Cool. See you at nine."

I click off the phone and toss it on the coffee table. I have no intention of going out tonight with my new, wannabe friend. The city. Teri. A club. Sounds too much all at once to cope with.

I slouch down, staring at the TV. Three hours later, I'm still on the couch, flicking through channels for about the twentieth time this evening. Rene is not home yet, and I'm starting to get pissed at her. She could have called. She can be so thoughtless sometimes.

I turn up the volume on the set. MTV. A music video. I love REM. I'm feeling uncomfortable from sitting so long. I lie on my side, stretching out on the couch. Maybe I'll just go to sleep. My lids start to droop.

The video on TV changes, and so does the volume level. It amplifies all on its own. There is a voice in the room. Low. Raspy. Just enough rasp that it brings my senses alive. *Alan.* I jerk up, pushing the hair from my face. Fuck, that's all I need tonight. How do you get over a guy when he's everywhere? I can't make it through a single day without seeing his face, hearing his voice somewhere.

I fight not to focus on the video and find myself doing exactly that. Why does he have to look so good? He's singing a new song. He must be recording again. I haven't heard it before. I hate it. It sounds angry. It's angry, mean Alan. God, even angry, mean Alan is beautiful.

I take a large swallow of my wine. Why can't I just forget Alan? I recall his burning, black stare and the intensity in the air just from being in a room with him. The way he looks in the morning, drowsy from sleep. The expression in his eyes after we have sex. How it feels to have those callused fingers brushing my skin with velvet care. *The taste of him. The touch of him. The smell…*

Crap. I grab the remote and click off the TV. Everything inside me is suddenly running loose and frantic. I go from nearly emotionally together to splintered with just one look at Alan.

I climb from the couch and wander into the kitchen. Dammit, Rene, why did you have to disappear on me tonight?

I check the clock. It's only eight-thirty. What am I going to do for the rest of the night? I'm wide awake.

Maybe I should just go to the city with my new friend Teri.

I start to compile a list of things to do that would be smarter than going clubbing with Teri. I go to my bedroom and open my closet. I start rummaging through my clothes. I don't know what to wear to a club in San Francisco. Two months and I haven't been to the city. Even Rene hasn't done the SF club scene.

I pull on a pair of jeans. I grab a black silk shirt with a halter tie and my sneakers. I plop down on my bed to put on my Chucks. I go to the bathroom and do my hair and makeup in record time. I tuck my license, my fake ID, the keys, a credit card, and some cash into my pocket. On my way to the front door, I debate whether or not to leave Rene a note.

Nope, forget her. She ditched me again.

~~~

I lean against the concrete wall outside the club, my hands shoved deep into my denim jacket. God, why is it always so cold in San Francisco at night regardless of the time of year? I stare at the line of bodies in front of me. The line waiting to get into the club is really long. We'll never get in.

"I'm glad you decided to come, Chrissie," Teri says. She shakes her head. She does an angry exhale of breath. "I don't know what happened to the rest of my friends. I so didn't want to stay in the dorms tonight. I'm really glad
~~~

you decided to do this."

I smile at Teri. "Me too."

It's the truth, I'm sort of glad I decided to join her. When I got to her dorm room at Sterns Hall, Teri was the only one there. It made me feel a little sad for her and happy I decided to go out tonight. Even though going out was all about Alan and not wanting to be alone thinking of him, and not at all about her.

I stare at the line. This looks like it's going to be a bust tonight. We haven't moved in half an hour, and the upstairs bar is packed. Still, it's better than sitting home alone.

I bounce against the wall. Finally. We get to move an inch.

"Where are you from?" Teri asks.

"Santa Barbara."

Her eyes widen, excited. "I'm from Ojai. We're practically neighbors. Maybe when we drive home we can share rides."

I smile. "Maybe."

Jeez, I hope the entire night isn't going to be boring small talk like this. No wonder her friends ditched her.

"Chrissie!"

I push off the wall and look down the street to see where my name is being called from. My eyes widen in surprise. *Neil.* I never expected to see him here and…*crap*…I never expected to see him looking so hot. He's just wearing jeans, flip-flops and a black t-shirt, but I don't know what it is; there's something different in how he looks tonight.

I'm unsure what he wants me to do, so I wave.

Neil shakes his head, as if exasperated, and waves me to come to him. When I don't immediately move out of line, his look of exasperation intensifies.

I tap Teri on the arm. "Come on."

"What?"

"There's a friend of mine at the front of the line. I think he's going to help us crash the club."

"Really?" she says, ridiculously excited and hopeful. "God, usually I wait in this line until after midnight. It's always so crowded here. Do you want me to wait here in case he can't get us in? I'd hate to lose our place in line."

"Come on," I say. "If he can't get us in, we'll go someplace else."

Teri gives me a slightly extreme look. "I don't want to go someplace else. There is a band performing here tonight I really want to see. And everyone is here."

I refrain from visibly rolling my eyes. "Then we'll get back in line if he can't help us." I tap the girl in line in front of me and ask if she'll hold our place.

I step out of line with Teri reluctantly following me. We're almost to Neil when Teri grabs my arm, stopping me. I turn to look at her.

"You know the super-hot janitor?" she asks, amazed and definitely too loudly. "He never talks to anyone. How do you know him?"

I stare. This is definitely intense and definitely weird. "His name is Neil Stanton. He's from my hometown."

Neil stomps out his cigarette. I can tell by his expression he heard Teri's booming *super-hot janitor* comment. He looks as if he wishes he hadn't called me out of line.

He stares down at me. "What are you doing waiting in line? Did you leave your pretty-girl magic at home?"

I give him a face, tilting my head. "Ha. Ha. Ha. Hello to you too, Neil." I nod toward Teri. "This is my girlfriend, Teri. Teri, this is Neil."

Teri blushes. She gives him a dewy-eyed look. *Oh my…* The girl looks overwhelmed and it's just Neil Stanton.

"Hello, Neil," she gushes.

Neil does a slight nod in her direction with his chin. I frown at him. Jeez, that was rude.

"What are you doing down here?" I ask.

Neil shrugs. "Just hanging out. I'm going to play a few songs next set with the band. Keeps my edge up."

My eyes round. So he's still working on his music. I don't know why, but that surprises me. I kind of thought it was bullshit, the way he talked about why he's living in Berkeley now. I guess I was wrong.

"Well, maybe I'll get to hear you if I can get inside tonight," I tease.

He doesn't take the hint. He looks like he's debating with himself about something. I stare at him.

Neil lets loose a sigh. "Come on. I've got to get back inside anyway." He crosses the sidewalk toward the entrance and nods at the bouncer. "Hey, Vince, this is Chrissie. She's with me."

It doesn't escape my notice that he doesn't mention Teri to the bouncer. We get our hands stamped and are waved through without paying cover, or even having our fake IDs checked.

I follow behind Neil on the stairs to the upstairs bar.

"Got a little pull here, huh?" I ask.

He stops, turns, and looks at me. "I play here sometimes. That's all."

Upstairs is a packed, smoky cave of brick and glass, high ceiling with open beams, and wall-to-wall college students. The crowd is so thick, I can't even see the band, but I can hear them. They're a thundering loud rock band.

"So what now?" Teri shouts over the noise.

I shrug. "I guess we find someplace to sit."

"The band has a table up by the stage," Neil says. "You can hang out there if you want, Chrissie."

I look at Teri. Her expression says she's more than eager to accept Neil's offer. We follow behind him as he cuts his way through the bar. She tugs on my jacket.

"Are you dating him?" she whispers.

My eyes widen. "Neil? No. I just know him from home."

"He's really cute. Do you…I mean, would it be OK…what I want to know is, if he tries to hit on me are you cool with that? Can I give him my number? You won't be pissed, right?"

She can hardly string a sentence together and is more rambling than usual. *Over Neil!*

"Sure. No problem," I repeat, but for some reason this entire exchange is irritating as hell. "We're just friends."

Teri's eyes are sparkly, really excited. "Good. He's freaking hot."

I turn back around and Neil is nowhere to be seen. Crap, I've lost him in the crowd. I start to cut my way through the bodies toward the stage. At the edge of the dance floor, I search the room. I find him standing beside a table.

I skirt along the edge of the dance floor until I reach him. I lean close to say into his ear, "Thanks a lot for just leaving me back there."

I make a face at him.

He ignores it. Abruptly, he says, "I've got to cut out."

I watch Neil walk away, wondering what's up with him. He's more weird than usual tonight. I pull off my jacket and hang it on the back of the chair.

I'm surprised when a waitress descends on our table after a short wait. "Hi, sweeties, what will you have?" she asks.

Teri looks at me eagerly. "What do you think, Chrissie? Pitcher of beer or margaritas?"

"I'll have a sparkling water with lime," I say, fishing for my cash from my back pocket.

The waitress waves me off. "Neil sent me over. The drinks are on him."

Teri's smile shifts in a flash to beaming. I guess she thinks this generosity means it's going to go well for her tonight with Neil.

I shove my money back into my pocket. It was nice of Neil to send a waitress to our table and offer to pick up the tab.

"I'll have a rum and coke," Teri says enthusiastically.

After dropping two napkins on our table, the waitress quickly moves on.

"You don't drink?" Teri asks.

I crinkle my nose. "Not that much. And I'm the one driving tonight."

Teri nods, as if she's only just remembering that I drove us here. "That was nice of Neil to buy us drinks."

She says it as if it means something significant for her. She's a sweet girl, cute, a little obvious in her guy craziness, but I don't think Teri has a chance with Neil. I don't see him with a bubbly, cute kind of girl. But what do I know? Maybe Teri is exactly Neil's type.

"He's a nice guy," I say, a touch surprised by my recent change of opinion of him. I never thought I would ever be friends with Neil Stanton. Are we friends? Strange. I don't know what we are.

As we wait for our drinks, Teri launches into a strategy conversation about how she should go about *making it happen* with Neil. Jeez, this girl has got it bad for him. The way she talks about him is very intense, and a little creepy. I wonder if Teri is still a virgin. Maybe that's why she's so over-the-top in the *wanting to pursue a guy* thing. I was sort of like this when I first met Alan. Unsure and obsessed and stumbling over every other phrase.

I shake my head. Stop it, Chrissie. Don't circle every thought back to Alan. Everything should not be a one-way trip to *Alan-ville*. Let it go already. It's over. Done. Past.

Shortly after our drinks arrive, there's a break in the music, and then I see Neil on stage, readying to play. Once Teri sees him, she swivels around in her chair, eyes fixed on him like a hawk, and I'm immediately forgotten.

I half expected him to look over at me, smile or do something, but he doesn't. He's tunnel-focused on his discussion with the bass player.

I study him. He looks good on stage. There is something very different about Neil, but I can't put my finger on what it is. It's more than how good-looking he is. He has a casualness mixed with sort of a shyness that pulls you in.

I wonder what he sounds like when he sings. Neil is like a still-water pond. No highs, no lows, just always rolling with the flow. His speaking voice is serene, pleasantly calm. I like his voice. It's sexy in its mildly husky quietness, its lack of forcefulness in delivery.

A flush rises to my cheeks. *Sexy? Did I just call Neil Stanton sexy?* I shake my head and swallow down a gulp of my sparkling water.

The rest of the band comes running back on stage and, without fanfare or even an introduction, Neil begins to play. The entire chemistry of the room changes. An intense assault of music, and then there's his voice. Raw. Raspy. Perfectly modulated. Perfect pitch. Velvety in an emotion-jarring blend of angst and sorrow, running with music that is a mixture of grunge and pure rock.

I'm pulled in before the first bridge and Neil never once looks out at the audience. He's in his own zone beneath his unruly waves of chestnut hair. I kind of assumed he was just another hopeful, wannabe rocker with a band destined to go nowhere. But no. He howls on the guitar. His voice is seductive and unique. He's an artist, and by the end of his set he's blown me away.

Who would have thought Neil Stanton would be incredible on stage?

When his set is done, Neil doesn't say anything to the crowd, he just unplugs and leaves. A few minutes later, he lumbers out of the back, his guitar case in hand. He runs a hand through his damp hair, brushing the shoulder-length waves back off his face. Sweat glistens on his tan forearms and makes his black t-shirt cling to his chest. For a guy who just put on a killer set, he doesn't look amped. He's just calm, quiet Neil.

He stops at our table, but doesn't sit down. Teri's eyes are huge as she stares up at him.

"You were awesome, Neil," she exclaims. She's gushing again.

Neil gives her a polite smile and gestures toward my glass. "What is that, Chrissie?" he asks.

"Just water." He takes my glass and downs half of what's in it. My eyes widen as my head tilts to the side. "Thank you for asking, Neil. Or do you just make it a habit of drinking other people's drinks?"

He gives me a strange look, part exasperated, part amused, and part something I can't identify. "We've kissed, Chrissie. Drinking from your glass isn't more intimate than that."

My entire face reddens. I don't know which disturbs me more. That Neil remembers our kiss at Peppers, that he mentioned it, or that Teri is now pissed at me.

Neil stares down at me. "You did drive here, didn't you?"

My eyes round. "Yep."

"Then let's get out of here."

"You don't want to hang out for a while?" I ask,

confused by his manner.

He smiles. "No. I'd rather be someplace quiet with you."

What the heck is happening here? Neil is a tough guy to read. He's definitely unpredictable at times, but this…?

I stare at him. "Are we going to your place or mine?" I ask flippantly.

"We can figure that out on the drive," he says, and before I know what he's doing, he's leaning into me, putting a full-mouth kiss on my lips. My body freezes, startled, and I'm a touch breathless when he pulls back.

More flustered than I care to be, I turn to Teri. "You want to cut out?"

Oh my—the look she gives me is not at all good. If stares were knives, I'd be bleeding now.

"Fine," she says, short, clipped, and decidedly not bubbly.

Neil finishes my drink. When I stand, he takes my hand and starts to guide me through the club in that *this girl's with me* proprietary way. I peek over my shoulder. Teri is following behind. Scowling at my back.

I lean into Neil. "What is happening here?"

"I'll explain later," he replies in a hushed voice. "I did you a favor in Santa Barbara. I did you another one tonight getting you into the club. I figure you owe me one. Be a really, really cool girl and just follow my lead."

I scrunch my nose at his embarrassing habit of quoting me back to me—*really, really cool…God, that was lame of me*—but I nod.

"Thanks," he says.

A few minutes later we're in front of the club. He stares down the street. "Which way is the car?" he asks.

I tug on his hand. "This way."

We're almost to the corner when someone calls Teri's name. She turns and waves, looking instantly awash with relief. There is a large group of girls across the street, calling out her name and gesturing for her. I wonder if those are the same friends who ditched her earlier tonight.

"Hey, my friends are here. I'm going to cut out. See you in class next week, Chrissie," she says quickly.

"Thanks for inviting me out tonight. It was fun."

She gives me a hard stare, doesn't reply, and is across the street in a flash.

Alone with Neil, I continue onward toward my car. "Since I'm pretty sure you've cost me the first friend I've made this semester, do you want to explain to me what is going on?"

Neil releases my hand and fishes in his pocket for his cigarettes.

"You should thank me," he says in irritation. "You don't want that girl as your friend. There is something seriously wrong with her."

My eyes widen. "Oh really? How would you know?"

Neil shakes his head in aggravation. "Because Teri is a fucking stalker. Her circle of friends isn't much better. They're in my face all day while I work. They don't take no for an answer. I'm getting really sick of the co-ed play with the janitor bullshit."

Really? He's upset because a whole bunch of girls thinks he's hot and wants to date him? I erupt into laughter.

"Poor Neil. It's rough being the super-hot janitor."

I'm laughing so hard tears are streaming down my face.

Neil stops. "No, it's not rough. It's a pain in the ass. They fuck with me so much it's going to cost me my job. Teri got me written up the second week of classes. Always hanging around. Trying to chat me up. One of the professors noticed it and informed my supervisor. I can't lose my job, Chrissie. I don't want to get into it, but it would seriously fuck up my life to lose my job."

The fierceness of his voice sobers me instantly. I stop laughing. My laughter-flushed cheeks suddenly feel unpleasant. He's very serious and very intense right now. "I'm sorry," I whisper. "Losing your job, that's not funny. You're right."

He sighs. "Thank you."

"So what was all that 'someplace quiet, kiss me' stuff back at the club?"

Neil rakes a hand through his hair. "I figured if they thought I had a girlfriend, Teri and her clique might let up a little. It's worth a shot. Talking to them doesn't work. Ignoring them doesn't work. Maybe if they think I'm unavailable they'll go away finally."

Suspicion leaps through my veins, followed by anger. "Is that why you've been nice to me? Making sure we ran into each other here. Popping up out of nowhere. You want them to think I'm your girlfriend so they back off?"

His expression tells me he knows how lame that sounds. "Not entirely. I like hanging out with you. You're different from most girls. No drama. No bullshit. I figure if it also helps get rid of Teri, what's the harm?"

My eyes widen in surprise. I'm a tad less angry with him. I fish in my pocket for my keys. I stop at my car and unlock the doors.

"A Volvo?" Neil teases.

Jeez, why does everyone say that? "Rene and I drove it across the country. My dad wanted us in something safe."

He shrugs. "It's a nice one. Top of the line. 760. Turbo. Leather. Fully loaded. Even if it is a Volvo."

I roll my eyes. What is it with guys knowing everything about cars, even Volvos?

"Where am I dropping you?" I ask.

"Just drop me at your place. I can walk from there."

OK, so why doesn't he want me to take him home? I sink down into the driver's seat, close the door, and buckle my seat belt. Neil settles in the front beside me.

I'm about to put the key in the ignition.

"I want you to know, I'm not using you," he says, quiet and sincere.

My lids go wide. "Did I say something?"

His green eyes fix intently on my face. "Just so we're clear. I hang out with you because you're OK. I wouldn't if I didn't think that you were an OK girl."

I turn the key and put the car in gear. "Wow. I'm OK. It's exactly what us girls hope to be."

He gives me a stare, shakes his head, rolls down the window and lights a cigarette in my car without asking. I should probably say something, but I don't. Rene smokes in it too when she borrows it. She doesn't think I know. And it is definitely not as bad as knowing she's had sex in both the Volvo and my dad's car.

Neil sits beside me, quietly smoking, staring out at the city lights as we cross the Bay Bridge. Jeez, he's a frustrating guy and really hard to read. He's full of coded messages, 24/7. That last one says friends; don't expect more. I wonder what Neil has going on in the girl department. I can understand him not being interested in Teri and her mob. Even working as a music department janitor, he's so out of their league.

Some guys have it. Some guys don't. Neil Stanton was born a babe magnet.

We're almost back to Berkeley when I smile and say, "Just so you know, Neil, I'm not using you either. I'm letting you ride in the Volvo because I think *you're* OK."

CHAPTER THREE

The practice room door opens and in pops Neil's face.

"Do you mind if I crash in here and eat my lunch?"

I look up from my book. "Why do you ask? You always ask and I always say yes. Knock yourself out, Neil. The floor is all yours."

He crosses the room and settles on the ground with his legs stretched out crossed in front of him, and his back against the wall. He sets his bag beside him and pulls out a sandwich.

"What are you reading?" He starts unwrapping his sandwich.

I don't look up. "History of the 60s. I have a final tomorrow."

Neil laughs. "Considering who your dad is you probably don't have to read that. I bet you know more about the 60s than the professor. Why bother?"

I smile and don't answer. *I bother because I'm nearly failing this class.*

I try to return my focus to my book. He takes from his bag a container of orange juice and starts to shake it. I don't know why, but it's impossible to study whenever Neil is here. I slap the textbook shut and shove it back into my bag.

He pulls off the top of the juice and takes a long swallow. "How many instruments do you play?"

"Six."

"Do you play the violin?"

"Yep." *What's with the twenty questions today?* Neil hardly ever asks me anything about myself.

He reaches into his bag, removes some chips, and rips them open. "I'm working on some new material. I've been laying down the tracks for a demo. Some of the music tracks I'm recording, I thought I might want to put strings on one if you're up for that."

That he asks me surprises me. He's never even heard me play. He doesn't even know if I'm good.

"Sure. Why not. Just let me know when and where."

He lifts his keys from his belt and gives them a shake. "Keys to everything. It's an after-hours thing. Way after-hours. The rooms here don't usually clear out until nearly midnight."

"Aren't you afraid you're going to get caught?"

He shakes his head. "I know my way around this campus better than you do."

I roll my eyes.

He laughs. Then he gives a quizzical stare. "Why are you at Berkeley? Why study music? Why don't you try to get something going for yourself? Record."

I shrug. *I did record once. With Alan.* I push that thought from my mind and say, "I'm thinking I might want to teach music. My dad has a foundation for children in South Central LA. I'll probably work there once I graduate. I figured I should know what I'm doing before I try to teach children."

"Might. Probably. Doesn't sound to me like you know what you want to do or why you're here." He takes a bite of his sandwich, then says, "I spent one summer at your dad's foundation. Scholarship. I was twelve. It was a fucking unbelievable summer program. Never met Jack, though. Some of the other kids did. Not me." He shakes his head. "Rich people. Only rich people get overpriced educations so they can take a job that doesn't pay anything."

I make a face at him. "Teaching is an important profession."

"Teaching for free is a hobby." He shoves the wrapping from his sandwich into his bag. "Jared asked about us."

I flush. Jared has shown some interest in me, but he hardly speaks to me, for all Neil said a month ago that Jared was working his way up to asking me out. I've been thinking I'd go if Jared asks, but he never asks.

"What did he want to know?" I inquire, trying to sound nonchalant.

"Wanted to know if you were available."

My eyes widen. "What did you tell him?"

Neil shrugs. "I told him the truth. We're just friends."

For some reason I'm a little irritated with that. I change course in the conversation and ask, "How are things with Teri and her Sterns Hall posse?"

He gives me a pained stare, his head tilting just enough to one side to make him look really adorable.

"She's pretty much leaving me alone these days. I

think all of them have gotten the picture I'm not interested. Thank God. It was a real pain in the ass."

I'm curious. I debate with myself whether to ask. Neil makes no sense. "Don't you date?"

"Nope."

I don't know what to make of that. It seems weird. Very strange. He's a really good-looking guy. A little full of himself. Definitely talented. Nice. But he doesn't date. Whenever he tells me that I always find it strange. But what the heck, I don't date either. Maybe we're both weirdoes. Maybe that's why we hang out together.

He crumples the remains of his lunch into a ball and tosses it into the trash can across the room. He springs to his feet. I'm a little disappointed he's leaving.

"That was a fast lunch. Why don't you hang for a while? I've got the room another half hour," I say.

He pulls his cigarettes from his pocket. "Got to be back to work in fifteen minutes. Got just enough time for a fast smoke."

I follow him with my eyes as he moves to the door.

"I'll let you know if I decide I want to put strings on some of the tracks," he announces.

"Aren't you even a little worried about how I play? You've never heard me play."

Neil shakes his head as if annoyed with me. "I've heard you play both the piano and the cello. I've also heard you sing during your labs with Jared. I used to make it a point to sweep outside your practice room. You're good. Real good. I'm not worried you're going to suck with the violin. You seem to do all things musical really well."

That compliment makes me feel more pleased than I ever expected to and, in surprise, I realize it is fast starting to matter what Neil thinks of me.

Instead of thanking him, I accuse, "Stalker."

Neil rolls his eyes and opens the door. "See ya, Chrissie."

~~~

A week later, I slap shut my blue book, check to make sure I've put my name on the front with the correct course code, and then tuck my pencil into my purse. I drop my final exam happily into the basket on Professor Lambert's desk. I've made it through my first set of finals. Done, that was it, and now I won't ever have to think of Lambert again.

I gather up my things, hurry up the aisle, and smile at Jared, who's sitting in the last row of the lecture hall. When I go to push open the door, I realize that somehow he's moved from his seat and is there to open it for me.

I step into the hallway and Jared follows.

He smiles. "Glad that it's over?"

I nod. "Very glad."

He opens the exit door of the building. "Since you're done with your finals, would you like to have coffee with me?"

I freeze in mid-step and turn to see a very nervous Jared waiting expectantly for my answer. I've been mildly obsessing about this since my talk with Neil. I have assumed I would say yes, but now that I'm here, at the point of him asking me out, I find I'm not at all excited about the prospect of a date with Jared the TA.
~~~

I smile. "I can't. Not today. I'm meeting a friend who borrowed my car and then I'm driving home for winter break."

"OK. Maybe some other time?"

"Definitely." I scan the road, looking for Rene and my trusty Volvo. I frown. Why is Jared standing there just staring at me? I look at him, my brows hitching upward. "Do you want my number so you can call me?"

He looks startled that I asked. He holds out the notebook he's carrying and I take the pen he offers and quickly write my number on the cover.

"Thanks. I'll call you next semester." He rakes a hand through his hair.

"Have a good winter break, Jared."

He points to my number on his book. "Next semester."

I smile and watch him leave. I check my watch and then the street again. Darn it, Rene, where the heck are you? Much longer and we'll get trapped in commuter traffic trying to get out of the Bay Area.

"What's got you so fidgety?"

I look over my shoulder to see Neil approaching me as he lights a cigarette. He's changed his bandana. It's blue today. I like the blue better.

"Rene. She took my car to the city. She's supposed to be here waiting for me."

"Probably just driving around the block. Can't block traffic waiting for you, Miss Parker."

I roll my eyes at the lousy Professor Lambert impression. I look down the street again. "I'm just anxious.

I haven't been home since September. When was the last time you were home, Neil?"

"Months. So you're off to Santa Barbara? I wish I'd known. I would have hitched a ride with you. I'm going home, too. I could have saved on the airfare."

I give him a pointed stare. "Who says I'd let you drive to SB with me?"

He gives me a thoughtful once-over. "You'd do it." He stomps out his cigarette. "Well, back to mops and brooms for me. At least until tomorrow. Maybe I'll see you around town, homegirl."

"Bye, Neil."

I watch Neil disappear. I'm kind of surprised he didn't ask me for my number since he's going home for the holidays, too. Maybe he doesn't need to hang out with me in Santa Barbara. He probably has tons of friends from high school. Tons of girls.

I shift my gaze back toward the street. *Finally.* I see Rene speeding down the road in my gray Volvo. She cuts into the curb in front of me. I open my door, drop onto the seat, and slam it shut.

"Where have you been?" I ask.

"Checking my O-Chem grade. They're not posted yet, but I got it from the TA."

I roll my eyes. I don't need to ask how she got the not-yet-posted grade. Rene can flirt anything out of anyone. "So? Was it as bad as you thought it was?"

She pulls aggressively into the thick, moving traffic. "A 74. Not good. Not bad," she says, annoyed.

"They curve it, right?"

Rene nods.

"So what's a 74?" I ask.

"An A."

I shake my head. I snap open the glove compartment, looking for my sunglasses. I find a pretty pink stack of parking tickets. I scrunch them up in my hand. "Rene, what are these?"

She's looking out the open window, gesturing with her arm for the traffic to move out of her way.

"That stupid van," she hisses, merging onto Bancroft Way. "Practically every time I come home he's in our space and I don't know why you won't let me call the management company to get him towed. I'd be doing a public service. Even if he wasn't a rude asshole, always parking in our assigned space. That van is hideous. It deserves to be off the road."

I laugh. The van is pretty awful: a 70s model, old blue extended cargo heap with yellow, green, and orange arrows painted on the sides, and those lovely hanging monkeys on the rear doors holding up their monkey fingers in the "hang loose" sign.

I put on my sunglasses. "Anyone with a van like that can't afford to pay for parking in Berkeley and certainly can't afford to get it out of impound."

Rene shakes her head. "God, you're such a softy. You get more like Jack every day." She stops at the light and exhales a deep breath. "OK, which way. East to the 5 or do you want me to cut through San Jose and 101 it all the way home?"

I slip off my flip-flops and put my feet up on the dash.

"If you expect me to drive any part of this trip take 101."

Rene blasts the horn and fights her way onto the 580. "I'm only driving as far as Salinas."

I nod. "You'll never guess who asked me out."

"Not Jared?" Rene sounds like she wants to gag.

I nod. "Yep, Jared. Wanted to do coffee today."

"Coffee? After three months of worshipping you with his eyes, that's the best he could do?" Rene jeers harshly. "So he finally got around to talking to you. What did you say?"

"I didn't go. Obviously. I'm here in the car with you."

"Did you give him your number?" Rene asks.

"I gave him my number."

Rene makes a face.

I stare at her. "I thought you thought it was unhealthy for me not to date."

"Well, not him. You can do better. Hell, Neil Stanton is a janitor and he would be better than Jared the bore."

"Neil is a not a janitor. He's an artist. He's working on his music. He's pretty incredible. You'd know that if you ever went out with me when I go hear him play."

She gives me the look, the *is something going on I don't know about* look.

I stare back. I fluff up my hair with my fingers. "Besides, I can't date Neil, we're practically going steady."

Rene grimaces. "Crap, you and guys, Chrissie. I hope it's not this weird forever."

~~~

Seven hours later, I pass beneath the high, black metal archway of our neighborhood: Hope Ranch. I drop Rene
~~~

at her mother's house.

Rene's house is completely decorated for the holidays. Jeez, Patty Thompson really went all out this year. It's ablaze with lights from the eight-foot stucco privacy wall surrounding the five acres Patty owns, to the tiled rooftop of that monstrous two-story house she had built that blocks out the view of the ocean for half the street. Even after twenty years, most of the neighbors haven't forgiven Rene's mother for that one.

I pop the trunk as she climbs out. I roll down the car window. "Call me later."

"Let's go to the beach tomorrow and just veg," she suggests. "Those finals really kicked my ass."

"Sounds good."

She nods, lugging her bag toward the front door. I hate that she's leaving the day after Christmas to visit her dad in Georgetown. It's going to suck being in Santa Barbara without Rene.

I put the car in gear, drive out of the Thompsons' driveway and then do a quick turn into my own driveway. I park my car behind Jack's.

I sit in the driver's seat for a moment, just staring at the house—a single-story, Spanish style, white stucco and red tile roof structure. It's good I can stare at the house and not feel all messy inside.

When I was younger I used to have mini panic attacks every time I came home, which was awful, because I really wanted to be home. There was a lot within those walls I didn't know how to deal with. My mom died of cancer in that house. My brother of a drug overdose in his bedroom.

It was a lot to work through.

Not even a hint of the emotional chaos comes. It feels good, really good to be able to just sit here, stare at my house, and not become an emotional mess.

Maybe that's the only reason Alan entered my life. Maybe that's why we crossed paths and then spun away from each other. We weren't meant to be forever. We were meant to cross paths to deal with our shit, and then move on. Alan had some intense shit to deal with last spring. I think he definitely worked through a lot of his shit being with me.

His life seems together. Good now. It's nice to think I'm a part of what got him there. It's nice to think our loving each other mattered in some private, significant way.

I pull the keys from the ignition and grab my purse. My dad's house is the only one on the street without Christmas decorations. Not even freaking lights. I bet Jack didn't even get a tree. Jack doesn't buy in to the commercialism of Christmas. It doesn't matter; we always spend Christmas Eve over at the Thompsons', and Patty Thompson is the queen of commercial Christmas.

I lug my duffel into the house, drop it on the tile entry hall, and kick off my flip-flops to rest with the pile of shoes by the front door. The house smells good. Maria is cooking. I follow the smell into the kitchen. I find her at the center island, surrounded by silver mixing bowls, busily making tamales. No traditional turkey dinner here. Jack likes Mexican food out on the back patio on the holidays.

Her round, matronly face brightens when she sees me. "Chica. You're home. ¿Cómo está mi niña?"

I smile. The way she says that makes it sound like I've been gone forever instead of three months.

"I'm doing great, Maria. How are you?"

"I'm good, chica. Señor Jack is good. He's going to be so happy you're home. Now give me a hug. I've missed my girl."

She steps out from around the marble countertop and holds her arms wide so I can hug her without getting dirty from the food all over her hands. She surprises me by placing a light kiss on my cheek. She's never done that before. Kissed my cheek.

She steps back. "Now go say hello to Señor Jack. Then come back. We have a lot of cooking to do."

I beat back a smile. She may be the housekeeper, but she rules me when I'm home and Maria is definitely making a mountain of tamales. I wonder if Jack has invited people for Christmas this year. This is way too much food for just the three of us.

"Are we having guests for the holidays?" I ask.

Maria shakes her head. "No. It's for Mrs. Thompson's party. It's a potluck this year so Señor Jack wants us to bring tamales, rice, and beans."

I start to laugh. That one should go over real well with Patty Thompson. Maria frowns at me, confused by my laughter, and I bite my lips to stop it.

"Do you know where my dad is?"

Maria rolls her eyes. "Silly question, chica. He's out back, sitting."

I go to the refrigerator, grab a Diet Coke, and then head for the French patio doors in the kitchen. The entire back wall of our house is nothing but glass so Jack can see the Pacific Ocean from every room.

All the lawn lights in the backyard are ablaze. It looks so stunning at night, with the walkways lit up and the view of the ocean directly beyond.

I don't see Jack. I step out onto the patio. I make my way around the pool, then head across the lawn toward the beach. I stop at the top step of the wooden stairs built into the cliffs, and look down at the shoreline.

I spot Jack about ten yards down the sand, sitting in the darkness, just staring at the ocean. We're so alike. Golden blond hair. Bright blue eyes. We're both just kind of loners. Jeez, as far as I know, my dad hasn't even dated since my mom died. I'm sure he has something going on, somewhere, but I don't know anything about Jack's love life. It would be too creepy to ask him and he never talks about his personal affairs. He's a really good dad that way.

Jack is not at all like Rene's dad. Mr. Thompson paraded an endless string of young women after his divorce from Rene's mother, right up until three months before he knocked up his junior law associate and decided to get married again. Those years of her dad being an *insensitive-jerk man-whore* still have Rene a little messed in the head.

Mr. Thompson is such an asshole. Jack was never like that.

I settle in the lounge chair someone dragged from the patio to the edge of the cliffs. Something in how my dad is sitting in the moonlight makes me not want to disturb him. Even the way we sit in the sand and stare at the ocean is the same. I used to think we had nothing in common, that we were not alike in any way, except by a strange quirk of genetics that made us look exactly the same. But we are so alike. It's strange how I didn't see that until this year.

I lean my head back against the cushion. I close my eyes. I am my father's daughter. And that's OK.

CHAPTER FOUR

I relax on a backyard lounge chair, staring out at the ocean. Christmas morning in Santa Barbara is sunny and seventy-four degrees. Jack and I had a quiet breakfast on the patio. The gift exchange lasted about twenty minutes. Since 9 a.m. the phone has been ringing nonstop for Jack with wishes for a Merry Christmas. I've only had one call. Rene.

A part of me, pathetic and definitely unrealistic, sort of thought Alan might call me today. Our time together was short. But it was significant for us both. I wonder where Alan is. I wonder if I haunt his thoughts, too.

My gaze shifts to the stairs over the cliffs leading to the beach. I haven't walked that stretch of beach since the one time I walked it with Alan last spring.

I take a sip of my coffee. He's probably having Christmas morning with Nia in New York. It's probably snowing outside and they're cuddled up in that big mahogany bed, with a fire roaring and the candles lit, and Alan being Alan in bed.

My eyes narrow and fix on a pelican skimming the water. Maybe Alan is stuck on the road somewhere. He's been on an aggressive worldwide tour since last May, and it's possible he's not even with Nia. No, Chrissie, no. Be happy for him. That's the voice of spite in your head.

"What kind of evil thoughts are you thinking, Chrissie? You used to have the same expression when you were little."

I lift my chin to find Jack standing beside my chair. "No evil thoughts. Just daydreaming."

Shaking his head, Jack sinks into the chaise beside me. "Nope, not buying it."

I make a face at him.

He reaches out and takes my hand in his.

"Was Christmas too boring for you this year, just being you and me?"

I smile. "No way. It was great after the craziness of finals."

"First semester at Cal go well?"

I shrug. "I survived. I'm pretty sure all Cs."

"Well, Cs get degrees. Who cares what the grade is? It's all about what you learn. The experience. The experience is as important as the education. Are you seeing anyone?"

That question makes me tense. This overly inquisitive dad kind of thing still feels weird to me.

"Not really. I've sort of a guy I hang out with, but it's not a dating thing. I don't really know how to describe it. But I did get asked out by one of the graduate teaching assistants."

Jack looks at me. "What does the sort of a guy do?"

I blush. *Sort of a guy*. Jeez, I phrase things so lamely at times. "He's sort of a janitor in the music department."

Jack laughs and closes his eyes. His entire face is alive with humor. "Date the janitor, Chrissie. I bet he's the guy who's interesting."

I crinkle my nose. "He's interesting. He's from here. He's from Santa Barbara. I met him when I was in high school. So it's not as bad as it sounds."

Jack opens his eyes and turns his head to look at me. There's a smile in his deep blue gaze. "I didn't think it sounded bad with him being a janitor. If he's got his head on straight, well, that's all that matters."

"He's a pretty OK guy."

Jack smiles. "Good. We've decided. Date the janitor."

I laugh and a sound makes me look over my shoulder. Maria is walking across the grass toward me. What is she carrying? A florist box? Jeez, who would send Jack flowers?

Much to my surprise, she sets the box in my lap. "This came for you, chica."

Stunned, I stare at the box. I've never gotten flowers before. This has got to be a mistake. The box is so perfect I don't want to open it. The ribbon alone is expensive: wide, silk, sparkly, and violet, tied into an elegant, elaborate bow.

I search beneath the ribbon for a card. I frown and look up at Maria. "There is no card. Did you drop it?"

Maria shakes her head.

"Are you sure they're for me?"

Maria nods.

Jack laughs. "I think they're from the janitor. He probably makes more money than the graduate TA and those look pricey." His eyes sharpen on me. "Is there something about your janitor you're not telling me?"

I blush. "Neil would not send me flowers. Neil is more

the minimart day-old burrito and coffee shop kind of guy."

Jack laughs again. "An interesting choice, Chrissie. Bring him around the house. I think I want to meet this guy."

I frown at Jack, shake my head, and open the box.

Jeez! I stare in disbelief. Long-stem magnificent roses, and more than a dozen. I'm not sure how many there are beneath the beautiful violet tissue. At least a dozen red surrounded by…I start to count…three, maybe four, dozen white roses. I rummage beneath the paper. No card in the box either.

I lean in to smell them. "I can't imagine who would send me these. I don't know anyone who can afford to buy me these."

The words clog in my throat before I'm done speaking. *Except Alan.* Did Alan just send me flowers for Christmas?

It's been eight months without a call, a letter, or anything. He married Nia, and from all accounts in the tabloids they sound like a perfect couple. No, it's too crazy of a thought. After all this time even Alan isn't weird enough to send me roses on Christmas Day without including a note.

"They're beautiful, whoever sent them." I take another sniff and hold them out toward Maria. "Can you put them in some water, please? Two vases. The red in one. The white in another."

Maria shakes her head. "One vase."

She says it as an imperative, as if I were doing something terribly wrong, wanting to separate my roses.

My eyes widen and I shift my gaze to Jack. He makes a face as if to say he doesn't get Maria's reaction either.

"Fine. One vase," I agree.

Maria smiles. "The note is the roses."

I stare at the flowers. The note is the roses? What the heck does that mean?

"Is it in Spanish? Can you read it for me?"

I make a playful pout, Jack laughs, and Maria rebukes me with her eyes. Those giant, dark eyes flash at me. Maybe I insulted her with the Spanish joke. My cheeks warm and my contrite face this time is sincere.

"I'm sorry I was rude. How is the note in the flowers?"

Maria turns the box and points. "The red roses are the man. He's passionate. He burns for you. The white roses are you, chica. Purity of love. Innocence. Beauty. The man in the center burns for you and wants to be surrounded by you, purity of love."

My entire body burns red. Jeez, how could Maria say that in front of my father? And how the heck did she get that all from a box of roses?

"Definitely put them in separate vases," Jack orders, breaking the heavy silence.

He laughs as Maria walks away, shaking her head.

Jack's eyes fix on me. "I definitely want to meet your janitor now."

The color on my face darkens. "They're not from Neil."

"Whatever you say, baby girl. I still want to meet him."

I pick up the ribbon from my lap and finger the pretty violet bow. The flowers couldn't possibly be from Neil. He wouldn't even think of doing something like this, and he definitely can't afford it. Logic says Alan, but my broken heart tells me that's not possible. But why do I feel suddenly alive and as if I've just been touched by him? Why am I suddenly burning in my own skin?

~~~

I pull over in the drop-off loop at the Santa Barbara Airport. Even though it is the day after Christmas, a busy travel day, there are only a handful of travelers in the departure area.

Rene springs from the car. I'm really going to miss her. The first five days of break have flown by and we had a good time together, visiting our local haunts and getting into what I consider only low-key trouble.

I join Rene at the trunk of the car and help her pull out her suitcases. I grab the handle of one of the cases and we roll toward the ticket counter. "I'm really going to miss you."

"Me too, Chrissie. Three weeks in Georgetown with Dad. Total nightmare. Be happy you don't have to split yourself between your split parents' homes."

I give her a fierce hug.

She steps back and taps on my chest. "Be good to you."

I nod obediently. "Call me when you get to your dad's."

She rushes off to the security area. Once through, she looks back and waves. "You stay sweet," she yells, oblivious to the travelers around her.

I smile and wave back. "You stay cute."
~~~

I climb back into the car and pull away from the curb. I suddenly feel anxious. I haven't a single plan for the next three weeks. *Not good, Chrissie. Not good at all.*

Instead of driving directly home, I take the long loop through the city. I head toward State Street, through downtown. It's my favorite drive. The road is narrow with a slight decline, so you can see the beach and pier as you cut through the heart of the city. It's always crowded with people, and traffic is slow because there's a stop light every block. Gives me enough time to people watch, look at the white buildings, the patio eateries, the pretty walkways with the small fountains and wood benches, the historic structures.

Fifteen minutes later, I'm at the waterfront and doing the last couple of miles back to Hope Ranch. I pull into our driveway and sigh when I check the dashboard clock. That killed all of thirty minutes. It sucks when you don't have anything to do.

Inside the house, I find Maria in the family room watching her favorite Spanish soap opera and folding laundry. I sink down on the couch beside her and put my head in her lap. For some reason I want to cuddle up next to Maria like I did as a little girl and have her rub my forehead. I've got all kinds of junk going on inside me and I'm not exactly positive it's just about Rene ditching me for the next three weeks.

I've been in a strange mood since the roses arrived. I can't describe it, and I can't shake it.

Maria puts her gentle fingers in my hair. "Why is my girl so sad?"

I shrug. "Not sad. Restless, I think."

"Do you miss your young man?"

I flush. I stare up at her. "I don't have a young man."

"You do in here." She taps my heart. "Do you love him?"

I look away. No one ever asked me *that* question. Oh, there were questions, lots of questions, last spring after my fling with Alan, but no one, not even Jack, ever asked me if I loved him.

"It doesn't matter how I feel," I whisper, feeling tears suddenly threaten.

Maria smiles sadly. "It's the only thing that does matter in life, chica."

In silence we watch Maria's soap opera and it's just gotten steamy when the phone rings. Spanish soap operas are very nasty things, and Maria is pissed that the phone is interrupting a very scandalous part. The irritation on her face makes me laugh.

I push up from the sofa. "I'll get it, Maria. But you have to explain what happens when I come back."

I jog into the kitchen so I don't disturb her, and grab the receiver off the wall. "Taco Bell. May I take your order, please?"

I hear a pleasant, familiar male laugh. "You've been in SB too long, homegirl."

I smile. "Hey, Neil, Merry Christmas one day late."

"What are you doing?"

I sink on a stool by the center island. "Watching Spanish soap operas and folding laundry." He laughs again and it's obvious he think I'm joking. I frown. "How did you get my number in SB? I never gave it to you and it's unlisted."

"I've had it since we met at Peppers. I got it from Josh. It's the number Rene gave him." Neil starts to laugh. "You should have been there the one time Josh called Rene and your old man answered. Your dad is a trip. Really gave Josh a full dose of shit."

I roll my eyes. Rene giving out my dad's phone number to guys she meets in bars. Good one, Rene!

"So what are you doing?" I ask.

"The family thing. But I think if I don't get out of here soon my head is going to explode," Neil says in aggravation.

I do hear a lot of background sound and people. "Big family?"

"Big enough. Three sisters and twenty cousins. All here. So noisy I can't think. What are you really doing?"

I laugh. "Watching Spanish soap operas and folding laundry."

Silence. I stare at the phone.

"So do you want to go kick around or something?" Neil says finally, after a long while. "Just hang out? Do some of those SB things? I just really need to get away from the family thing for a while."

I make a face at the receiver. Hang out? SB things? Is Neil Stanton finally asking me out on a date? I can't really tell for sure. Or is this just more of our buddy stuff from Berkeley?

I shrug and wonder why it even matters. It's not like I've anything else do to. "OK. I'm up for kicking around.

What time are you picking me up?"

"Picking you up?" Neil repeats. More silence. "I don't have a car here. I flew down. You're going to have to pick me up, Chrissie."

"Ah, so what you really want is transportation," I tease.

"If that's what you think, don't bother," Neil replies, a harsh edge to his voice. "You're a very difficult girl to be friends with. Do you know that?"

Coldness crawls across the surface of my face, and then heats rapidly. Jeez, why so touchy? I exhale a breath I didn't realize I was holding. "Where do you live?"

A long pause. "The lower eastside, one block over from Milpas Street."

I frown. Neil says that like I should know where it is. "How do I get there?"

"My house or Milpas Street?"

I scrunch up my nose. "Both."

"What kind of homegirl are you? Go south on the 101 and there's Milpas Street. You want to go left, not right toward the beach. Left toward the eastside."

Well, that sounds simple enough. I grab a pen and a piece of paper. "What's the address?" I write it down and repeat it to Neil since I've never heard of the street before. "Is that right?"

"Perfect. Now, when you get here, just pull into the driveway and honk the horn. That's what Josh does. It makes everything easier."

I don't like the sound of that. "What? You embarrassed to have your family meet me?"

"No," he replies with irritation. "I don't want to be trapped here for another hour while everyone insists on meeting you."

I laugh. "It can't be that bad."

"I don't bring girls home, OK? Like seriously. You'll be the first one."

I frown. That's odd. Neil is a really good-looking guy. He must have had tons of girlfriends in high school.

"Didn't your parents ever want to meet your girlfriends?"

A loud exhale of breath. "Yes. And I should point out, you're not my girlfriend." Another long pause. "Fine. Walk to the door. Find out for yourself. When can you get here?"

"When do you want me?" I blush. That didn't come out right.

"About eight hours ago," he says with humorous desperation.

I smile. "Give me thirty minutes."

"You may be saving my life, Chrissie."

I hang up the phone. OK, a date that is not a date, hanging out and doing something Neil calls SB things. What do I wear? I pull a pair of jeans and a black tank top from my drawers, and grab from the closet my Converse and a pink sweater to tie around my waist. It's warm now, but the weather could change in an hour and I don't know where we're going.

After I dress, I go to the bathroom, brush my teeth, and put on a touch of mascara and some lip gloss. I brush out my hair, puff it with my fingers, and give it a light spray.

In the driveway, I find my car blocked in by Jack's. I

go back into the house and down the hallway to my dad's bedroom. Jack is on the bed, reading.

"Can I borrow your car, Daddy? I'm blocked in and I don't want to play musical vehicles."

He looks up over the top of his book. "Where are you going?"

I have to fight not to make an *are you kidding* face at him. In high school Jack never questioned where I went, but that was pre-Alan. Crud, I'm nineteen, I go to Berkeley, and I'm getting the parental treatment over an afternoon in SB with Neil Stanton. If it wasn't so weird it would make me laugh.

I sink on the bed. "Just out to kick around and do some SB things with a friend."

"Male or female?"

I roll my eyes. "Male."

"Janitor or TA?"

This time I do make a face at him. Jack is just teasing me. "Janitor, if you must know. May I take your car? Where are the keys?"

His eyes return to his book. "In the kitchen. You know where. Don't be late."

~~~

I go south on the 101 searching for Milpas Street. I can do this. I stop at the streetlights for the downtown freeway cross-through traffic. I wonder if I missed the off-ramp and I'm not familiar with south of the lights on the 101. It's like a demarcation line. I never drive past the lights on 101.

The light turns green and I continue frantically reading
~~~

the signs. So there *is* a Milpas Street. I pull off onto the ramp and make the left turn toward the eastside.

Jeez, I've never been on this street before. I didn't even know there were buildings with bars on the windows in Santa Barbara. What kind of neighborhood does Neil come from? I tighten my fingers around the steering wheel. I should have played musical cars and taken mine. The Volvo would have definitely looked less out of place than my dad's shiny new black Porsche.

I stop at a light and read the street sign. I haven't a clue where I am. Two blocks down I find my turn and make a right. One block over from Milpas Street was what Neil said. I look at the address I scribbled down. Two-twelve, two-twelve, where is two-twelve? Why is nothing in Santa Barbara logically laid out?

There! No wonder I missed it. The house is set back from the street, with a long driveway and a smaller structure before it. Well, this isn't awful. It's charming. It makes me curious about Neil's family.

Neil's parents' house is a lively blue California bungalow with white shutters and a pretty front porch, crowded with plants and rattan patio furnishings. It's an old house, but then most houses in the downtown area are old, and it is small. Neil said he has three sisters. How do they all fit in there?

I pull into the driveway, lift my hand to honk the horn, and stop myself. Nope, I want to go inside. I want to meet Neil's family.

Neil is, if nothing else, an enigma. As friendly as he is, he is never personal. He never talks about his family, his days with Josh and the band, his music, or even casually about his love life. If I take Neil at only what he shares, I would have to believe that this superhot guy doesn't date. Why is Neil so private about everything?

I climb from the car and I can hear the sound of lots of people from the backyard. I walk up the four concrete steps onto the porch, pull back the black iron security screen door, and knock beneath the wreath of eucalyptus on the heavy oak door.

I take a last, anxious glance over my shoulder at Jack's car, having second thoughts about this. It didn't occur to me until I knocked that Neil might get pissed about this. He doesn't introduce girls to his family and he didn't want me to come in. I'm sort of invading his personal space. Personal space is definitely an important boundary to Neil, and I don't know how he's going to feel about this.

The door is jerked wide. Too late.

"May I help you?"

The man standing before me is tall, tan, and very fit for what looks like a man in his fifties. His expression is warm and strangely intimidating simultaneously. Sandy brown hair, big green eyes, baggy board shorts beneath a t-shirt: Neil's dad.

"Do you need help?" he says, this time louder.

I blush. Crap, I didn't answer him the first time. I just stood there studying him. Neil's dad looks over the top of me and notices the Porsche parked in his driveway. A curious stare fixes on me and the color on my face deepens.

"I'm here to pick up Neil," I mutter and then kick myself mentally because that was lame. I smile. "I'm

Chrissie."

Now his expression is one of surprise. "It's a pleasure to meet you, Chrissie." His gaze shifts to the car again. "Would you like to come in?"

Another tall male, clearly a Stanton by the looks of him, and by his age probably one of the twenty cousins, is in the doorway now with his arm around Mr. Stanton's shoulders. "Is that your car?" he asks.

I nod.

"This year's model. A Carrera. Right?"

I shrug. "I don't know. It's my dad's. I drive a Volvo."

Mr. Stanton laughs. "It's good that your dad has his priorities straight. I see too many pretty young things like you wrapping cars like that around poles these days." He makes a slight gesture with his head. "Come on in. I think Neil is in the back with the rest of his cousins. I'm Robert Stanton. You may call me Robert. Or Mr. Stanton. Or if you haven't guessed yet, Officer Stanton—"

"Or Officer Robert," the guy at his side interrupts with a grin.

Mr. Stanton frowns. "Come on in, Chrissie. The rest of them are not as obnoxious as Taylor here."

I laugh. Mr. Stanton is intimidating, must be that cop thing, but he's friendly enough, and I can see where Neil gets his dry humor from.

The door is closed behind me, and the living room seems to shrink around me and the very tall men. It takes only a half dozen steps to get across the room to the patio doors.

My eyes widen as I step out onto the simple brick

patio. Jeez, Neil wasn't kidding. His family is enormous. The yard is a pretty nice size for a city lot, but it seems to strain from the sheer number of them. And crud, this is a family barbecue I've crashed and I don't even see Neil here.

I'm quickly surrounded by four men that I can tell are Mr. Stanton's brothers; the same coloring, approximately the same age, and the same smile.

Mr. Stanton places an arm lightly around my shoulders. "Everyone, this is Chrissie. She's here for Neil." That elicits an interesting assortment of reactions. I flush. Mr. Stanton smiles down at me. "I'm going to do this once."

"And there'll be a quiz before you're allowed to leave here," jokes Taylor, and everyone laughs.

"This is my wife, Michelle," Robert announces proudly. "She's modern. She likes to be called Michelle."

The woman in the chair in front of me stands up and offers her hand. Her smile is quick and pretty, and she is tall, blond, and curvaceous. It's clear that the Stantons adore each other.

"It's a pleasure to meet you, Chrissie."

"It's a pleasure to meet you, Mrs. Stanton."

She shakes her head, smiling. "I'm Michelle. Always Michelle. Mrs. Stanton is my mother-in-law."

I laugh and Robert takes me by the hand and introduces me to the rest of them. I can't keep up with the names, and there's an undercurrent of affection in the fast flowing words around me, the quick exchange of quips and comments tossed around the yard by the Stantons like a rapidly kicked hacky sack.

Neil's sisters are young, the oldest only in tenth grade, and they're pretty, long limbed, and green-eyed like their brother. I can't help but smile at everyone's boundless enthusiasm at meeting me. Neil's family is delightful. Why wouldn't he bring his girlfriends here?

I'm directed by Mr. Stanton to sit in a chair beside Michelle.

"What would you like to drink? Diet or regular?" Taylor asks.

"Diet Coke if you have it."

Mr. Stanton settles in the chair on the other side of me. "Where are you from, Chrissie?"

"I'm a local. Born and raised here."

"So what high school did you go to?" Michelle asks.

I take the plastic cup from Taylor. "Saint Catherine's Academy."

One of the cousins laughs. "Boarding school, huh? Which were you? Troublemaker or divorced parents?" she asks, eyes bright with curiosity.

"She's with Neil. Troublemaker," another of the cousins jokes.

They all laugh.

My entire face burns.

Michelle rolls her eyes. "Don't take them seriously, Chrissie. The Stantons have a weird sense of humor, Mia and all present company included."

They all laugh again.

"So what does your father do?" Neil's Uncle Richard asks.

I tense. I hate that question for a variety of reasons. There are some people who adore Jack for his politics and music, some people who hate Jack for his politics and music, but I've yet to find any people who have no opinion on Jack, and the Stanton brothers are law enforcement. Neil comes from a family of cops. I never expected that one.

I take a sip of my Diet Coke. "My dad is sort of retired."

"Nice work if you can get it," Neil's Uncle Greg laughs.

"Really nice work," a loud female voice exclaims. I turn to see a woman carrying a grocery bag crossing the yard toward me. "You should see the car parked in our driveway." She drops the bag by the picnic table and extends a hand to me. "I'm Carol." She points to Neil's Uncle Richard. "I'm married to that one and you must be the reason Neil is pissed."

"So where do you go to school now?" Greg Stanton asks. "City College or UCSB?"

"Are you and Neil staying for dinner?" Robert asks.

I struggle to keep up with everyone. "I don't know…"

"I doubt it," Carol says loudly right over top of my sentence.

I look at Greg Stanton. "I go to Cal."

"Smart and beautiful," Richard announces. "Why are you dating a janitor? Hey, Robert, isn't that what Neil is doing these days? Not music. Janitorial profession. You should date this one here."

Uncle Greg squeezes the shoulders of a tall replica

cousin of Neil. "My son Tony. He's a starting fullback at USC."

"Go Bruins!" someone shouts.

"Go Bears," Taylor counters, and gives me a wink.

They all laugh.

I blush.

"What are you studying?" Michelle asks sweetly.

"English and Music. I want to teach."

"Neil, keep this one around. Smart, beautiful, head on straight, and knows where she's going," Robert advises, his voice loud, his face turned toward the patio doors.

I look over my shoulder to see Neil crossing the yard. There is no smile in his eyes. I don't think I've ever seen Neil without a smile in his eyes. Oh crap, he's pissed at me.

Neil doesn't say hi to me. He drops down in front of a cooler and begins to stock it with cans from the bag he carried out from the house. "I warned you," he mutters, shaking his head. He scrunches up the empty bag and looks at me. "I told you to wait in the driveway and honk."

I flush scarlet and shrug. "OK. And you said you'd be here, and you weren't when I arrived, so we're even."

I stand up and fish the keys from my pocket.

"Aren't you staying for dinner?" Michelle asks, sounding disappointed.

"We're not staying," Neil says, dropping a kiss on his mom's head.

"That's a lousy way to say hello to your girlfriend," Richard jokes, tossing a burger on the grill. "You should at least kiss her on the head like you did your mom."

Neil rolls his eyes. "Can we go please, Chrissie?"

Robert rushes across the yard. "It was a pleasure meeting you, Chrissie. Now that you've braved meeting us, don't be a stranger, dear."

I smile and do a quick wave to everyone. I have to walk double time to keep up with Neil. I catch him on the front porch.

"Well, that was rude," I exclaim.

Neil stops on the steps, turns, and exhales a ragged breath. "Sorry. I just don't like people in my shit. I don't bring girls home because I don't want them in my shit."

I frown. "I don't get it. You have a great family. They're nice. They're fun. They're—"

"They're obnoxious. First they grill you about who you are. Then there's the background check. Then the drug test. And then they'll throw condoms at you. One of them has probably got the plate number of your car written down. You don't know what it's like growing up in a family of cops."

He has to be joking. I laugh. "Not really?"

Neil's eyes widen, but there's a little of the usual sparkle in them. "Really. Ask Tony. He'll tell you."

I make a pouty face. "I'm sorry."

"Can we go?"

I follow Neil to the car. He opens my door and the gesture makes me smile. I lean my arms across the top and stare up at him. "You're twenty-three years old and you have really never brought a girlfriend home?"

"Yep."

I sink into my seat, stare through the windshield, and laugh. Taylor and Tony are watching us from the living room window.

Neil drops down in the passenger seat and frowns. "Why are you laughing?"

I bite my lip and shake my head. "Nothing. I just think funny thoughts sometimes."

I put the key in the ignition and put the car into gear.

"Where are we going?" I ask.

"Anywhere. I don't care."

I stare at the intersection, trying to remember how to get back to the freeway. "Can you give me some idea of where you want to go?"

He runs a hand through his hair. "Anywhere. Someplace quiet. It's always so loud there."

Red light ahead. I downshift. "OK, how about the pier? Hendry's? The mall? I might even consider a movie."

Neil grimaces. "The pier, Hendry's Beach, and the mall? I thought you were up for just chilling and doing some SB things."

"Those are Santa Barbara things."

He turns the air conditioner off and rolls down his window. "Why do you have the air conditioner on? We have ocean air."

"Boy. I guess I just do everything the wrong way. There's the freeway. Right or left?"

"Let's just do something outdoorsy. Let's go up to Devil's Playground and just sit."

Devil's Playground? I haven't a clue what he's talking about. "OK, so do I go right or left on the freeway?"

Neil frowns. "Don't you know where Devil's Playground is?" He points to the onramp. "There. We go north. Chrissie, there's no right or left on the freeway. We go north."

I roll my eyes. "Be nice. Beggars wanting transportation should not be overly rude."

Neil gives me a smile. "I'm sorry. Give me five minutes to decompress. I'll be chill again, I promise."

"Whoever said you were chill before?"

He laughs, reluctantly at first, and then with a more natural flow. I smile. I've amused him. Good. He was entirely too grim and keyed-up before, and I make a mental note to myself to figure out what's up with that. The dots don't connect: the Neil I know; his family; his reaction to his family. Nope, the dots don't connect.

"If you want quiet, we should go to my house," I say, shifting gears.

"And if you want to bring your dad's transmission home not stripped, you need to learn how to shift gears," he teases.

Neil points at a sign. "Get off here."

This exit I know. It's one I sometimes take to get home. I slow down for the stopped traffic ahead, concentrating on correcting my downshift.

"Right or left? Since this is State Street, I assume I can say right or left."

"Straight. We're going up 154."

I push down on the brakes too hard and we make an abrupt stop. "Up the mountain?"

Neil frowns. "Of course. Unless you know another way to get to Devil's Playground from here."

I go through the intersection and pull into the parking

lot of a strip mall. My fingers tighten around the steering wheel and I turn to stare at Neil. "I'm all for fun and I'm all for outdoorsy, but I'm not driving up the mountain. That road is dangerous."

He gives me an *are-you-joking* look. I put the car in neutral, set the parking brake in place, and climb from the car.

"What are you doing?" Neil asks through his open window.

I open his door. "You drive."

He holds up his hands in front of him. "Whoa, I'm not driving your dad's car. I can't even afford a windshield wiper if something happens to it."

"Well, we're not going to get there if I drive since I don't do hills well with a stick shift. So unless you want to go to Hendry's, or the pier, or the mall…"

Neil climbs out. "Fine. Maybe you can watch while I shift and learn how to do it so you don't fuck up your dad's car."

I smile. "Maybe."

We sink back into our seats, Neil adjusts his for driving and I lock my seat belt in place. "Just don't hit anything," I admonish, fighting to keep the smile from my face.

Neil gives me a look and I sink my teeth into my lower lip not to laugh. He shifts into gear and we exit the parking lot fast enough to make the tires squeal. A quick right turn and we are on our way up the mountain. I watch without letting him see me as he maneuvers Jack's car through traffic. It's effortless for him, but I've never been a stick shift girl, no matter how much time Jack has spent trying to teach me.

I lean my head back against the rest, close my eyes, and enjoy the feel of the air swirling through my hair. "Can I ask you something, Neil?"

"Sure. Anything."

I open my eyes to look at him. "So why did you call me today? What's up with that? You're a hometown boy. You must have lots of people to hang with. A girlfriend. Why me?"

He frowns at me, sort of startled by the question, and quickly shifts his eyes back to the road. "We're friends. I thought we were friends."

He says it as if he's confused. His answer does nothing to help my confusion over what *this* is. I smile. "Yep, friends. I just wanted to make sure we were both on the same page."

"Trust me, Chrissie. Same page. More than you know. You don't have to worry about anything else."

OK, what's up with that, and what is that I hear in his voice? A part of me feels rejected, a part of me relieved, and a part of me just wants to slap him. God, what a stupid combination of emotions to feel, especially since it's not like I *want* to be more than friends with Neil. Maybe it's just knowing he doesn't want more that makes the female ego react contrarily, even when I don't want Neil to be interested in me.

I peek at Neil out of the corner of my eye. Or maybe it's just because he's so freaking good-looking, even if he's all full of himself in that hot-guy way. Tousled sandy brown hair, bright green eyes, strong features, and perfect white teeth to top off his perfect tan. Nice body, too. Tall, long limbs, lean defined surfer-type muscles. And he's always so attractively understated and just a touch messy in how he dresses. Like the clothes he puts on don't matter, and yet every garment he puts on loves him. He looks good in everything, even that stupid jumpsuit on campus he's forced to wear while working.

That's probably why my female ego felt a little prick after the *you don't have to worry about anything else* comment. I probably wouldn't have had any reaction if he wasn't so damn good-looking.

Near the top of the mountain we exit the highway onto a winding road that heads toward the ocean and begin a series of blind turns down a one-lane road, heavily shaded by trees and cutting through rocks. Some of the giant boulders are covered with vivid green moss. It looks entirely different than the rest of Santa Barbara. Where are we? I've never been here before.

"I love it up here," Neil says, and makes another left onto an even narrower, only gravel-lined road.

We stop. All I see is forest and giant boulders. "Devil's Playground? This is Devil's Playground?" I asked, surprised.

Neil laughs. "I can't believe you've never been up here. What kind of local are you? Josh and I spent half of high school up here. Smoking weed. Writing music. It's my favorite place to get my head clear."

He climbs from the car and quickly comes around to open my door. I stare. "So what do we do here?"

He points at the rocks. "There's a path across the rocks to the cliffs. I guarantee you've never seen a view of Santa Barbara like this."

My eyes grow wide. "You want to hike across rocks to a cliff?"

Neil laughs. "Yep. Something tells me you'll love it, Chrissie."

He takes my hand and guides me to a rock. Effortlessly, he climbs atop. He offers his hand and I take it, but I'm not feeling at all sure about this. He pulls me easily up beside him. Jeez, it didn't look that high, but it feels a lot higher standing on top of it.

"Just do what I do, Chrissie. It's no big deal."

Neil hops to the next rock. I follow. Neil hops. I follow. Jeez, they're getting higher, the ground is farther away, and each hop a little tougher.

I stop. I stare across the gulf beneath me. "I don't think I can make it."

Neil smiles reassuringly. "Sure you can. My sister Kristy can do it. I haven't lost anyone yet."

I take in a deep breath and hop. I smile up at Neil. "You bring your sisters up here?"

"I used to. When I lived at home. Don't see very much of them now that I'm in Berkeley." He hops onto the next rock. He turns to wait expectantly. "I miss them, though. My sisters."

I can see the edge of the mountain.

"Three more rocks and we're there," Neil says with heightened encouragement and enthusiasm.

I start to laugh. He sounds excited, like a little boy, and

all we're doing is jumping rocks to a cliff. He hops. I follow. He hops. I follow. He hops, and then I'm on the rock at the cliff.

Oh my God. I see what all the fuss is about and instantly understand why Neil loves this place. It's like being on the edge of the earth, surrounded by no one, only forest below, then Santa Barbara in such detail I can see the streets, a hundred-mile view of the Pacific Ocean coastline, and each Channel Island so clearly I can see the topography. Home looks entirely different from up here.

Neil sinks down to sit, hugging his knees. "Awesome, isn't it? I can't believe you've never been here."

Smiling, I sink down beside him, sitting cross-legged. "It's incredible. Thank you for bringing me here."

He reclines on an elbow and hip, long limbs relaxed, and the smile on his face is breathtaking. "The best things in Santa Barbara are free. Most people never get that."

I laugh. "Why do they call it Devil's Playground?"

Neil's gorgeous green eyes twinkle. "Because if you miss a rock, you're pretty much screwed, Chrissie. It's a lot farther drop than you think."

I hit him and he rolls away, laughing. I lie back against the rock, arms beneath my head, copying his posture.

"Why did you really quit the band and end up in Berkeley?" I ask.

Neil exhales heavily, exasperated, and then leans back up on his elbow. He studies my face.

"A relationship," he admits haltingly. "I've had one of those on-again off-again things going since I was fifteen. Worst kind of relationship. The kind you can't seem to make work or make end. We were on again, so I left the road for San Francisco and we were off again right after we got there. I'm still getting over it, Chrissie. Shit got crazy this time. It kind of fucked me up for a while."

I smile. It surprises me that he told me this. "I'm sorry. It sucks to care about someone you can't make it work with." I study his face. "Why did you tell me this? It's the first personal thing you've told me."

He brushes the hair back from my face. "I wanted you to know it's not you. That's not why I'm not interested in anything. If I wanted a relationship with a girl, it would be you. You're pretty cool."

I blush, the compliment throwing me completely off balance. *Cool.* I never expected that to be what Neil Stanton thought of me. I always feel terminally uncool. An outsider.

He looks away and settles back against the rock. "I also figured you'd get it. You're still hung up on Alan Manzone. We're both in love with people not good for us. People we can't be with. I think that makes us perfect together. I figure if we hang together, we'll end up really good friends."

CHAPTER FIVE

I wait in the driveway as Neil walks to the car. He sinks into the passenger seat and slams his door shut.

I smile. "Where to?"

"Up the mountain. Everyone is up at Knapp's Castle. We can just go there. Hang out. If you want to."

Everyone? OK, Neil, who is everyone? And what the heck is Knapp's Castle? Never heard of it. I put the car in reverse.

"OK. Sounds fun."

He says nothing. I start driving down the road. Fine. Just sit there silently beside me, Neil. It doesn't bother me any longer.

We've spent every day of the last three weeks together. I've given up making suggestions on how we should kill time. I wonder if that's all Neil is doing being with me; killing time until he returns to Berkeley. It should probably bother me, but it doesn't.

I've really had a good winter break with Neil, and when it started I thought this month would be miserable. A new Chrissie low.

I roll to a stop at an intersection, pleased with how well I'm shifting my dad's car these days. It took an entire afternoon in a parking lot, but Neil finally got me into the swing of things with a stick shift so I wouldn't bring my dad's car home *without its transmission.* Neil is a really patient guy. Even Jack couldn't teach me this.

I merge onto the freeway and Neil is still silent. He seems tense, and a touch preoccupied. He hasn't even looked at me once since we pulled from his folk's driveway. He just sits there, staring out the window.

We roll to a stop at the lights in the downtown stretch of freeway. I glance at him out of the corner of my eyes. All the time we've spent outdoors has darkened his tan to a rich bronze. It makes his bright green eyes just pop from his face. There are more sun streaks in his brown hair, probably because of all the saltwater and surfing. I like that he never pulls the long waves into a ponytail. Some guys are made for long, messy hair. Neil is definitely one of them. Even *that* outfit seems to make him look better. He's wearing a pair of faded shorts, a baggy t-shirt, and flip-flops. He looks hot today, even sitting there all distant and jerk-like.

A honk makes me return my focus to the road. Crap, green light. I wonder how long I sat there checking him out.

I put the car in gear and start driving again. Ten minutes later, I turn onto the highway to the mountain.

"This may surprise you," I say, a touch sarcastically, "but I don't know where Knapp's Castle is. You're going to have to start talking soon if you want us to get there."

Neil rakes his hand through his waves, lets out a poorly concealed long, slow breath, and then turns to look at me.

"Sorry. Just got a lot of shit on my mind," he says.

"Good or bad?"

He shrugs. "Depends on how you look at it."

He pulls out his cigarettes and lights one. He adjusts how he's sitting, as if uncomfortable in his seat, and my eyes follow his hand as he adjusts himself *there*.

I look quickly away.

Neil points. "Turn right, there at Old San Marcos."

I turn onto an unfamiliar road that is extremely intimidating. Narrow, curving, and a sharp uphill incline. I turn out on the shoulder before I enter the one-lane nightmare.

I unbuckle my seat belt. "You drive."

Neil gives me an irritated stare. "You give up too easily. You can do this if you try. It's not that bad."

I climb from my seat and slam the door. "I don't know where we're going and I'm not driving up that."

Neil climbs from the car. He holds my shoulders, shaking his head, his green eyes full of amusement at me. "You could have done it if you'd tried. You're such a scaredy-cat," he says.

I watch him move to the driver's side of the car.

Quickly, I mock, "Did you just call me a scaredy-cat? Scaredy-cat? Such a girlie thing to say for such a manly guy."

I make it a point to laugh obnoxiously loud at him.

He arches a brow. "Fine. Would it have been better if I called you a pussy?"

The blood jolts in my veins. He's pissed, suddenly out of nowhere. I always insult, we always trade barbs. They bounce right off him most of the time. Why did that one piss him off?

I sink onto the passenger seat. Neil is confusing and weird today. He turns the ignition, puts the car in gear, and speeds away from the shoulder with more acceleration than I think is necessary.

After the first three hairpin turns I'm really glad I made him drive. The road is intense and slow going, and I'm definitely not a fan of the blind turns as we move up and up the mountain. But it is pretty up here. Lots of old oak trees and tall, brown grass-covered fields.

I wonder what it would have been like to grow up like Neil. Always having to invent your own ways to have fun, surrounded by a big family, lots of friends, doing nothing at all, and belonging somewhere. Normal, instead of how I was raised. It's probably why he's so comfortable in himself. It's probably why I'm never comfortable in me.

I lean my head back against the seat and close my eyes. *No, Chrissie. No. Don't go back into the lockboxes. Things are better this year.*

After the long drive, the car stops. I open my eyes. There's nothing here. A dirt road blocked by a rusty fire gate. But there are cars parked all over the clearing.

"Knapp's Castle?" I ask.

Neil laughs. "I can't believe you've never been up here. What the hell did you and Rene do for fun in high school? Just clubbing and the beach?"

I ignore that. It's not worth pointing out that I was locked away for eight years in boarding school. It's also not worth pointing out that *clubbing and the beach* are normal things people do in Santa Barbara.

He climbs from the car. "It's a short hike. Not bad. It's worth it when you get there."

A hike? So we're hiking today. He moves on toward the gate without even waiting to see if I follow. He plants his hands on the top rail and effortlessly pulls the rest of his body over.

I stop at the gate. I stare. There is a no trespassing sign.

"Ignore that," Neil says. "Everyone comes here. It's open to the public. I don't know why that sign is there."

I start to work my way through the wide spread bars, but he shakes his head, amused. He makes an aggravated gesture with his hand for me to move closer to him. Without warning, his hands take hold of my sides and he lifts me easily over the bar.

He sets me on my feet. "It's easier my way," he says.

I glare up at him, adjusting my clothes back into place. I'm really regretting the clothes I put on this morning because my shorts suddenly feel too short-short. They rode up for some reason when he lifted me. And I'm definitely not loving this tight tank with bikini top underneath. My boobs also got all out of whack being manhandled over the barrier.

I look up to find Neil watching me, looking annoyed. I stop fiddling with my clothes. He shoves his hands into his pockets and starts walking.

"Come on," he says.

We start walking up the dirt path to whatever is at the end of it.

"There are a lot of cars parked at the gate," I say. "This must be a popular place. Is it always crowded up there?"

"Nope. Never crowded. Hardly anyone ever comes up here." Neil sighs. "As for the cars, I should have told you, but this is sort of a family thing with my cousins. We all take off this weekend. They go back to school. I go back to mops and brooms. We always just get together here at the end of a holiday. Just sort of a family thing we do."

My eyes widen. A family thing with his cousins. It surprises me that he wanted me to tag along with him today. He hasn't let me within ten feet of his family since that day I met them.

"So what is Knapp's Castle?" I ask.

Neil shrugs. "Just some mansion that was built. I don't know when, around the early nineteen hundreds. Then there was a fire, like thirty years later, and ever since it's sat there, in ruins. It's cool, though, trust me."

A burned-out mansion. Interesting.

"Lots of people believe it's haunted," he says, amused. "People get swept away with such bullshit, but we used to come here on Halloween when we were in high school."

"Why haunted?"

"The rumor is some rich guy built it for a woman he loved. She never came to him here. So when it burnt down he left it that way and now he haunts it."

I smile. "I like that story. It's romantic."

Neil's eyes darken. "Only a girl would see that as romantic. Building a house for someone who doesn't want you and then losing everything by fire."

I roll my eyes. "Well, it doesn't sound romantic the

way *you* put it."

Neil frowns. "It's not romantic any way you put it. There is nothing romantic about loving someone who fucks up your life." He says that practically through gritted teeth.

I focus on the path as we continue to walk. I wonder if it's *her,* if she's what has him acting grumpy and weird today. I don't know Neil's ex-girlfriend's name. He's never mentioned it. We don't pry into each other's shit from the past. I stare down at my feet. We both have shit from the past.

I freeze when we get to the top of the hill. It *is* only a burned-out mansion, but it's incredible. The edge of the cliff is covered with old sandstone and wood, arches that were something once, steps, and some walls. Just ruins. Neil was right about that. But through the arches is pouring the sun, and everything has a stunning orange patina.

The sound of lots of people floats downward from somewhere.

Neil gives me a slight smile. "I thought you'd like this, even if all my cousins are here. I should have probably asked if that's OK with you before I brought you here."

"Don't worry about it. I like your cousins."

Casually he drapes an arm around my shoulder. "Come on. There should be food. Music. If we stay after dark there'll be a fire. It's usually pretty chill when we get together up here. I promise. It won't be awful."

I laugh. It almost sounds like Neil is dreading this.

When he reaches the stone steps, his arm moves from my shoulder, and he takes my hand. Carefully this time, he guides me upward with him.

At the top step, I stop. Beyond the pillars are rolling green foothills, the city, the ocean, and the islands. But that's not all I find. The dirty, speckled wood floor is set up for a lazy afternoon in the sun, and practically overfilled by people. It's not just the cousins. It's a couples' thing, and I'm instantly confused why Neil brought me here.

I don't have time to figure out *that one*. Mia Stanton's eyes have locked on me. Her pretty face is awash with excitement. She starts hopping on her feet pointing at her brother Taylor and saying, "Pay up. Pay up. Pay up."

Taylor shakes his head. Mia laughs. She looks at me. "I knew you were the girl Neil doesn't talk about. I knew he would bring you today. I won the bet."

Neil closes his eyes and shakes his head. "Fuck, Mia, can you be less tactful? I really want to know. Does it get worse than this?"

Mia shrugs, unaffected, and laughs again. "I won the bet. You brought a date. I deserve some gloating time."

She focuses her trademark Stanton green eyes on me.

"He never brings anyone. Not since we started doing this in high school. Not one time. Neil is so weird about his girlfriends."

"Why would I bring a date here? You guys are all such jerks," Neil says, but in a good-humored way.

Mia laughs. Unruffled. Her eyes fix on me again. "Are you really Jackson Parker's daughter?"

I smile, but it surprises me that Neil talked about me to his family. "Yep. That's my dad."

Mia's eyes widen, sparkly. "The family practically shit

a brick when they heard that one." Then she teases, "What the hell are you doing with, Neil?"

That earns Mia another aggravated grimace from her cousin. "Is the whole day going to be like this, Mia? Just tell me now so we can leave," Neil says.

"Why don't you go away and get something for Chrissie to drink? You don't have to hover over her like you're protecting her from us." Her gaze shifts back to me. "He thinks we're obnoxious."

"You are obnoxious," Neil corrects. "Do you want something to drink, Chrissie?"

I notice more than a few beer cans and wine coolers around me. "Just a diet soda if you've got one."

I stand with Mia as Neil ambles away. As soon as he's out of earshot, her gaze grows curious, sparkly again. "Did you really have a thing with Alan Manzone?"

I blush. "We dated. Briefly."

She laughs. "Dated, huh? Crap. How can you be so cool about everything?"

I change the subject, remembering something Mia said. "Haven't you ever met any of Neil's girlfriends? He must have had tons of them in high school. You should see how crazy the girls at Cal are over him."

Mia's eyes widen. She shakes her head. "It must be slim pickings at Cal if they're crazy over a guy pushing a broom. Now I know I made the right decision choosing UCLA." She laughs, then blushes. "Sorry. That was kind of a crummy thing to say to you. You're dating Neil."

Her gaze shifts to Neil as if making sure he's safely out of distance not to hear.

"He had a long-time thing all through high school. Never met her. Neil has just always been sort of off from the rest of us. In his music. In his own world. Private about everything. I always just assumed she was part of the music thing. Other than Josh Moss, I never met any of the guys in Neil's band. He didn't bring them around the family either. I figured he just didn't want to get more shit. God, his dad gives him such shit about not going to college and the music thing."

"Mr. Stanton shouldn't give him shit. Neil is an incredible musician."

Mia's smile is beaming. "That's what I think, too." She shakes her head. "But the family. They think he's being irresponsible and fucking around in his life."

Mia takes my hand, pulling us toward the rest of them. "We're going to be great friends. I just know it. Now I've someone to hang with when I'm in Berkeley."

Seven hours later, I'm lounging on a blanket, the party is still raging, and I'm trying to follow Mia's nonstop talking.

Neil sinks behind me. He startles me by pulling me between the V of his legs, easing me back against his chest, and surrounding me with his arms. He's been very boyfriend-like today. Keeping me close to him. Never leaving me for a moment by myself with his cousins. Touching me randomly. Making sure I always have what I need.

Why is he doing this? It feels odd. It's almost like he wants his cousins to think we really are a couple.

A small fire flickers, pops, and dances from a portable

fire pit, and it is dark on the mountain. The laughter, drinking, and music hasn't stopped all day. The cousins definitely like to party. Some of them are drunk. Some of the cousins are a little high.

It surprises me Neil didn't take a hit from the weed being passed around. He seems like a guy who would smoke weed. But no weed. No booze. There is still a lot I don't know about Neil.

I smile at Tony as he crosses the wooden floor, hand outstretched with a joint.

"Come on, Neil. You're more fucking fun when you're high."

"Get that away from me," Neil says, brushing him off.

Tony laughs. "I get it. I get it. Want to keep sharp tonight. I definitely would if I were you."

He leans into Neil. I can hear him say something, but I can't catch the words. Every muscle in Neil's body hardens at once. I'm looking over my shoulder just as Neil gives his cousin a hard shove back.

"You're fucking wasted, Tony. Get out of my face."

Tony laughs and goes back to his girlfriend.

After about five minutes, Neil's face moves until his cheek is warm against my neck, his lips almost touching my ear. "Let's get out of here," he says in a low, angry voice.

I search his face. Shit, what happened here? Neil is keyed-up and fuming.

He doesn't wait for my answer. He pulls his arms and body from me and springs to his feet.

"We're going to head out," he announces to no one in particular.

Mia, sitting on the other side of the blanket, sits up in alarm. "No. Don't go. It's still early."

Neil holds out a hand for me. "We're out of here," Neil snaps in a harsh and angry way.

My eyes widen, trying to figure out what changed everything. His rude manner with Mia makes no sense.

Without saying goodbye to the rest of them, Neil starts pulling me toward the stairs. I send quick waves here and there. Over my shoulder I see Mia hold up her hand, pinky and thumb, wiggling it by her ear. She mouths: *Call me.* I nod. Of all of Neil's cousins, Mia is my favorite. She scribbled her number in black ink on my wrist four hours ago.

He starts tugging me faster along behind him. We're on the path going back to the car. It's dark. I can hardly see where I'm going, and it's really hard to keep up with him.

I shake my hand from his and stop. "Slow down. I can't walk that fast."

Neil turns toward me. "I need to get out of here. Like now, Chrissie. Or I'm going to go back there and punch my cousin."

My eyes widen.

"OK. But I can't walk that fast."

With his hand, he rakes back his hair. "I'm sorry. I'll walk slower."

We walk the rest of the way to the car. Neil unlocks my door, opens it, and then sprints around to the driver's seat. He's practically running for his door when he usually lumbers. I barely have my seat belt latched before he's maneuvering us quickly down the mountain.

I push back in my seat, turning just enough toward him so I can see him. The tic in his cheek is working double time. His jaw is tense. He shifts through the gears aggressively, not smoothly. He's silent. He's pissed off.

When we get to Neil's parents' house, he doesn't park in the driveway. He pulls ahead, under a tree, out of view of the front windows.

He turns off the car. Silence. He takes several hard breaths, in and out, as if he's trying to calm down.

"I fucking hate them sometimes," he says on a ragged exhale of breath. "I'm sorry I did this. I'm sorry I took you there."

My eyes widened. He sounds really upset. "Your cousins are nice. I had a good time."

I watch his expression change several times. Finally, he looks at me.

"Tony said something about you before we left. Did you hear it?" Neil asks.

He looks nervous about this. Worried. Furious.

I shake my head. His expression tells me I don't want to ask what Tony said. Tony was really wasted tonight. I can't imagine what could change Neil from calm, smiling Neil to anxious and enraged Neil.

I take in a breath. "No."

His jaw and mouth tighten and untighten, several times.

"Tony was wasted," I say.

"Tony is an asshole. He thinks he knows things he doesn't. He says things he shouldn't. He's an asshole."

God, he's really angry, and for some reason, really

distraught by a rude comment made by his wasted cousin.

"I had a good time today, Neil. Don't let Tony ruin what was a pretty fine day. He's your cousin. Let it go,"

Neil's eyes shift toward me. He searches my face, and then a ragged exhale of breath pushes its way from his chest into the air. He starts to unbend.

"I had a good time with you," he says. "I always have fun when I'm with you."

"I have fun when I'm with you."

The last of the tension eases from Neil's face. "Who would have thought we'd ever end up friends?" he teases.

I smile. "Definitely weird, but I kind of like it."

He touches my face. He looks surprised by it, too. "So do I, Chrissie."

Then something changes in Neil's eyes. I don't see the movement of his body toward me, me being pulled into him, his face lowering to mine, and his arm lifting so he can bury his fingers in my hair, moving my face with the movement of his kiss.

Whatever I imagined kissing Neil would be like before this night is shattered with the first touch of his lips. This is no feather-light, tentative first kiss. It's hungry and demanding. He plunders my mouth with his, and the taste of him is delicious and new, making me pulse everywhere, in time with each stroke of his tongue.

I melt into him, my too-long-denied senses greedily absorbing the taste, the feel, the heat in him. We're both moaning loudly. We're both fucking each other's mouth. We're both straining and wanting.

My anxious hands roam and touch him everywhere,

learning the feel of him, eager to get closer and closer to him.

The kiss breaks. I'm breathing hard. I'm wet and wanting *there,* for the first time since…I push the thought away.

My gaze fixes on Neil. His hair has tumbled forward, hiding his face, but I can see he's trying to collect himself.

"Oh fuck," he exhales, his fingers tightening around the steering wheel.

I stare at him. My body surprises me by how strongly I want Neil.

Neil looks up, his gaze heated as he meets my stare, the lines of his face tense. "Give me a minute, Chrissie. I can't get out of the car yet."

I lean into him, putting my mouth back on his, and my hand drifts lower. I can feel his erection thick and straining within his shorts. I push into him as much as I can from my seat. My tongue attacks his. My fingers brush him *there.*

He starts kissing me back, matching my fever, and our bodies are both moving urgently as if trying to figure out how to get closer to each other in the car. I'm about to climb over the center console, when Neil grabs my wrist, stopping me.

He pulls free his erection from his shorts. There's a little bit of cum already on it. He rubs it along himself, and then guides my hand to him, showing me how to stroke him. He swells in my fingers, moves my hand faster, then moves his own hand to feel his balls and squeeze before he returns to control my hand running up and down the length of him. Faster. Faster.

My arousal heatedly courses through my body. The feel of getting him off with my touch, feeling him surrender to my fingers, has my body going full throttle. The way he's moaning. His mouth is punishing as he kisses me. Every part of me is desperate to have him in me.

He stretches back in his seat. He's shaking and groaning. He pulls his lips free. Eyes closed and head back, he breathes, "Oh fuck, oh fuck, oh fuck…" and then my fingers are a sticky and warm mess. His shakes quiet into quivers. His ragged breathing takes on a steady rhythm.

I stare at him, the blood pulsing through my body, urgent in my sex, and he's trying to recover from his passion-empty cock.

"Oh fuck," he murmurs again, this time in distress, not pleasure.

He doesn't look at me. He covers his eyes with his forearm. "I'm a fucking asshole, Chrissie. I don't want to fuck up our friendship. Our friendship matters to me. I don't want to ruin it by complicating it."

My scalp prickles as my body goes cold. He sounds angry. I've just given him a hand job. He wanted it. And now he's angry.

He looks at me. "That was a really selfish, prick move to make, but I've had a fucking boner every time I've been around you for the last three weeks."

My eyes widen. He always plays it so cool. Why doesn't he make a move on me?

He reaches past me into the glove compartment and starts searching through my dad's things. He finds a packet of tissues and pulls out a handful, hands some to me, then proceeds to clean himself off before he tucks his dick back in his shorts. He crumples the tissue in his hand as he unbuckles his seat belt.

He closes his eyes and shakes his head. He makes a face. "I can't believe I just came in Jackson Parker's car."

He says it like it's disgusting.

"Are you OK?" he asks.

I nod, fighting to keep my emotion from my face.

"Are you pissed?"

I shake my head, and he climbs from the car as I ease myself over the center console into the driver's seat. He stares down at me from outside the open door.

"I'll call you tomorrow," he says quietly.

I struggle to talk. "Sure, Neil."

"Night, Chrissie."

He shuts the door. I watch him walk to his parents' porch. He pauses there, staring at me. I turn the key in the ignition and accelerate away from the curb.

By the time I reach the house my mind is a torrent of conflicting thoughts and emotions. I'm too wired to go to sleep.

I cut through the front entry hall toward the kitchen. I stare through the wall of glass. Jack is on the patio, sitting on a chaise, still awake, and waiting up for me.

I go out the French doors and settle on a lounger beside him. I hug my knees with my arms.

"Did you have a good time tonight, baby girl?"

I nod. I lay my cheek on my knees so I can meet Jack's gaze. "Daddy, why are guys so complicated?"

Jack laughs. "I don't know that we are. We're pretty much what you see. What we say, what we do, is what you get."

I bite my lower lip. I debate. I feel so lame wanting relationship advice from my dad.

"Neil likes me. Like *into* me, likes me. But he doesn't want to like me and I don't know why. What's wrong with me that a guy wouldn't want to like me, when he already does?"

Jack's blue eyes soften. "There is not a thing wrong with you. If he likes you, it'll happen. You don't need to make it happen. It just will. Maybe he's got some shit to work through. People have shit, Chrissie. It doesn't have anything to do with you."

I hug my legs tighter against me. Last spring Linda Rowan said the very same thing to me. It's strange to hear the exact same words out of Jack today.

I turn to stare out at the ocean. Being with Neil feels so much different than it felt being with Alan. No easier for me. No less confusing. Different. No less weird.

CHAPTER SIX

By four in the afternoon, I'm pissed. Neil said he would call and then didn't. What a jerk. And I'm really annoyed with myself that I've spent an entire day wondering what the heck happened last night.

The more I replay it in my head, the less it makes sense. It was weird. There is no other word for it. But then there's a lot about Neil that is just plain weird. What kind of guy admits to your face he's had a boner over you for three weeks and never tries to make a move on you?

I shake my head, frustrated with my thoughts. It's an unexpectedly emotionally taxing process to try to figure out a guy who doesn't want to have sex with you.

The phone rings. I don't move from my seat on the couch. Maria can answer it. It's probably not even Neil. The phone rings nonstop all day for Jack.

I'm disappointed to realize I'm straining to hear Maria's voice in the kitchen. And I'm also disappointed to realize I'm more than a little anxious wondering if it *is* Neil. Crap, we're not even dating and I'm a fucked-up mess over him.

Finally, Maria exits the kitchen carrying the phone. So Neil did decide to call, after leaving me hanging all day.

I take the phone from her hand. "Hello."

"Hi, Chrissie."

I purposely don't say hi back to Neil. A long pause. I can hear him breathing into the phone. I run my tongue along my dry lips and then pucker them tightly.

I wait.

"I'm sorry about last night," he says quietly, an edge of contrite misery in his voice.

"It's all right. No big deal. Just forget about it."

I shake my head in frustration. Why all the apologies? I don't know why he keeps apologizing or why the apologies make my emotional messy messier.

"It's not all right. I was an asshole. No guy should treat you that way."

I struggle not to respond. God, this is awful. From completely comfortable with Neil to completely *not* comfortable with Neil, and all I did was give him a hand job in the car. My emotions turn; my stomach feels sick.

"I have to go, Neil."

I start to hang up. I hear, "No! No, wait."

I hold the receiver back against my ear.

"Are you still there, Chrissie?"

"I'm here."

Another pause.

"Are we cool, Chrissie? Is everything OK between us?"

"Yep." It's the only word I can work out of my mouth.

More silence. Then he says, "I'll pick you up in about an hour."

That wasn't even a request.

I don't answer him.

"I'll pick you up in an hour," he repeats.

I take in a ragged breath. "OK." I quickly click off the phone.

I toss the phone and then run my fingers through my hair. I rest my forehead in my palms. Why am I letting him pick me up? Talking on the phone with Neil was bad enough. Seeing him is going to be just unbearable.

The doorbell rings exactly one hour later. I sit on the bed and let Maria answer it. I've been dressed for over half an hour, but I'm not going to hurry out there. Neil wanted to pick me up. He can cool his heels with Maria for a while.

I go back into my bathroom and give my hair and makeup one last check. I stare at myself in the mirror. At least I look together on the surface. I'm anything but together internally.

When I went to my bedroom to dress, I started to wonder why Neil wanted to see me. Belatedly, it occurred to me he might want to tell me to my face he doesn't want to be friends with me anymore. It surprised me how much the thought of that hurt me, and has made me more than a little nervous over the possibility that is why he wants to see me today.

Getting dumped when you are not even a guy's girlfriend would be a humiliating thing.

I let fifteen minutes pass. I head for the living room. I stop in the entry hall and stare. Neil is across the room with Jack. They're standing in front of the glass guitar cases, talking quietly. Neil's stance tells me he's engaged in the conversation with my dad. They're probably all consumed in music talk. Musicians are always comfortable talking music together.

My brows hitch upward when I take note of how Neil is dressed. Nice jeans. A V-neck, long-sleeve, gray wool sweater. A white t-shirt peeking from beneath the collar. Not even flip-flops today. Sneakers. I've never seen Neil in anything but his work clothes and casual-messy attire. It's almost like he dressed for a date.

"Why didn't you tell me your janitor was a musician?"

Jack's amused voice pulls me from my thoughts.

I flush. "He's not my janitor."

I regret that comment the second it's out because something flashes in Neil's eyes, too quickly for me to read it, but it makes me feel bad anyway.

I drag my gaze away from Neil by focusing on walking into the sunken living room. I feel Neil's eyes following me as I sit on the arm of the sofa. I let out a nervous breath.

"Are you ready to go?" Neil asks.

I nod.

"Where are you off to tonight?" Jack asks.

God, even this is weird. Until I saw Neil standing with my dad it didn't register in my brain that I haven't had a guy home to meet Jack since I was thirteen.

"Probably just dinner," I hear Neil say from across the room. "I'll have Chrissie home early."

Early? What the does that mean?

"Are you ready to go?"

I look up. Neil has crossed the room to me without me noticing.

"You already asked. I already answered," I say, rolling to my feet.

After Neil says his goodbyes to Jack, we walk in silence out of the house and across the driveway toward his car. I don't know why I'm being so combative and petty. It's just dinner. I'm not exactly sure why I'm going with him. I'm definitely not sure of Neil's motivation in this.

Neil unlocks and opens my car door. He studies me cautiously. "I can't read your mood. Are you pissed off? Are you upset with me? Or do you want to tell me to fuck off and go away?"

I drop into the passenger seat. I peek up at him through my lashes. He looks nervous as hell. That surprises me, and for some reason it makes my mood soften.

"I don't know yet," I say. "This feels odd."

Neil lets out a heavy sigh. "I don't think odd covers it, Chrissie."

He shuts my door. I try to look at him as he moves around the front of the car and then settles in the driver's seat.

"Whose car is this?" I ask.

It's nice. It's a brand-new BMW. It seems like such a non-Neil thing to be driving an expensive car.

He turns on the ignition. "Mia's. She doesn't usually toss me the keys. I told her I fucked up last night. She practically hit me in the face with them when I asked to borrow it tonight."

I exhale a long, ragged breath. "You seem really close to Mia."

Neil nods and flicks on a turn signal. "I am. Mia and I've always gotten along. I don't really fit in with the rest of the cousins."

I nod. I could feel that last night at Knapp's Castle.

He turns onto the freeway heading south. I debate whether to ask him where we're going.

Neil lights a cigarette and takes a long drag.

"Are you hungry?" he asks.

I shrug. "I don't know yet."

Neil exhales. I can feel his eyes on me. "Are you going to stay pissed at me the entire night?"

"It depends on why you're doing this. What this is. If it's going to be awful, we should probably pass on dinner. I probably won't eat."

He searches my face. Then he smiles and laughs. "I don't know if it's going to be awful, Chrissie. I haven't been on a date in a really long time. I could fuck this up too."

Date? I stare at him.

"What do you mean date? Since when are we dating instead of hanging-out buddies?"

He looks at the clock on the dash. His eyes are amused. "Since about twenty minutes ago. Why do you think I borrowed Mia's car to pick you up? I have three sisters. My dad's a cop. I can't date a girl without meeting her father."

I stare out the window. I try to contain my rapidly churning emotions. My anger at his arrogance. My frustration over how emotionally volatile I am tonight with Neil. And the sudden, unexpected flash of relief. He's not dumping me; he's trying to date me.

Neil surprises me a second time by driving out on the pier. My stomach somersaults as he pulls into the valet lane in front of one of my favorite restaurants. Neil hates the pier. He thinks it's touristy. He brought me someplace I would like.

He takes my hand and guides me into the restaurant. We sit upstairs on the outside patio staring at the water, the boats, and the people around us.

Once the waitress has taken our dinner order and left the table, Neil asks, "You're very quiet, Chrissie. What are you thinking?"

I shrug. "I was just thinking that I've never really been on a date before."

Neil smiles and takes a sip of his ice tea. "What do you mean you've never been on a date before? You must have dated a lot in high school."

He's staring at me in a way that tells me he thinks I'm joking.

My cheeks redden. "I've had boyfriends. Well, two. But I haven't been on a real date. You know. Pick me up. Meet my dad. Take me out and then take me home. A date-date."

He studies me quizzically, and then gives me a small smile. "How do you think it's going so far?"

I laugh. "I don't know. I'll let you know when it's over. But it's going OK so far."

We both laugh this time.

We're not talking a lot as we eat our dinner, but I think the laughter made it all less uncomfortable than it was when we first got to the restaurant.

After dinner, we take a walk along the pier. At the end, I lean over the rail, staring at the water. Out of the corner of my eye, I catch a quick peek at Neil. He looks as awkward in this as I feel, and I never expected that from Neil. He's always so calm, so sure of himself. He always has an air of popular-guy superiority about him. It's kind of sweet that Neil feels awkward on a date with me.

Wind and dampness brush my skin. I shiver.

"I should get you home. I promised your dad I'd get you home early."

I nod. It's been a good night. Something in me doesn't want to push the evening further.

I turn from the rail and start to walk. We stop at the valet, and we wait for the car to be brought around.

"Do you still have it?" he asks.

I frown. "Have what?"

"The half dollar?"

Our silly bet. I can tell by the way he's looking at me he doesn't think I kept my half of the dollar. I rummage through my bag, pull out my wallet, unzip the pocket, and hold the half dollar beneath his nose.

"Do you still have yours?" I ask.

He stops and lets go of my hand. He pulls his wallet from his back pocket and fishes it out.

I stare up at him. I would have never bet in a million years Neil had kept his half of the dollar.

"Why'd you keep it?" I ask.

He shrugs. "I don't know. I'm just like that. I keep all sorts of things."

When the car arrives, he opens my door before the valet can come around. He stares down at me. "Why'd you keep yours?"

Those green eyes are fixed on my face.

"I don't know."

It's the truth. I don't know why I kept that silly half dollar, made in a bet, from a guy who wasn't even interested in me.

I watch Neil climb into the car beside me. We drive back to my dad's house in silence, only I like our silence this time. He pulls into my driveway, parks, and turns off the car.

"I had a good time tonight, Chrissie."

"I had a good time, too."

"So do you think you might want to do this again?"

I smile. "It would be all right."

He leans in and gives me a feather-light kiss. He pulls back quickly and climbs from the car.

He opens my door. I climb out. When he closes the passenger door, I lean back against it. I should go into the house.

He runs a hand through his hair. "Good night, Chrissie."

I stare up at him.

Neil steps into me, his hands planted on either side of me, and I'm flattened against the car, and he's kissing me passionately. Across my face. My cheeks. My lips. His lower body pushing into me in time with the thrusts of his tongue. The hungriness of the assault makes my head spin, because I can feel raging desire and need in how he's kissing me. And I can feel it inside me as I match each kiss and thrust.

I lock my mouth to his and the twisting urgency of my

body moves against his fully erect cock. He's grinding into me, as if he can't get close enough. I feel my body building and building. My flesh heats. My heart accelerates.

Neil breaks off. He steps back. We're both breathing raggedly.

"Shit," he says, leaning forward. He looks dizzy, disoriented, aroused.

I stare at him. "Don't leave yet. You can stay for a while, Neil."

His arms are quivering. He's trying to calm himself. "I've got to go, Chrissie. I can't stay here with you. Your dad is in the house."

My eyes widen and my cheeks flush. Neil always plays it so cool, but he's as hot for me as I am for him tonight.

"I want you to stay," I repeat.

I'm shocked by my admission. Neil looks undecided, almost vulnerable as he exhales another long breath and stares at me.

I take his hand and start pulling him with me around the house to the side.

"What are you doing?" he asks.

I peek around into the backyard. Jack isn't on the patio. I tug on Neil again, this time at a running pace, and drag him into the pool house. I lock the door behind me. I lean back against it.

Neil stops in the center of the room, his gaze does a fast float across the fully appointed bedroom, and then he stares at me.

"No one ever comes here," I say.

My voice sounds strange. Excited, and lower than

usual. I can feel everything in my body. The blood pumping through my veins. The pulse in my sex. The rise and fall of my breasts. Even the wayward strands of hair teasing my cheeks as I breathe.

"Are you sure?" Neil asks.

I'm not sure what he's asking me.

"That no one ever comes here? Or that I want to go to bed with you?"

"Both?" he asks.

My lids flutter wide. "I'm sure about both." And I'm surprised how sure I feel about everything this second.

Neil starts to move toward me. My breath catches in my throat. In a moment, he's back on me, pushing me into the wall, his cock rubbing me, eager and demanding. I moan into his mouth, parting my lips so his tongue can invade me. The touch of it against mine brings the urgency singing through my limbs. There is something hard and immediate in Neil's kiss. I've never been kissed like this. Not in this bludgeoning desperation. Not even by Alan in his most passionate moments. Neil is all consuming, in want of flesh and nothing else.

I close my eyes against the disorienting, leveling assault of sensation running through me. His hands close on my wrists and he starts to move us toward the bed. Between kisses and grinds, we shed our clothes, dumping them in a trail on the floor.

I feel his erection searching against me. I open my eyes as he takes us back upon the bed. Between kisses and brushes against my sex, he works at tearing open a small foil package. For some reason, seeing that heightens my arousal; the thought that he brought it, and perhaps planned through dinner how he would get to use it with me.

He eases enough away from me to slip it on, and then he's in me, hard and searching at first thrust.

"Oh fuck, Chrissie," he groans into my mouth, pumping, filling, searching in my flesh.

The thrusts are good. I'm almost there. My hips start to move in their own rhythm, using his body to hit all my spots of inner arousal. I'm moving in my own dance. He's moving in his own dance. Looking for release. Separate, bodies joined, and yet it is strangely right that it should be this way with Neil. The command of our bodies for our own pleasure. Me taking him as I want. Him taking me as he wants. No emotional convolution. Just sex and want and need.

My head starts to sway on the pillow. My breathing matches his own ragged inhales. I'm nearly there, painfully wet and tight around him.

"Oh fuck," he growls. And then there's the sensation of Neil, overwhelmed by his climax, the intensity of his release, flooding my veins as he pours into me.

It takes me a moment to realize his body has stopped. My body still wants. It continues to seek even after that last *oh fuck*.

I open my eyes. He's still in me. On me. Balancing on his arms, breathing heavily, his features awash with almost relieved contentment.

I'm pulsing and close to the edge. He looks down at me and pulls out, easing off me. He takes the condom off, tossing it carelessly on the floor.

I stare. I pant in. I pant out. I brush the passion-damp hair from my face. I fight to ignore my still overly alert body.

I don't know what is on my face, but Neil's expression changes, a slight reddening moving across his features. He lays his head back on the pillow. He covers his face with his forearm. He looks really cute flushed with embarrassment. It makes it almost OK that I didn't get to come.

"I'm sorry. I've been thinking about this for three fucking months. I'm not usually so…" His voice trails off.

"Quick," I whisper, biting my lower lip.

He laughs. He lifts his arm from his face. His eyes are smiling when he looks at me. "It's been a long time. I haven't been with anyone since my ex."

I curl into his sex-damp flesh, laying my cheek on his chest. His skin feels good against my flesh. I rub my nose against him. I even like the smell of Neil.

"How long ago was that?" I ask.

"Six months."

My eyes widen. "You haven't had sex in six months?"

"Nope." He holds up his hand. "All these calluses are not only from playing guitar."

I flush and he laughs. He curls into me and starts to kiss me. "If you give him a blow job, I bet he'll come back really quickly also."

I crinkle my nose.

"No?" he whispers between kisses.

"No."

He starts moving down my body, his kisses roaming from my neck to breast to the full underside. My alert sex ticks upward in need. With his hands, he eases me onto my back, his lips roaming lower. To my navel. My pelvis. My mound. He kisses the inside of my thigh. My fingers curl around the sheets.

And very slowly, teasingly, he brings his tongue to that spot on my clit that makes me crazy. Then it is nothing but breaths and fingers, tongue and tantalizing strokes. My back arches. My body tightens in record speed. Damn, he's good, really good at this. For some reason, I didn't expect Neil to be.

My legs start to quake and I grind into his mouth. He doesn't pull back. He doesn't toy with me, bringing me to the edge and then taking it from me. He takes me directly there. I come hard and fast against his face.

I'm panting heavily, trying to calm my scattered senses. He kisses his way back up my body, claiming my mouth with his, his tongue swirling in me so I can taste myself on him. His finger lightly glides over my still pulsing sex.

"It sucks that you're so quick," he whispers into my ear.

My lids fly wide. It's then I see the grin on his face.

"It's been a long time," I say sheepishly.

Neil reclines on his side, looking down at me. "Since Alan Manzone?"

I don't correct him. For some reason I don't want to tell Neil about my one-night stand in August. And in truth, I don't even count that, because that sexual experience didn't even touch me.

He lies back on the bed, pulling me against his body.

"What's with that scar on your wrist?" he asks quietly. "And the ones on your stomach and leg."

My gut churns. I should have prepared for that question. I didn't. I didn't expect Neil to notice the burns on my body, or to ask. And I'm really not prepared for it, emotionally. I've only talked about this to three people: Linda Rowan, Jack, and Alan.

I take in a ragged breath. "I used to have problems, Neil. I used to be a pretty fucked-up girl."

Neil's eyes widen, answering in sympathetic heaviness. He turns on his side, moving me into the spoon of his body.

Into my hair, he says, "I used to have problems, too. I was pretty fucked up."

I debate with myself if I should ask what kind of problems. "Are you OK now?" I ask instead.

His chest shimmies with a hard exhale of breath. "I don't know, Chrissie. I'm trying to be."

I kiss his arm. "I don't know if I am either."

We lie together, sexually spent, emotionally messy, and in this companionable sadness hovering in the room, we feel good. Really, really good together.

~~~

A sound wakes me and I turn over in bed to find Neil grabbing his clothes from the ground and quickly dressing.

"Where are you going?" I ask.

Neil looks at me, continuing to dress. "Fuck, Chrissie. We fell asleep. I should have been out of here hours ago."
~~~

I rub the sleep from my eyes. I stare at the window, the light pouring in through the shutters.

He stops at the bed. "What do you think is the best way out of here? I don't want to run into Jack. Do you think he's still asleep?"

My eyes widen. His nervousness and anxiousness makes me start to laugh.

"I wouldn't count on Jack being asleep. He wakes at dawn every day. He's probably sitting by the pool already."

Neil's expression is priceless. I bury my face into the pillow, laughing until I'm nearly in tears.

I peek up at him.

"Fuck." Neil runs an anxious hand through his hair. His eyes sharpen. "What do you think he's going to do?"

I shrug. "I don't know." And I really don't. I didn't think that far ahead last night.

I sit up, tugging the blanket with me to cover my naked breasts.

"Just leave," I suggest.

Neil's eyes widen. "Like that. Just walk out there."

He's staring at me like I'm out of my mind.

His gaze softens. "I had a good night with you, Chrissie."

My flesh warms. "I had a good night with you."

He goes to the bathroom, comes back with a handful of tissues, and starts picking up the condoms off the floor. I lie back against the pillow on my side watching him.

"When do you go back to Berkeley?" I ask.

"This afternoon."

He balls up the condoms and tissues, almost tosses

them in the trash, then thinks better of it and shoves them into his pocket.

I stare up at him. "I leave today, too. Don't fly. Drive back with me."

It looks like he's debating with himself and a whisper of hurt moves through me since I can't figure out why he would debate that. Free transportation over a high-priced plane ticket? A no-brainer. Does he want space from me?

He sinks down beside me on the bed and kisses me.

"What time are you leaving?" he asks.

"I want to get on the road around eleven."

Neil nods. "I can get Mia's car back to her and packed up by then."

I smile. I watch him move toward the door. He puts his hand on the knob. He shakes his head. He leans his brow against the wood. He says, "Oh fuck," and then he passes through the door.

CHAPTER SEVEN

Spring Semester, 1990

As I pull off the freeway to start making my way across Berkeley to home, I peek at Neil out of the corner of my eye. He's quiet, troubled, and a little grim. He's been that way since he climbed into the car in Santa Barbara.

I flip on my turn signal. "I'm not letting you out of this car until you tell me what happened."

Neil closes his eyes, doing a slight shudder, and then looks at me. "It was the worst fucking ten minutes of my life. I'm not repeating it by telling you about it."

I pucker my lips to keep from laughing. Jack only talked with him for ten minutes. It's rattled Neil in a big way. Ten minutes. How bad could it be?

"Jack seemed fine when he talked to me," I say, turning down my street toward the condo.

Neil stares. "You're his daughter. I'm some asshole he caught sneaking out of his house."

"You're not an asshole."

"I feel like an asshole. He made me feel like an asshole."

I laugh this time. I can't stop it. Neil is a deeply sensitive guy. He's also very respectful in a sweet, quiet way. Very different than how I expected him to be under his layer of hot-guy arrogance.

I turn into my driveway.

Neil rakes a hand through his hair. "Do you really want to know what Jack said?"

I nod eagerly. I stop without going all the way to the carport. I turn in my seat to face him.

Neil takes a deep breath. "I only remember the highlights clearly. The rest is a blur. He told me *If you hurt her, I will kick the shit out of you.* And then he said nothing for like five minutes. He just sat there staring at me, and I don't know what it is, but it's fucking unnerving to have Jackson Parker stare at you. Then he said *Don't be a fuck-up. No one can make you a fuck-up unless you're willing.* And then he walked away."

My eyes fly wide as laughter explodes from my chest, throaty and deep. I curl my fingers around the steering wheel and lay my head against it, trying to contain my humor.

"It's not funny," Neil says, but he's laughing a little himself. He smiles. "What did he say to you?"

I glance up at Neil. "Six words. I wrote them in my journal and counted them afterward. *I hope you used a condom.*"

Neil grimaces.

"Your dad is an interesting man."

I nod. "Jack is interesting."

I start inching forward toward my parking space in the lot and turn the corner at the carport row. I slam on my brakes.

"Crap," I exclaim, my fingers tightening on the wheel. "I've been on the road for seven hours. I'm tired. I don't need this. Can't he pick on someone else for a change?"

Neil looks at me. "What?"

I shake my head. "That freaking van. Every time I turn around it's in my spot." I push back in my seat. "Rene wants me to have management tow it. I'm towing it tonight."

Neil points. "Don't go all princess-ape-shit. There's a spot over there. Just park over in guest parking."

I clench my teeth. "I don't want to park in guest parking. I want to park in my spot." But I park in the vacant space anyway.

I stop the car. I turn to look at Neil. He's smiling. He lightly brushes my lips. "You're so cute when you're snooty and angry," he whispers, leaning in to kiss me again.

I melt into his mouth and, between the light play, I say, "And you're so cute when you're freaked out over Jack."

He stops kissing. He stills. "That was a mood kill."

He opens his door and gets out of the car. I climb from the driver's seat. I stare at him across the roof of the car as he stretches. I don't know what I'm supposed to do now. Neil didn't have me drop him at his place; he just had me come straight home.

"Do you want to come up for a while?" I ask.

He reaches in for his bag. "No. I should probably head out. I've got some stuff I need to do before work tomorrow."

Stuff? I frown. *Why so secretive here, Neil?* I watch him

lift my duffel from the trunk and set it out on the ground. He goes in for his guitar case.

"I'll call you." He drops a light, quick goodbye kiss on my lips.

I stare up at him. "You can't call me. You don't have a phone. You don't know my number."

He grins. "I can get your number from Jared."

I flush.

"He was really stoked that you gave it to him, Chrissie."

Shit, I'd forgotten I'd given my number to Jared. I wonder if it matters to Neil. I'm not sure what *this* is to him or to me. It's too new.

I stand beside my car, watching Neil walk away. At the exit of the parking lot, he turns back and waves, and I smile.

I grab my duffel and make my way to my top floor condo via the elevator. I hate coming home to an empty house. Rene won't be home from her dad's for two more days. Neither of us has classes starting until Wednesday. I had planned to stay in Santa Barbara up until Rene returned, but Neil leaving for Berkeley today made me change my plans on the fly. I sort of thought Neil would spend the night.

Not one of your smarter calls, Chrissie. Stuff. He has stuff to do. Crap, why doesn't anything with Neil go as I expect it to?

I drop my keys onto the table by the door, switch on the lights, kick off my flip-flops, and toss my duffel across the room toward the bedroom door. I click on the TV just so there's sound in the room and wander into the kitchen.

I grab the phone, the refrigerator magnet with the telephone number for the management company, and sink down in a chair at the kitchen table. Snooty-princess is about to go ape-shit and get that ugly van towed.

I punch in the numbers. Ring. Ring. Ring. Recorded voice. No one will be in the office until Monday. Great.

I put the magnet back on the fridge, grab a Diet Coke, and stand at the kitchen patio doors, staring out at the view. I love how the city looks at night, all the sparkling lights from San Francisco bouncing off the water of the Bay. *A million dollar view* or so Mr. Thompson said in that *you girls don't live in the real world* way he has from time to time. He may be a reformed man-whore now that he's remarried, but he's still a jerk.

Poor, Rene. Poor, poor Rene. She's going to be a grumpy, emotional mess when she returns after three weeks with her dad.

The phone rings. I reach for the cordless on the counter. "Hello."

"I asked you to call me when you reached Berkeley. I don't like it when you drive up the coast alone," Jack says.

I roll my eyes. I'm about to say *I didn't drive alone*, but I don't know if that one will go over well today.

"I made it back to school in seven hours. A little bit of traffic. Not bad." I take a sip of my soda. "I'm sorry I forgot to call. It's just, there's this stupid van parked in my carport. He does it all the time. I was going to call the management company to have him towed, only no one is there. Do you think if I call the police they'll tow him?"

"Don't get him towed," Jack says. "Try leaving a note on his windshield. Most people will do the right thing if you just ask them to. Have you tried leaving a note?"

"Nope."

"Leave a note. If that doesn't work, then have him towed if he does it again."

"OK, Daddy. I had a good Christmas with you. I'm glad I came home."

"Come home more often. I like having you here. Just…" There's a long pause. "…no overnight guests. Show respect when you're home. Leave that behind in Berkeley."

My entire face covers with a burn. It's the closest thing to a reprimand Jack has ever said to me.

"Don't get me wrong," Jack continues. "I like Neil. He seems like a good guy. Head on straight. Let me talk at him. Never talked back. Respectful. But there's nothing wrong with taking your time in getting to know someone, Chrissie. That's all I wanted to say."

Oh, thank God. My heart is racing. I'm relieved when I hear the click. I sink down onto my chair and take several rapid breaths to compose myself.

I stare at the kitchen, trying to remember what I came in here for. Find a pen, Chrissie. Write a note to the incredibly rude van owner. I reach into the drawer behind me and pull out a notepad.

I stare at the paper, tapping my pen. I know what Rene would write. *Stay out of my spot, mother fucker, or you're toast.* But that's not me. I tap the pen again. I write: *Please don't make me have you towed. Park somewhere else. Thank you.*

I toss the notepad back into the drawer and grab the tape. I'm going to tape it on his windshield so it doesn't blow away.

At the front door, I pull on my UGG boots, grab the house key, and make my way to the elevator and then the ground floor. Outside, I run a hand up and down my arm. It's suddenly gotten chilly. I should have grabbed a sweater.

As I near the van, I pull a nice length of tape off the roll. I pass between cars to get to the windshield. I hear a sound. I freeze.

Crap, somebody is in the van. I stare at the closed side door. I debate whether to run, tape the note, or knock. I spring back. The rude van owner inside must have moved. It rocked a little.

I'm about to run back into my condo and forget the whole thing when, suddenly, there's music from inside. Guitar. Oh shit. I know that riff. Some musicians can play a riff and have it be like a signature. I'd recognize this anywhere. I've definitely heard this musician before.

More than mildly pissed off, I pound on the side cargo door.

Quiet.

I roll my eyes. "Don't pretend you're not in there, Neil. I heard you playing."

A few seconds of silence, and then the door swings wide. Neil's face comes into view. "Hey."

Really, that's all he has to say? Hey?

"Why are you hanging out in my carport? Why are you always stealing my spot?" I exclaim in unmistakable irritation.

Neil shrugs. "It's complicated. Can't you let it go at it's hard to find an overnight parking place in Berkeley?"

"No. I can't."

I search his face. He looks so miserable right now that some of my temper cools.

He rakes a hand through his hair. "I really don't want to get into it."

I climb in, sitting on the bed in the van. "I've got all night. You've clearly got all night. Explain it to me."

His eyes flash at the *clearly all night* remark. OK, that was a touch snotty. I look around the interior. Clothes. His musical gear. Books. Sleeping stuff. Is he living in his van?

I search his face. "You don't have an apartment in Berkeley, do you? That's why I never drop you off at home and why you can't give me your number."

He meets my stare. "No, I don't."

My eyes widen. "And you live in your van?"

Neil gives a short, rough laugh. "You make it sound worse than it is. I've been all across the country in this van. Betsy has probably been to more states than you have. I've slept in it hundreds of times. It's OK."

I frown. "This doesn't make sense. You've got a good job. The university must pay you enough so you don't have to live in your van."

Neil sighs. "I've got bills. Big bills I want to pay off as quickly as possible."

"What kind of bills?"

He studies my face. Every part of him screams he'd rather die than explain this to me.

He does another long intake of air. He lets it out

slowly. "I told you, Chrissie. Shit got fucked up last time with my ex. Can't we just leave it at that?"

My lids flutter wide. I stare at him, hard. "No. Not if I matter to you. Not if you want to stay friends."

He shakes his head. He sucks in a full chest of air. "I have probation, restitution, and court fees I need to pay off. About another eight thousand dollars is left on my account. That's why I'm really serious about not losing my fucking job on campus. I got it through county probation. I need to pay my fees so I can get off probation. Get back to Seattle. Get back my life. And worse than that, if I lose my job, I violate my probation and I could go back to jail."

"Back to jail?"

Neil's been in jail. Shit, do I even know Neil at all?

"I did thirty days in June at county," he admits, with a reluctance webbed with something I can't decipher.

"What for?"

He looks away from me. "I left the road to try to make it work, and I came home and found another guy in my bed." He lets out a long, emotion-ragged breath. "I fucked him up pretty good. Only fight I've ever been in and I end up hurting him into a twenty thousand dollar hospital stay. He pressed charges. So I got thirty days in county, probation until my fees are paid, and ninety days of anger management."

It's too much to process.

His eyes come back, locking on mine. "That's everything, Chrissie. You know everything." His stare liquefies. "I didn't want to ever tell you any of this. Can you blame me for not wanting to tell you this? It's fucking humiliating."

He looks so sad, so achingly sad. I can't get my head around this. It doesn't match the Neil I know. But then we're all a little crazy when we're crazy in love. I was certainly crazy over Alan.

I don't know why I do it, but I move from my side of the van and curl into him. He instantly surrounds me with his legs and arms, easing me back against him. I feel a long, shuddering breath release from his chest.

He buries his lips in my hair. "I'm sorry, Chrissie. But I never lied to you. I told you I had problems. I was pretty fucked up."

I melt into the feel of him, his hands gently caressing my arms, his lips in my hair. I should be angry that he didn't tell me this before we got involved. I should be wary of Neil. I should probably end *this*—whatever we are—right now. I should do a lot of things other than what I'm thinking.

I turn in his arms until I can face him. "Grab your stuff, Neil."

His green eyes go wide. "No, Chrissie. I'm not going to move in with you."

I arch a brow. "And I'm not asking you to. But I'm not going to let you live in my carport. I have a couch. You can sleep there. I'll get an extra spot from the management company for the van tomorrow."

"No." He shakes his head.

"Neil, grab your stuff and stop being a jerk about this."

I start grabbing at things. I don't know what I'm

rummaging through. It makes him move. It makes him stop me.

Once we've gathered some of his things, we walk in silence back to the elevator. I insert the key, turn it, and hit the call button.

I look over my shoulder at him. He looks emotionally frazzled, miserable, and a little overwhelmed.

"Why can't you go back to Seattle, if that is where you want to be?" I ask.

The tic in his jaw twitches. "You can't leave the state while you're on probation. It's a violation. I have to pay off my fees before I can move back and try to put something together with Josh and the guys again."

I nod.

We step into the elevator. I hit the button for the top floor.

"Is this why you're so uncomfortable around your family?" I ask. "The being in jail? The probation thing?"

He lets out a shuddering breath. "Partly."

Partly? I wonder what else there could be.

I slide the key in the lock of my front door.

"I'm not staying here forever," he says stiffly from behind me.

I make a face at him. "I'm not letting you stay here forever. We have a guest bath in the hall. There are linens in the closet. There's the couch. Unless you'd rather take the floor."

I go into my room and shut the door. It's only nine, but I put on my pajamas and climb into bed anyway. I just lie there. I'm wide awake for hours. I look over at the clock.

Crap, it's 1 a.m. and I can't sleep. I feel anxious and out of balance. A strange reaction to having Neil sleeping on my couch.

I roll over in bed and stare at the ceiling. We had a good night last night in Santa Barbara. At least I thought so. The sex was different than it was with…I stop myself before I think *his* name…but the sex was good in its overheated sort of exuberant in-artfulness.

I like Neil. I always have fun with him. Even though he drives me nuts sometimes. Like he is now, doing nothing but sleeping on my couch.

Shouldn't he have wanted, pushed a little, to be in here in my bed? We've had sex. What's up with the couch?

I sit up in bed, push the hair from my face, and stare at the door. Maybe Neil thinks I don't want him with me in my room because I made a point of offering him the couch. What's the worst that could happen? He could say no?

I pad across the bedroom, open the door, and peek out into the living room. It's dark. I can't tell if he's asleep. Neil is stretched out on the couch. He's over six feet. That can't be comfortable for him.

I switch on the hall light and make my way to the sofa. I can feel his eyes on me. So he's awake, too. I settle on the arm of the couch, the opposite end from where Neil's head lays, and set my feet in the space between his legs.

"This feels really stupid. Do you know that?" I say into the darkness.

Neil turns, sits up and switches on the light on the end table.

"I'm sorry," he says.

I take a deep breath. "We're sort of dating. We've slept together. It feels really awkward having you sleep on the couch."

Neil frowns. "Do you want me to go?"

"No. Sleep in the bedroom. It's dumb having you out here."

He lifts both hands in front of me, fingers spread wide as he shakes his head. "No, Chrissie. I'm not doing the living together thing. Especially since I'm a charity case."

"Neil, you are not a charity case. We're good friends. Friends help friends. And I'm not asking you to do the living together thing."

He shakes his head again. "No. I want to take it slow with you. I've been lying out here all night wondering if even the couch is a mistake. When things go too fast, they get too intense and all fucked up. I don't want that. Not with you."

I stare at him. Alan and me were the prototype of too fast, too intense, and all fucked up. Neil is right. We shouldn't do this. Still, I really want him in my room and not out here. I like how I feel when Neil is close to me.

"Why don't we just move you to the bedroom and see how it goes? You do your junk. I do mine. None of that relationship bullshit. Just two friends living together until you can get your shit together and go back to Seattle. Clear, defined arrangement…" I do a meaningful lift of a brow. "…with a few benefits for both of us."

He laughs and rakes a hand through his hair. "It won't work. It's going to get fucked up and I don't want to fuck up everything with you, Chrissie."

"Then don't fuck it up."

He gives me another tired, ragged laugh. "This couch is miserable."

I sink my teeth into my lower lip to keep back my smile.

I stand up. "Come on, Neil. Grab your stuff, again."

He lugs his possessions into my bedroom and sets them by the door.

"I'll clear out a section of my closet and part of my drawers for you," I say.

He shakes his head. "I don't need closet space or drawers."

"Well, I don't want your crap sitting on the floor messing up my room."

I climb into bed and wait for him.

He stares at me. "Why are you doing this?"

I shrug. "I don't know."

I watch him climb into bed beside me.

"I always get the left side," I say, reaching over to switch off the light.

"I want to move slowly with you, Chrissie."

"OK, we'll move slowly."

"I don't want to mess up your life."

"I'm just offering you a place to stay. Don't worry it's something it's not. You're not going to mess up my life."

"Good night, Chrissie."

He stays on his side of the bed, with a ridiculously large space between us. I can hear him breathing quietly, but he's awake. Then he turns into my body. He kisses me beneath my hair on my neck. His arm slips around me. I scoot into him, my backside brushing him *there*. And that's all it takes before Neil rolls me over and we start fucking again.

~~~

I lie on the bed, my cheek on the pillow, nose to nose with Neil.

"I don't want to go," Neil whispers.

"Then don't go."

"I have to. I have work today," he says.

"Then go to work."

"It's kind of hard when you have a boner."

I flush and bite my lower lip. "I'm a little sore."

He makes a small pout, but his eyes are gleaming. He kisses me. "Sore, huh? Is it bad?"

My eyes widen. "A little. I like it, though."

That makes him smile. Then he rolls away from me, stretching back on his pillow and running a hand through his hair. He sits up.

"I've got to hop into the shower and get out of here."

He starts rummaging through his things for his work clothes.

"What are you going to do all day while I work?" he asks.

"Probably sleep. My classes don't start until Wednesday."

He laughs. "Fine. Gloat. Rub it in."

He tosses his clothes on the end of the bed.

"Do you have juice? Coffee? Anything?"

I sit up. "Everything." I watch him walk to the door.
~~~

He's butt naked. Jeez, he's got a beautiful body. I like that there's no ink on it. "Bring me some coffee."

"You're such a princess. You don't even ask. You demand," he says, but there's a smile in his eyes.

I lie back in bed, curling around his pillow. The first night of being together—*without being together*—wasn't bad. I start to doze, and then a door slamming jolts me awake.

From the living room I hear Rene exclaim loudly, "Oh fuck." I sit up, reach for my shirt from the floor, and quickly pull it over my head.

Rene runs into the bedroom. She's furious. She stops and stares at Neil's pile of things by my door.

"What the fuck are you doing?"

I frown. "I thought you weren't going to be back until tomorrow."

She stares at me, hands on hips. "What is Neil's stuff doing all over our living room and your bedroom? What's going on here?"

"Neil is just staying here for a while," I say matter-of-factly.

She drops heavily on the bed beside me. "Without asking me what I think, you've decided to move in Neil Stanton?"

I roll my eyes. "Jeez, Rene, you have guys overnight all the time. I don't ever say anything to you about it."

"I don't have them move in." Rene does a harsh shake of her head and then her eyes settle on me and widen. "I know you're unhappy at Cal, Chrissie. But you don't move into our condo some guy you don't really know. This isn't how you fix it."

My cheeks burn red. Now I'm furious. "That's not what I'm doing. I really like Neil."

She gives me *the look*. "I can't believe you did this." She springs from the bed. At the door, she turns back to give me another heated, pointed stare. "This is fucked up."

Rene slams the bedroom door behind her. From the hall I hear her scream, "Put on some clothes when you're out of the bedroom."

"OK, Rene. Oh, and Josh says hi," Neil bites off.

Silence. No comeback from Rene. She slams her bedroom door. In a minute Neil is in the room with me. He sets my coffee on the nightstand.

His face grows all serious and he sighs. "I don't want to cause problems between you and Rene. Maybe I should move out right now."

I stare up at him and shake my head. "She'll get over it."

"It doesn't sound like it's going to happen anytime soon."

"I don't care, Neil. Stay."

CHAPTER EIGHT

I sit in the passenger seat of the Volvo, staring at Rene as she fights her way through traffic toward campus.

"When are you going to get over this? It's been four months, Rene. I'm really tired of you being pissed at me."

Rene's eyes flash. "How about when you have Neil move out?"

"Why do you dislike Neil so much?"

"I just do."

"He's a really nice guy. You could cut him some slack. You don't have to stomp around being rude to him every chance you get."

Rene stares at me, her eyes intense. "He's a moocher. He's using you. And like all guys, he'll stick around when he needs you and walk away when he doesn't."

The legacy of Mr. Thompson is here in the car with us today, coloring Rene's opinion of Neil.

I sigh. "He's not like that."

"All guys are like that," Rene snaps.

"Why don't you like him? For once, just tell me why."

She lets out a long, hard breath. "I don't like him."

"You don't need to like him. I like him," I say, more than a little miffed.

"I don't trust any guy who doesn't check me out."

Oh jeez, not that again.

She's so damn female-competitive. It's indisputable that Rene is drop-dead gorgeous with her dark hair, dark eyes, perfect olive complexion, and long limbed five-foot-nine frame. Why does she need every guy on the planet confirming that for her?

"Neil isn't a jerk. Probably because he has three younger sisters. He doesn't ogle girls in that jerk way most guys do."

"Ha." Her eyes widen, sparkly and disapproving. "All guys look. All guys check. I don't trust a guy who doesn't."

"Alan never checked you out," I say before I can stop myself.

She stares at me, arching a brow. "I don't like Alan Manzone either."

"You don't like any guy who has an interest in me."

There. It had to be said.

Her eyes go wide like an overinflated bullfrog. She clamps her mouth shut and fixes her stare on the road.

I look out the window. This conversation is going nowhere. There is no point in repeating it, but I repeat it anyway. "You should be happy for me. That's what a really good friend would do. Be happy for me because I'm happy."

She makes an angry jerk with her hand to flip on the turn signal. "I'm a really good friend, Chrissie. I care about you first. I can't be happy over this. There is something about Neil I don't like."

She pulls over to the curb to let me out. I gather my things and then open the car door.

"I'm out of here the day after finals. I've decided to spend the summer traveling the UK with my mother," she announces through the open passenger door.

Well, that's mature, Rene. Ditch me for three months to reinforce that you're unhappy with me. As if it's not obvious 24/7.

I don't say anything.

"What are you going to do this summer?" she finally asks.

I shrug. "Stay in Berkeley. I need to take summer classes if we're going to graduate together. I can't do twenty units a semester like you do."

She gives me a look that screams *bullshit.* She shakes her head. "You should go home to Santa Barbara. Cool things down for a while. You're moving too fast with Neil, Chrissie. But you never take my advice. Have fun all summer with Neil."

My brows hitch up. "Have fun with Patty."

Her eyes flash, and I regret that comment. Rene's relationship with her mother isn't any less emotionally complex than her relationship with her father. All of Rene's relationships, except her one-night stands, are emotionally complex.

She does a slow shake of her head and looks away first. I close the door and watch her speed off.

I cut across campus to the concrete slabs with the statues of the bears, the place where Neil and I reconnected at Cal.

I spot him casually sitting on the slabs, long legs dangling—customary work clothes, boots, and bandana covering his unruly waves of chestnut hair—smoking a cigarette. I notice that more than a few girls check him out even in his easy to identify janitor uniform. Janitor or not, Neil is a gorgeous guy.

I stop, standing between his legs, and lift my face for him to kiss me. I ease back, looking up at him. "Have you been waiting long?"

He shakes his head, smiling. "Nope. Five minutes."

He slips off the concrete and takes my hand. We start to walk toward the food court.

"I've only got a half-hour for lunch today," he says.

"Why's that?"

"I want to get off early. There's some junk I've got to do."

Junk? *Why always so private, Neil?*

"Good junk or bad junk?" I ask.

He shrugs and doesn't answer me.

I make a face at him as he opens the door to our hippie vibe natural café. I don't know why we eat here. Neither of us are vegan or vegetarian.

We order our food and settle on a patio table.

"I have to go see my probation officer," he says unexpectedly halfway through lunch.

I look up from my sandwich. "Everything is OK, right?"

Neil leans back in his chair. "When I got paid last week I paid off the last of my fees and fines. I'm supposed to get the paperwork today confirming that my probation has terminated. My PO suggests that I carry it with me. That it takes time, sometimes, for court records to update. So I should carry it with me if I decide to go back to Seattle."

He's done with probation. He's free to go back to Seattle, back to the band and his life.

"That's great news," I say, pleased that my voice sounds happy for him and not at all like I feel.

"Yep, even if I'm still a janitor. Only now I'm a broke janitor. Cleaned me out. Every cent. But a fucking relief to have it done with."

"So what do you want to do now?"

He laughs. "Honestly? I'd love to have a beer and smoke a bowl tonight."

"Very funny. I was talking big picture. Be serious."

Neil shakes his head, amused. "I'm serious. I keep forgetting you've lived a completely sheltered life. Probation does random drug tests. I've had random drug tests for twelve months. I haven't been able to drink or get lit once. Not if I didn't want to risk having my probation revoked."

"Oh." I've wondered why he never drinks. It was silly of me not to just to ask him.

He points at my lunch. "Are you done?"

I nod. He collects our trash and tosses it away. We walk back onto campus. We stop at the concrete bears again.

I feel Neil's eyes on me, studying my face.

"You OK? You're really quiet, Chrissie."

I smile. "Just a lot on my mind with finals coming up next week."

"Speaking of Rene," he says in that *Rene is a pain in the ass* tone of voice he has.

"We weren't speaking of Rene," I point out, interrupting him.

"I'm sorry having me around gives you so much shit with her. I try to keep everything chill. It's impossible."

"It's not your problem. It's hers." I stare up at him. "Besides, guess who's going to be gone for the entire summer?"

Neil's eyes widen and then start to shimmer. "Oh, please don't be messing with me. Three months without Rene? You better not be messing with me."

I smile. "She's spending the entire summer with her mother. She leaves the day after her finals."

He laughs. He sets his nose to mine. "We can fuck without someone pounding on the wall acting like the sound police," he whispers. "You can make your little squeaks without her getting pissed off the next morning. If we're on the couch and want to do it, we just can."

I blush and toss him a playful glare. "I don't squeak."

"Yes, you do. It's such a turn-on. It's giving me a boner just thinking about it."

He pulls me into him for a deep, open-mouthed kiss that makes my blood start to pump warmly again.

Neil steps back. "I'll probably be home before you're done with class."

I smile. "OK."

He makes a lush sigh. "God, I can't wait to have sex without Rene in the next room." He checks his watch. "I've got to get back to work."

I stand by the concrete bears, watching Neil disappear across campus. Neil wouldn't be happy about Rene taking off for the summer if he wasn't planning on staying here in Berkeley.

~~~

I should be studying.

My head sways and I move my body slowly up Neil's erection. I stop just before he's out of me, planting my hands on his chest and opening my eyes to look down at him. His face is flushed, passion-taut, in that way he has when he really wants to come and is fighting not to.

I slam down, taking him as deep as I can. He groans and my muscles clench, getting wetter. I love when I ride him. I can make myself come when *I* ride *him*. It doesn't happen when he controls the fucking, but it always does when I fuck him.

I do another glide up. Another slam down. I'm there, on the edge. I do a slow swirl of my hips, keeping him buried as deeply as I can. I reach for his hand, guiding him to clutch my nipples in a way so that it's the callused tips pinching and stroking me. I move again.

My head goes back. Heat runs across my surface. "Ah…ah…ah…" punctuates my breaths as I shake with my climax.

I'm panting, consumed by shudders, my limbs too weak to support me. Neil lifts up, propped on an arm stretched behind him, his other arm encircling my waist as he pounds into me, harder and harder with each thrust. They're gloriously painful.

I'm no longer here. My body has no sensation. Every part of me is numbed by fucking, and I'm nothing in this brief moment but tissue and bone Neil thrusts into.
~~~

His face presses against my neck beneath my hair. His tempo builds. His breath is warm and rapid.

Everything in his body tenses. "Oh, Chrissie…I love you…" He erupts, spilling into me. "I love you…"

~~~

I sit on the bed in my Cal t-shirt trying to focus on my textbook.

Neil is naked and reclining beside me. He's been sitting there for over an hour, just picking at something on his guitar.

I look at him. "I have a final tomorrow. Can you go into the living room if you want to play? It's very distracting."

He sets down the guitar. "Ah, so you're finally talking."

"What's that supposed to mean?"

"You haven't said a word since we fucked."

I make an exasperated face and then look down at my book. "I need to study."

He leans in and brushes my lower lip with his thumb. "Why are you pissed at me, Chrissie?"

I take in a deep breath. "I'm not pissed."

Neil's brows go up. "Bullshit, Chrissie. I know you better than that."

I struggle to hold back my words and emotions. Finally, I toss the book away.

I don't look at him. "Don't say that you love me. Not even in that bullshit way guys say while screwing. I don't want you to say you love me."

He sits up then, more than a little perplexed. He
~~~

frowns. "It's not bullshit, Chrissie. I do love you."

I can feel Neil studying my face. I suck in my lower lip, biting it hard, and shake my head.

He turns my chin so I have no choice but to meet his eyes. "God, you're really frustrating at times. I just told you I love you. Don't you have anything to say?"

I stare at him, pretending not to comprehend him.

"Chrissie? Do you love me?"

I make an aggravated shake of my head. My eyes go wide. "Fine. Yes, I love you."

"Jeez, why can't you just say it without making even that difficult?" He folds me against his chest, kissing my hair, my brow, and my cheeks. "Why don't you want me to say I love you?"

I kiss his jaw. I curl into his chest.

"I'm fucked up that way," I whisper.

Neil shakes his head. "You're not fucked up in any way."

He lies back on the bed with me draped atop him. There's a sweet kind of expression on his face and his eyes are warm as he stares at me. I muster a smile and lay my cheek on his chest.

If I'm not fucked up, Neil, why did I just tell you I love you when I don't?

CHAPTER NINE

Summer 1990

I park in the carport and reach over to the passenger seat to grab my purse.

I've just spent two frustrating hours stuck in traffic from San Francisco Airport. Why can't Rene book her flights out of Oakland? She can be so thoughtless at times.

I make my way to the elevator. I've got two weeks off before summer classes begin, a Rene-free condo, and I'm going to make the most of it. When the doors open on the top floor, a blast of music rolls down the hallway.

I rush into the condo, spot Neil lying on the couch, eyes closed, and without asking I turn down the volume. "Neil, you're going to get us in trouble with the management company." I start picking up the junk scattered across the floor. I see a stack of demo tapes by my sound system. I pick one up and turn to Neil with my hand outstretched. "What is this?"

Neil sits up on the couch.

"Two weeks ago Josh brought down from Seattle some instrument tracks the band has been working on."

Two weeks ago? That was about the same time Neil told me he'd finished his probation.

"Josh was here in Berkeley? Why didn't you tell me?"

Neil shrugs. "I don't know. Didn't seem important at the time. The band has a new guitarist, Les Wilson. I don't know him. He's from Laguna Beach. His band just broke up. They're looking for a front man. Josh wanted me to work on some lyrics."

I sink down on my knees beside him. "Why didn't you tell me you were working on this?"

Neil shrugged. "Wanted to think it through on my own."

I stare. "Think through what?"

Neil sighs, running a hand through his hair. "Josh and the guys. There's a lot of history there. A lot of shit that wasn't good. They're not sure they want me. Josh made that clear. Still, he wanted to see what I could do with the instrument tracks." He shrugs. "I sent some tapes back to them this morning. We'll see what happens. Maybe nothing will happen."

"How many tracks did you finish?"

"Fourteen."

Fourteen? This must have taken up every free minute he had for the last two weeks, and for some reason he deliberately didn't share this with me.

I feel my body flood with a chill and uncontained hurt unfurls within me.

He leans in and kisses me. "Let's go down to the beach. I can smoke a bowl. You can tell me not to. And then maybe I'll get laid."

He pulls me up until we're lying on the couch with me on top of him. I exhale a long breath that does nothing to calm my inner distress. "Forget the beach and the weed, Neil. Why don't we just stay here?"

~~~

I walk home from the campus bookstore.

Taking only two classes in summer definitely makes it easier to lug the books home. I hurry across the street, away from Cal, then up the shaded road to the condo complex.

I spot Neil's van in the parking lot. He's home from work early. He hardly ever gets home this early. I step into the elevator, hit the button with my elbow, and wait for the world's slowest set of doors to close.

After more time than seems necessary, the metal springs open on the top floor. I hurry down the hall. Struggling to balance my books in my arms, I manage to get the key in the lock, turn it, and push the door open with my leg.

I dump everything on the floor as I kick off my shoes. I step into the kitchen just as Neil hangs up the phone.

I cross the room and give him a kiss. "You beat me home. That's a nice surprise. Why are you home early?"

"Josh wants me to come up to Seattle for a week," he says. "Jam with the guys. See how it works, what we can create. Maybe do a live gig."

I sink down on a chair in front of the table.

"That's great, Neil. How long will you be in Seattle?"

I force a smile and wait while he collects his thoughts.

He sits down at the table across from me. "Why don't you come with me, Chrissie? There is no reason why you have to stay in Berkeley. I don't want to go up there without you."
~~~

I sit back. "I can't, Neil. My classes start soon."

"They don't start until next week. I told Josh I want to go right into the studio. No messing around. Get to work and get out of there."

"I've got to be back by next Monday, Neil. I can't miss even one day in summer school or the class will drop me."

He rakes a hand through his hair. "We'll be back in time. I probably can't push calling in sick to work for more than a week without getting fired, Chrissie."

Two hours later, we're on a flight from Oakland to Seattle.

Once we land, we go to the baggage claim area to grab our suitcases and Neil's guitar, and then make a rushed detour to the rental car counter. We make a fast stop at our hotel to check in, dump our bags, and thirty minutes later we're making our way across the city again.

Neil has been in a strange mood since we boarded the plan. Anxious and quiet in a way I've not seen before. For a guy who wanted me along with him this week, he couldn't be any more remote if he tried. It feels like being in Seattle affects him in some deep, emotional way.

History with the band? Shit? Or maybe this is where his ex-girlfriend is from? I wonder what parts of Neil's life in Seattle he hasn't yet shared with me. He's a careful guy about what he discloses about himself, and never more vague than about his ex. Jeez, we've been together six months, if you count it from the day he found me crying outside the music department, and I still don't know her name. Shouldn't I know her name by now?

I ignore Neil's silence and just stare out the car

window. I've never been to Seattle before. It would be nice to get to see a little of it. Our hotel is near Pike Place Market. Other than the Space Needle, I don't know what else is supposed to be interesting here.

As I watch Neil maneuver our rental car through streets that don't look at all like anything in Southern California, it's obvious he knows his way around here. He can probably tell me what else is worth seeing in this city.

I stare up through the car window at the city lights. It's a pretty city and it edges the Pacific. In a lot of ways Neil is like me. I can't imagine either of us living away from the ocean. When he's not at his job, working on his music, or in bed with me, he's at the beach surfing.

Neil parks in front of a dilapidated building that sells art supplies. Josh Moss rented the basement as rehearsal space. The street looks a lot less safe than the one where our hotel is located.

Josh is leaning against a brick wall smoking a cigarette. I've only seen him the one time, that night at Peppers, but I didn't remember he was such a good-looking guy. Though I really don't like his long, wiry build. Definitely more Rene's type than mine.

Neil says, "I don't know how long this will be tonight, Chrissie. Whenever you want to cut out, take the car. I'll have one of the guys drive me back to the hotel."

"OK."

I watch him open his door and climb from the driver's seat. I wonder if, now that he has me here, he's changed his mind about me sticking around.

Neil walks around the car and opens my door. Strange,

but the two guys haven't even said hello to each other yet. I wait at the curb, feeling awkward, as Neil retrieves his guitar and Josh just stands there smoking and staring at me.

Finally, Josh pushes up from the wall and tosses his cigarette into the road. "The convict is back," he says.

"Fuck you, Josh," Neil says, but he's smiling.

Then they're hugging each other in that guy way, hard pats and a firm clutch. They shake each other and then step back.

"You look good, man. You good?" Josh asks, taking in Neil with a thorough glance. The way he says that makes it sound more significant than a casual inquiry.

Neil nods. "It's all good, Josh. Nothing to worry about. Like I said on the phone, I'm here to work. Then I'm going back to Berkeley with Chrissie."

Josh shakes his head. "You had me fucking worried there for a while."

Neil tilts his head toward the building. "Did the rest of the guys send you up here to make sure I wasn't a fucking nutcase before you let me through the doors?"

I listen to the conversation, trying not to let my expression surface on my face. *Nutcase?* What the heck does that mean? Neil is the farthest thing from crazy I know.

Josh laughs, lighting another cigarette. "Yep. Told them you looked good when I saw you in Berkeley. They're not sure about you yet. You fucked up Andy pretty bad. Everyone is still blown away about that, trying to figure out what set you off enough to fuck him up so much you put him in the hospital. Fuck, Neil, we've all been friends since grade school. Why the hell did you fuck him up instead of talking to me?"

Andy? My eyes search Neil's face. He's tense and edgy with anger. *Andy*...and then I remember the night at Peppers, the guy Neil was pissed at, the guy who stared at me so strangely while I danced with Neil. Is that the same Andy? The guy Neil caught in bed with his girlfriend? Getting fucked over by a friend; is that why Neil flipped out and did such a non-Neil thing?

Josh's eyes sharpen on Neil's face. "Andy is back in Seattle. Did you know that?"

Neil shakes his head, but his tension intensifies. "I don't talk to that fucker and I never will."

"There are not going to be any problems are there? There's no way to avoid him here."

Their eyes lock in an intense stare, full of meaning I can't begin to decipher.

"Like I said, I'm here for a week to see what we can put together, but I'm not moving back. I'll come here to work. I'll go on the road. Nothing more. Then I'm back in Berkeley with Chrissie."

I'm startled out of my thoughts by the feel of Josh Moss's eyes on me.

He says, "I know you. We hung out together once. You have a friend. Rene, right?"

I flush, but before I can say anything Neil laughs and gives Josh a little shove in the chest. "You're such a prick. I told you not to mention that to Chrissie. Not cool, man. Don't fuck with my girlfriend."

For the first time Josh smiles at me. "I'm just messing

with you, Chrissie. Rene was hot. I was hoping you could give me her number." His gaze shifts to Neil. "Girlfriend, huh? You didn't tell me this when I was in Berkeley."

"I didn't think it mattered in making a decision to let me rejoin the band. Is there a problem?"

Josh moves to open the store door. He shakes his head. "Neil Stanton and Chrissie Parker."

The tic twitches in Neil's cheek. "Don't say it like it's fucked up."

Neil's sudden temper and the tone of his voice send an instant chill through me.

Josh freezes and turns to look at Neil. "Don't be so fucking intense. I didn't mean anything by it."

"You better not have," Neil counters harshly. "Chrissie goes pretty much everywhere I go. If it's going to be a problem, you tell me now."

Something in their exchange makes me flush. I stare at Neil, but he doesn't look at me.

Josh shrugs loosely. "No problem, Neil. You just surprised me."

They start walking. I tug on Neil's shirt. He stops.

I stare up at him. "What was that all about?"

Neil jerks a hand through his hair. He's very agitated right now about something.

"Nothing. Josh is an asshole sometimes. Blow off anything he says."

"OK." But I don't really get what just happened here. It feels strange, disturbingly so, even though I can't make sense of it. I stare up at Neil. "Andy. That's your friend from Santa Barbara, right?"

Neil nods.

My eyes widen. "Why did you leave that part out when you told me about the guy you beat up in San Francisco?"

Neil shrugs. "It wasn't important."

"Getting screwed over by a friend is kind of a significant part."

"Jeez, Chrissie. Stop with the fucking third degree."

My body goes cold. I take a slight step back from him. He feels peculiar.

Neil's shakes his head. "I'm sorry. I'm really tense right now. Can we just wait to do this until I'm done here?"

Neil walks off toward the basement. At the bottom of a narrow flight of stairs is a storage room filled with canvas, paints, and raw materials. The basement is dark and dirty, the air has an unpleasant odor of cleaning supplies and dust, but the area is large and the equipment is already set up.

I've seen everyone in the room once before except the lead guitarist, Les Wilson. They were part of Neil's gang at Peppers the night we met and, later, part of the upstairs party we went to for Kurt. Old friends. A Santa Barbara mob. It makes the tension in the room that entered with Neil a doubly odd thing.

Nate Kassel, drumsticks in hand, gives Neil a wraparound arm pat and then lifts his chin toward me. Pat Larsen is a little friendlier in greeting Neil, but not much. And Les, their new lead guitarist, isn't really a part of this tight-knit group from Santa Barbara, so he's sort of just here, like I am.

I sink down onto an old, dirty couch pushed up

against a wall of shelving and, for once, I'm grateful I've been rapidly forgotten in a room. The strain between the guys is palpable. It almost looks like none of them know how to act around Neil. So strange. Calm, smiling Neil is the awkwardness in the room.

It isn't long before they're plugged in, playing and really gelling. Neil started with this band. That's the way they're playing, like musicians who have played together forever. And there's definitely something in the music they create. Something raw, powerful, uniquely their own.

Four hours later, they're still jamming. I move to lie on a pillow. My lids drift open and closed, over and over again, and as I watch Neil and the guys I just know it doesn't matter what shit Neil brought with him to Seattle. Neil's band is a band again.

~~~

I am exhausted. Our six days in Seattle have moved at a grueling tempo. Hours in the rehearsal space. Sex. Late nights in the thriving music scene here. Sleep. Then the cycle all over again, numbing me until I can't feel, too tired even to sleep.

The band played their first live gig together in an old theater that looked as though, at one time, it had been scarred by fire. The corridors, the performance area, everything had been packed. Normally this kind of nightmare I would avoid—new places, new people—but it wasn't a difficult thing for me. And I'm glad I went. Neil and the guys were amazing live on stage.

It feels like everyone here is sort of different, an outsider probably everywhere but here. By extension it
~~~

makes everyone belong. Being strange, being different, is normal in this underground world of hungry and creative musicians. It's a surprisingly good feeling to feel I belong simply by being here. The easiness of it all is seductive. I understand why Neil loves life here. It's so different from what my life has always been in the judgmental world of money and pretty rich girls.

In spite of the first day's tension, everything else has rolled in an easy flow. Neil is subjected to the occasional jeer about having fucked up Andy. Good-humored taunts about his jail thing always flitter through the air wherever we are. But for the most part, it's the music and the scene everyone focuses on in this alternate universe of not normal.

There is only one moment I would label bad if I had the strength to write in my journal today. In the corridor after Arctic Hole's first live gig—Arctic Hole, the name of Neil's recreated band, was lifted from a joke he made about jail being an arctic hole—I came face-to-face with Andy. He just showed up out of nowhere and was there; cocky, long blond hair, an unattractively small and thin guy with blue eyes, always staring with a glint that makes it obvious he's an asshole. He didn't seem at all like a guy who would have ever been a friend of Neil's.

I didn't really want to talk to Andy. There is something in the way he looks at me that puts my nerves on edge. But he started talking to me and I didn't know how to get away from him.

When Neil spied us from across the room during the after-performance party, something changed on his face.

Jealousy over me? Hatred of Andy? I couldn't tell for sure. The mixture of anger and other emotions was something new and strange on Neil.

I thought they were going to come to blows right there in front of half of Seattle. It was an ugly scene. Neil snarling in Andy's face for him to stay away from me. Then dragging me, like a caveman, from the party, barking at me: *You don't talk to him. You don't look at him. You don't go near Andy.*

Neil's nerve in ordering me had my temper fully lit by the time we got back to our hotel room. We would have had an enormous fight, except Neil had me on the bed the second we stepped into the room. The sex was pounding, emotionally void, rough, and painful. It was messed up, but it made my blood boil; the unrestrained acts of his body.

I curl into the blankets. It's been an intense week. Tomorrow we're supposed to return to Berkeley. It's our last day here. I wonder when Neil is going to tell me we're over and he's not leaving Seattle with me.

CHAPTER TEN

I zip closed my duffel bag. My last final of summer session is done. I'm out of here for three weeks.

The phone rings. I click on the cordless. "Hello."

"Hey, Chrissie. You got everything arranged to come up here?"

Neil. I smile. "Yep. Bag packed. Ticket booked. Are you ready to meet me at the airport tomorrow?"

"More than you know," Neil says in a husky growl. "You can count the new calluses on my hands when you get here."

I laugh. Neil staying one extra week after me in Seattle slipped into all summer in Seattle for Neil. But it wasn't as awful as I feared it would be, being alone in the condo for eight weeks.

There was a weird sense of relief, getting a breather from both Rene and Neil. A loss of tension in the air. A loss of tension in me.

I lie back on the floor, curled around the phone. "Have you missed me at all?"

A long sigh. "You know I have."

"I've missed you, too."

A pause. "Chrissie?" Neil's voice has changed.

"Yes?"

"You don't just sit around down there alone in the

condo without me, do you? You should be having fun. Going out."

"You can be such a conceited jerk at times, Neil," I say flippantly, though the emotion running through me is uncomfortable.

I wonder if Neil has just told me, in a guy roundabout way, *he's* fucking around. And I'm pissed off with myself because I realize *I'm* pretty much just sitting around when I don't have classes.

"What time is your flight?" Neil asks, ignoring my jibe.

"I get to Seattle at 3:30."

"Are you staying the whole three weeks until fall semester begins? Or are you going to go to Santa Barbara as well?"

"Nope, the entire three weeks you're stuck with me."

"Good. You're not going to get out of the apartment for days," he whispers.

"I'm counting on it, Neil," I whisper.

I try not to let the shabby apartment Neil is living in, unpleasantly located in a cheap-rent neighborhood of Seattle, form clearly in my head. He shares it with Josh Moss and Les Wilson.

A two-bedroom rat hole above a store, with walls so thin that knowing the guys are in the next room when I visit Neil definitely doesn't put us, sexually, at our best. I wish Neil would come to Berkeley instead of me always going to him.

I hear the guys in the background calling for Neil. "I've got to run, Chrissie. Night."

Click.

I take the cordless phone to the kitchen and drop it into the cradle. I wander to my glass patio doors. I stare across the Bay to the city. Alan is there. Blackpoll's San Francisco concert date of his world tour. It's the closest we've been to each other for over a year. I wonder if Alan is standing across the Bay thinking of me.

~~~

When I wake, I'm on my couch and the living room is filled with cruel morning light. My head hurts. My mouth is dry. I can feel that I drank too much last night. I fell asleep without making it to the bedroom.

I roll over, stretching and yawning, trying to rally my muscles into action. I definitely need more than my share of coffee today. I look at the clock on the wall. Crap, it's midmorning. I've got to get to the airport for Seattle by one.

I wander into the kitchen and grab the instant coffee. As the water heats in the microwave, I down a tall glass of orange juice and I run my finger over the newspaper lying on the counter. It's folded with the block ad of Blackpoll's West Coast concert schedule glaring up at me. Portland, Seattle, Vancouver, then away.

After giving it a good crumple, I toss it in the trash. The only thing more foolish than having that darn thing lying on my counter for two weeks is spending an entire night thinking of Alan.

It's over, Chrissie. He's out of your life. Married.

I stir the instant coffee into my cup and head for the bathroom. An hour later I'm in my bedroom, dressed in a simple black sundress, trying to decide if I've packed
~~~

everything I'll need for three weeks, when there's a soft knock on my front door.

Groaning, I move toward the hallway. Rising up on my tiptoes, I look through the peephole. A large body is so close to the door that I can't make out who it is. I undo the chain. I open it a crack and my heart drops to my knees.

Oh my God! I don't move. I can't speak. I can't find a single word in my head.

The perfect lines of Alan's face change from enigmatic to amused.

"The correct moment to say hello passed about three minutes ago. Are you going to invite me in, Chrissie?"

I flush. Crap, how long have I been standing here doing nothing but staring at him?

Alan doesn't wait for my response. I clutch the door for support as he moves around me into my condo. He tosses his leather jacket on a chair and then sinks onto the sofa.

I try to still my spinning emotions by focusing on closing the door and locking it. I'm feeling more than a little flustered and more than a little stupid, but in my wildest dreams I never would have believed that Alan would cross the Bay to drop in on me, uninvited.

I step from the door, and then do a fast scan of the room with my eyes for a place to sit. I drop down onto the chair where he tossed his jacket.

"You're looking good, Chrissie," he says softly, shattering the acutely silent air.

My vision ignores my will and fixes on him. "You look good too, Alan."

It's petty, but I hate that he does. Alan looks even better than he did during our spring together. Fit, tan, rock star chic. He's stylishly dressed in the kind of clothes he wears for interviews: a flowing black shirt and leather pants. His long, wavy hair is just the right amount of tousled. Must have wanted to give his fans a dose of fuck-me hair in the morning.

"Are you enjoying school? What are you studying?"

I inhale a long breath. God, this feels weird. "Music."

I drag my gaze away from him. In spite of how many times I've imagined this moment, I never expected it to feel like this. Miserably uncomfortable. But then we didn't exactly part as friends and having him here sitting, strange and distant, forces me to remember he's married.

"Jack bought you a nice condo, I see," he says casually, fishing his cigarettes out of his pocket. He lights it without asking if he can, takes a long drag, and stares at me through the smoke. "I've wondered what it would look like. The place you chose over me."

My face burns. Only Alan could make a glib pejorative directed at himself a cutting insult. If there had been a hint of anything in his voice—kindness, gentleness, affection—that comment would have played so much differently. But it held only the clip of meanness.

I stare at him. Elegantly mean Alan. Emotion rockets through my veins, raw and unwanted. It's mean Alan who is sitting in my condo with me today.

"If there's a reason why you dropped by, tell me and then leave," I whisper, in spite of my resolve to stay emotionless. "Otherwise, your being here is ridiculous, and

I should go to the airport for my flight to Seattle."

He arches a brow. "Seattle?" he repeats in a rough sort of way. "Why are you going there?"

Normal question in not normal context.

I stare at him without answering.

He casually studies my living room and then shifts his gaze back to my face. "How long have you had a guy living with you?"

I tense. How does he know that? My gaze focuses on Neil's surfboard and wetsuit propped against the wall.

"I don't see as how it's any of your business how long I've been living with Neil."

His eyes flare and widen. "And I don't see why you care if I know." He stomps out his cigarette on a plate I left on the coffee table. "It was a polite question. Conversational. Nothing more."

That comment hits me like a slap on my face.

I force myself to look at him directly. "I think you should leave, Alan. Why did you come here?"

He takes out another cigarette, lights it, and takes a long drag, staring at me through the smoke again. "I'm in San Francisco. But you know that."

I pretend not to understand what he means.

He says, "It seemed *ridiculous*…" There is just enough edge in "ridiculous" that my scalp prickles. "…not to cross the bridge to see you."

I change course. "So how is Nia?"

"I don't know. I don't care."

I blink at him.

What does that mean? Are they getting divorced?

Maybe the stories in the press aren't true. Maybe they're not deliriously happy together.

"Where's your boyfriend? Seattle? Is that why you're going there?" he asks.

"Yes."

It's probably a stupid question, but right now it feels like the most important question in my life. "If you don't know or care where Nia is, why did you marry her?"

His simmering gaze locks on me, and I feel the punch even before he bites out through clenched teeth, "To forget you."

I can barely breathe. Weird, convoluted, harshly spoken, Alan honesty. I don't know how to deal with him when he's this way. I'm relieved when his eyes move from me to focus on stomping out his cigarette.

"It didn't work," he adds on a rasp. "I still think of you, always."

"Were you thinking of me when you married Nia, four months after I left New York?"

I watch the dark light in his eyes change. His gaze clouds into something painfully harsh.

"I think of *you* when I fuck *her*," he says in a brutal, quiet voice that is deafening. "Is that good enough for you, Chrissie?"

I flush deep crimson and my eyes fix on his face. I fight to recover from the shock of him saying that, and realize he's watching me and expecting some kind of reaction. He's assessing every change in my expression. I don't know what has slipped onto my face, but his features lose their harsher arrangement.

"Do you ever think of me?" His voice is so quiet I can barely catch his words.

"I think of you every day, Alan."

His posture and expression change in a flash. For some reason my answer kicked up his anger. I can see something powerful coursing through him.

He stands up, pacing the room as if struggling to contain something. He takes a deep breath, stops, turns, and then stares down at me.

"Then can you do me the courtesy, Chrissie, of explaining why you haven't responded to a single phone call or letter? One returned call would have sufficed to tell me directly to fuck off."

The last of that is said through gritted teeth. *Calls? Letters?* What is Alan talking about?

"You called? You sent me letters? I don't understand," I choke out.

His gaze burns into me. "What don't you understand, love? That even the worst cunt would have picked up the phone once, or answered at least one letter?"

My face snaps up. I feel shaky inside. My heart stops.

Oh no…cunt. I see it on his face and I don't want to. Alan isn't here because he loves me; he's here because he hates me. Oh God, he hates me. Alan is here because he hates me.

"I understand you leaving New York, Chrissie. What I can't understand is why you had to be such a bitch after you left."

Everything inside me collapses in a fast free-fall.

I spring from my chair and race to the kitchen. I don't

want Alan to see me cry. My fingers curl around the edge of the sink, my head lowered as I struggle to breathe in and out.

He thinks I'm the one who walked away from us. It's too much for my emotionally undone senses. That I haven't a clue why I never received a phone message or letter from him doesn't matter. Alan hates me. It would have been so much better if Alan hadn't come to Berkeley. If I had never known this.

Alan's voice sounds behind me, void of emotion, but at least no longer angry.

"Why are you crying, Chrissie?"

"You can be so mean sometimes, Alan. Why did you come here if all you wanted to do is insult me and call me names? I would have preferred to pass on that."

"I would prefer not to be here as well." He says it coldly.

"Then why did you come?"

"I don't know," he admits. "It *did* seem ridiculous to be in San Francisco and not to see you, Chrissie. So I came here."

"You sent me roses for Christmas, didn't you?" I whisper.

A long pause; I can feel him staring at me.

"Yes," he says, the edge returning to his voice again.

I push my lips tightly together, fighting a fresh wave of tears. I knew they were from Alan. I knew it in my heart. I felt it in my skin.

"Was there a card with the roses?"

"No," he says in a rough way. "I had given up sending

you cards by then."

"How long after I left New York did you continue to call me? Send me letters?"

"I don't see as how that's important now."

"It's important to me."

He takes a minute.

"A year."

Another heavy silence falls between us, and the emotion warring in the room isn't only my own.

"Why didn't you call me, Chrissie?"

The room is suddenly overfilled with the feel of Alan. His anger. His hurt. I'm dizzy and confused.

"I didn't know you tried to reach me. If I'd have known you called me, I would have called you back. But I didn't know. I didn't get your messages or anything else. I thought when I left New York we were over. Clean break. You told me we were over if I left. What was I supposed to think?"

"I was angry. It was bullshit to get you to stay. I didn't mean it when I said we were over. I regretted saying it the moment you walked out the door."

Time stops around me, heavy and silent.

"Where did you go the summer after you left me?" he asks in a worried way. "Linda wouldn't talk to me about you. It got me concerned. And Jack doesn't take my calls since New York."

Concerned. I can't begin to process that one, or what I hear in his voice.

"I drove across country with Rene. An after-graduation road trip we'd planned all through high school.

Jack thought it would be good for me. So we went."

"So you weren't in Santa Barbara?"

"No."

"I traveled to Santa Barbara two weeks after you left to try to reach you. Went to your house. Maria said you weren't there. I've always wondered if she lied to me."

My senses slowly grow aware that I'm still facing the sink with my hands clutching the counter, the only thing keeping me on my feet.

Two weeks. He only just missed me. "I wasn't there."

Another long exhale of breath. "Chrissie, look at me," Alan orders.

I can't move. If I let go of the counter I will drop to the floor.

"Please, look at me, Chrissie."

He brushes the hair from my neck. I want to turn into him. I want him to hold me. My entire body feels vacant with shock, like I've been run over by a truck. All this time, I thought *he* ended it with *me.*

"I apologize for being an ass earlier," he murmurs, his voice pulling me from my thoughts. "I didn't mean a single word. Not the cruel ones. I've been nervous since I walked through the door."

My fingers curl tighter around the rim of the sink. "I'm really glad you came to see me. It's been hard wondering why we ended not at least as friends."

Alan's body eases closer into me, not touching, but close enough to surround me with the feel of him anyway.

"It's been hard for me, every day, not being with you," he whispers.

I hear him swallow.

"I love you, Chrissie. I never stopped."

"I need you to go, Alan."

He places a feather-light kiss on my neck. It ripples along my nerves, and then jolts in my sex.

"Are you still in love with me?" he murmurs.

"I want you to go."

"I have two days, Chrissie. I don't have anywhere I have to be for two days."

Two days. The blood starts pumping even more fiercely through my body. That unrelenting pull. The electric current. The want. Here, now, over a year later in Berkeley.

"Do you really want me to leave?" Alan whispers.

I hesitate.

He turns me around, away from the sink, and eases into me, one hand planted on the counter, holding his body just beyond me. I lift my face and his mouth lowers. The touch of his lips is just a brush, gentle and yet a sharp reminder of how we used to be. I feel his finger lightly on my cheek, nothing more, but the feel of him is all across my flesh.

I part my lips and he deepens the kiss in slow degrees, giving the feel of him, inch by inch. I'm about to melt in my skin. He slowly pulls back.

I open my eyes to find him staring down at me.

"Tell me now, Chrissie, if you want me to leave."

His expression betrays nothing. He hovers over me, watching my shifting emotions as my brain, my body, fills with my need.

"Please, tell me you want me to stay," he says softly.

I take in a steadying breath. I say nothing and he leans into me. His lips touch my neck and my breathing increases, my head tilting back as my heart accelerates. I don't stop him. Then I'm pinned against the counter and he's kissing me passionately.

I lock my mouth on his as we devour each other's lips in an almost desperate, frenzied way. I let him press my body against him, lifting me into his pelvis, molding us together, giving me the feel of him *there.*

He lifts me from the floor, never breaking contact with my lips, and he carries me from the kitchen. Somehow he knows where to take me and eases me back on my bed. I don't resist as he undresses me and I lie still as he gazes down at me. The cool air of the room touches my flesh, and the warmth of his fingers brush it away.

He starts to remove his clothes.

A kiss on my arm; my heart skips a beat.

A touch on my shoulder; tears in my eyes.

He covers my entire body with a kiss and a touch, but he doesn't say the words whispering through my memory. He doesn't need to. A kiss: *I'm sorry.* A touch: *I love you.* Soon, all I'm feeling is him and I'm out of my mind with the feel of him.

His clothes are in a pile on the floor. He's naked, standing there staring at me. He exhales, a ragged shudder through his limbs, and then he's in me. I close my eyes and I revel in the feel of him, the taste of his mouth, the bite of his fingers as he holds my hips, easing out of me slowly, and then slamming into me again harder.

He moves faster and faster. I wrap my legs around him. I rake his back with my nails. I bite his shoulder. I run my tongue along his flesh. I feel myself tighten and tighten. I'm whimpering and he's overfilling me as I melt around him.

He lifts up onto his knees, taking my hips with him, going as deep as he can go inside me. I come quickly, calling out his name. Alan follows with another hard thrust, and the surface of his flesh is claimed by trembling as he pours himself into me.

Slowly he quiets, lowering us to the bed until he's on top of me, his face in my hair. I kiss his head. My fingers wander the surface of his back. We're both quiet inside, and I'm lost in Alan again.

CHAPTER ELEVEN

A sound, distant and faint, pulls me from sleep.

My slowly focusing senses finally identify what woke me. Oh crap, the cordless phone in the kitchen. I never went to Seattle. I never called Neil.

I check the clock on the nightstand and it's after midnight. I lift my face from Alan's chest and ease away from him. I gaze down at him, blinking. It still feels just unreal enough that he's here in my condo in Berkeley that I almost can't take my eyes off him.

After the second time we made love, Alan fell asleep quickly. I stared at him for hours afterward before sleep finally made me stop doing it.

There's enough light in the bedroom that I can see the perfect lines of Alan's face. He looks so peaceful in sleep right now, younger and less intimidating than he did when he brushed past me into the condo yesterday. I want to run my fingers along his features and memorize, with my touch, how he looks at this moment. But I don't want to wake him.

I slip from the bed, take Alan's shirt from the floor, and tug it in place as I quietly go from the bedroom to the kitchen.

I grab the cordless from the counter and click it on. I

slide downward, my back against the counter to sit on the floor. "Hello?"

"Chrissie…" My name is said in a long, amused, aggravated growl. Neil. Silence. Then he says, "What happened?"

I scrunch my nose. "I missed my plane."

Laughter. "Obviously. I waited at the airport for two hours before I figured that one out. What happened?"

The tension uncurls, just a smidge, from my body. He isn't angry.

"Do you want to hear the highlights or the lowlights?"

"Oh, definitely the lowlights," he says, amused.

"I drank too much last night and passed out on the couch. I woke up late. Can we just leave it at that?"

Neil laughs. "If you want to."

I definitely want to, I think to myself, feeling really shitty, even though we have an understanding. An expressed understanding. When we're not together, it means we're not together.

Neil's rule, not mine, delivered before I left Seattle, surprisingly tucked into an overly long non-Neil-like discussion about how he doesn't want me ruining my college years waiting on a guy who spends most of his life on the road. It was just a touch arrogant. A touch conceited. Totally Neil. Totally sweet.

My fingers tighten around the receiver.

"Why didn't you call?" he asks. "I've been worried."

"Trying to figure out how to fix everything. Then I fell asleep."

"You're still coming, right?"

"In a few days. There are some things I should really take care of."

"Chrissie." Another growl. "I want you here now."

I laugh, but I don't feel like laughing. "I'll be there soon."

"Call me with your flight info."

"OK."

"Night, Chrissie."

Click.

I hold the phone in my hands and just stare at it. I spring to my feet, turn the ringer off on the cordless, grab a glass of ice water, and leave the kitchen.

When I enter the bedroom, I freeze. The light is on and Alan is sitting up in bed, smoking.

"A little late for someone to call. Everything all right?"

I tense, searching his eyes, wondering if he could hear me from the kitchen. "That was Neil. He wanted to know why I never made it to Seattle today."

"What did you tell him?"

I shrug. "That I missed my plane."

Alan stares. "Why is he in Seattle?"

"Work. He doesn't live with me anymore."

I climb onto the bed and sit facing him.

His eyes soften with amusement. "What is he? A broke musician?"

There's enough edge in the way he says it that it should piss me off, but it doesn't.

"A brilliant, broke musician."

Alan laughs. "I wouldn't have expected anything less if he's got you interested, Chrissie." His finger lightly traces my cheek. He leans into me. "Give us a kiss, love. You were gone too long."

I melt into him, into the play of his fingers, the feel of his lips, but he holds the space between us. His mouth leaves mine in a slow disconnect, and then he pulls back the rest of his body.

"So what's he like?" Alan asks.

My heart stops in my chest. I can't believe Alan just asked me that.

"Neil?" I repeat stupidly.

Alan lights another cigarette. He laughs, amused. "Yes, Neil. What's he like?"

I shrug. "The exact opposite of you. Very low-key. Outdoorsy. Likes to surf."

He watches me, unruffled. "Did you meet him in Berkeley?"

"No. Santa Barbara."

"Before or after me?"

I have to give it thought. "The same night I met you. We bumped into each other on campus and have been sort of hanging out together ever since."

I put my water on the nightstand. God, that sounded lame.

Alan laughs. "Why is it the girls who are everything wrong for you are the ones you cannot forget? He probably couldn't forget you either, and bumped into you on purpose. You're probably all wrong for him, too."

My body grows cold and I fight to keep from my face that that jab hurt me.

"Why do you think I'm everything wrong for you?"

He takes me in his arms and moves me until I'm curled in bed beside him, my head and arm on his chest. "Because you won't run away with me," he whispers, and I know the voice, the silky ribbons of theatrics. "Tell me you will and we can leave Berkeley together."

I feel his words in my center, but my calm inside suddenly vanishes. This night has been so much more for me than I thought it would be, and it hurts how much I wish I could leave here with Alan.

"You look really good, Alan. Better than you did…"

I break off, unable to finish. I give him a fast once over, and then I pause at the ink on his wrist. I don't recognize it from the details of Alan I carry in my memory.

I trace it with a finger. I'm not sure what it is and I don't remember it. "Is this new?"

"New. I got it last year. After you."

I run the line with my finger again. I look up at him. "What is it?"

He closes his eyes and laughs. "You don't recognize it?"

I frown. "It looks like barbwire, but it's too fragile and the artist forgot the spikes."

"Infinity symbols. The artist made them the exact size of the clasp on your bracelet."

My eyes fly wide. Into my silence he just stares, beautiful, enigmatic and sad.

He lifts a curl from my face. "Linda gave me the bracelet to return to you when we left The Farm. I kept it. It was the only thing you left behind in New York."

He pulls his shirt from my body and his fingers start

moving along my arms, then tracing and touching everywhere. My lips. My neck. My breasts. Stomach. Lower. Even my scars. Everywhere. His mouth begins a slow trek. My nipples harden in urgent anticipation as I'm bathed in the exquisite slowness of Alan making love to me.

My mouth presses against his flesh, kissing randomly and not caring where. I run my hands up his powerfully muscled arms. I kiss his wrist. "I like the new ink."

His face changes. "I hate it. It makes me think of you, and I don't want to."

His mouth closes over mine, trapping my words within me before I can answer him. I feel his flesh searching at my sex, then buried deep within me. The feeling of him inside me is overpowering this time. I arch up, meeting him, pushing him deep inside me.

He lifts his face above me and his eyes are blazing. "It's the only thing you left behind in New York other than me."

Then I'm held tightly beneath him, and he is pounding into me. My heated blood moves through my body. I writhe. He isn't gentle, but there's no pain. There's nothing in my body, my veins, or my senses, except Alan.

~~~

I lie on Alan's chest, wishing away the soon to come daylight.

His arms tighten around me. "I've been out of my mind since you walked out on me in New York."

I lift my face. "I didn't walk out on you. Stop saying that. I told you that when I left New York. I had to go back
~~~

to Santa Barbara. I wasn't leaving you."

An emotional shudder rolls down his arms. "By the time I landed in San Francisco I hated you, but more, I hated myself for wanting you. I hated you and I came to you anyway."

I kiss his chest. "I left New York because of me. Not you."

He stares, the emotion sparks in his eyes changing too quickly for me to read any of them.

"So now that we're together, where are we, Chrissie?"

I lay my cheek back on his chest. "I don't know."

I can feel Alan's stare, intense and indecipherable as it burns into me. After several minutes he leans in, capturing my lips, and starts kissing me again.

~~~

I open my eyes and then shoot upright in bed. The stillness in the air makes reality cruelly inescapable. I'm alone in the condo. Alan is gone.

He left while I was sleeping without so much as a goodbye. *Why would he do that?*

Then all the reasons it is better this way, one by one, flitter through my head. Nia. Neil. That it would hurt too much for me to watch Alan walk out my door.

I lie back down and curl around his pillow. It's better this way. An ending we both needed. The dangling strings tied up. One last goodbye, understood, with the least amount of pain.

My eyes fix on an object on the nightstand. Alan's silver lighter. I recall that day in New York when he threw one at me and it hurt so much seeing it lying on the floor.
~~~

I pick it up. He left it behind by accident, but maybe not since I'm never sure of anything with Alan. I run my finger along its cool surface, feeling its coldness without bite. It's just an oversight, nothing more, but touching it hurts me anyway.

CHAPTER TWELVE

I catch a plane for Santa Barbara instead of Seattle.

I exit the terminal and find Jack waiting at the curb in the drop-off loop. "Hey, Daddy. Thanks for picking me up."

Jack smiles, taking my bag and putting a kiss on my cheek. "I was surprised when you called this morning. I thought you were going to Seattle with friends."

I cringe internally. I'm almost twenty and I still fib to my dad about guys. *How lame is that?* Really lame, since it's obvious Jack must know Neil is sort of living with me. Alan figured it out in two minutes.

"I'm still going to Seattle," I say, climbing into the car as Jack puts my bag in the backseat. "I just wanted to come home for a few days."

Jack climbs into the driver's seat and turns on the ignition. "Everything all right?"

I tense. "Great, Daddy. Homesick, I guess."

Jack smiles. "I miss having you around, too, baby girl. Get homesick any time you want to. I like having you here."

We drive for a while and I stare out the window. Now that I'm here, it isn't as easy as I thought it would be. And I suspect I was wrong thinking it would be easier in person instead of on the phone.

I take in a deep breath. "Daddy?"

"Yes, Chrissie?" he says with humorous exaggeration.

"Have I gotten any letters or anything at the house? Anything you've forgotten to give to me?"

Jack's brows hitch up. "No. Are you expecting something?"

I search his face. "I don't know. Maybe. I've been applying for internships for next year. I haven't gotten any responses. I thought, maybe, I put the wrong address on the forms."

I turn to look out the window again. Jeez, that sounded stupid.

Jack shakes his head. "We haven't gotten anything for you here. But ask Maria. She always knows everything."

Jack laughs and I force myself to laugh, too.

"So how's Neil?"

"I don't see him very much. He's on the road a lot."

"That'll keep you out of trouble," Jack says in a way that makes my entire face color.

"God, Daddy."

Jack laughs again.

"You doing OK at school?"

"Great. It's been weird having Rene gone for the summer, but I think it's been kind of good, us having a break from each other."

Jack parks the car in our driveway. I climb out and wait while he retrieves my bag.

Inside the house, I ask, "Where's Maria?"

Jack shrugs. "I don't know. She's home somewhere."

I move down the hallway, poking my head into rooms,

and then into the kitchen. OK, not here. I turn around and make my way down the far hallway, past my bedroom to the door at the end, and knock.

"Yes?" Maria calls.

"It's Chrissie. Can I come in?"

The door opens and Maria smiles at me.

"Come, chica." She gestures me in with her arm. "I'm only resting. It's hot today, but it is nice to see my girl."

Maria closes the door and I sink on her bed, waiting until she sits in her chair.

"Maria, have I gotten any letters, anything, you haven't given to me?"

Maria stares and my entire body feels covered in needle pricks. I can tell, I can see it. Before she speaks it is on her face; it was she who kept Alan's messages and letters from me.

I stand up, angry now. "Maria, answer me."

Her face changes. "Oh, Chrissie…" and then the room is flooded in a rapid torrent of Spanish and English, the words too quickly spoken for me to fully understand. Something about protecting me. Something about me being like her own daughter. Something about Alan that I'm not even close to being able to translate.

Maria is crying, wringing her hands, worried and miserable.

"Please, stop talking," I beg anxiously. "Why did you do this to me?"

"I love you, Chrissie. I did not want you hurt."

"Well, you hurt me, Maria. More than you know," I exclaim harshly.

"Señor Jack..."

"Don't blame this on my father," I say, cutting her off. "My dad would never have done this to me. He may not have wanted to give me the messages and letters, but he would have given them to me."

She brushes at her tears and her face changes. "I kept the letters, Chrissie. I sent the gifts back. But I have the letters. I have them all. If you want them, the letters."

She's at her armoire, rummaging through things. She pulls out some kind of metal tin and hands it to me. It's an old cookie tin, the kind we get fancy shortbread cookies in.

Seeing the tin makes me think of when I was little, watching Maria save everything—used tinfoil, paper towels, half-eaten meals—and that she *is* the only mother I've ever really known.

"I'm sorry I got really angry, Maria."

She hands me the tin. "I did not think it good for you to give you this last year. So much was happening all at once. You and Señor Jack, both so unhappy."

Her face is so sad that now all I can do is nod.

"Are you going to tell your father?" she asks.

I shake my head. "No, Maria." I kiss her on the cheek. "I just wish you hadn't done this."

And before she can say anything else, I'm out the door toward my bedroom.

I sink on the bed, staring at the tin, afraid to open it. A year of my life in an old cookie tin. A year that cost me Alan forever. I'm not sure I should even look.

I lift off the lid. My eyes widen. There are dozens of letters. I pick them up, my hands trembling. I start laying them on the bed by date. I wipe my nose, dripping with tears. I rip open the first letter and lie back on my bed.

I'm emotionally exhausted when I finish the last letter. They're surprisingly long. Painfully loving. Achingly angry at times. In the last letter, a two-page rant about what a bitch I am, below his name Alan still scribbled a phone number and wrote: *I can't breathe. I can't work. I can't think. Please, Chrissie, call me. Even if it's only to tell me you're OK.*

New tears start and I didn't think I had any more in me. I left New York. But nothing, not time, not even the angry letters Alan sometimes penned among the beautiful ones here, changed a thing.

I'm still in love with Alan, and he's still in love with me. The only thing to change in a year is that Alan is married and we are no longer possible.

CHAPTER THIRTEEN

Spring 1991

I lie on my bed, trying to focus on my book, but I can't.

Neil is reclined with his back against the footboard, sitting in his boxers, facing me. He's listening to music on his Walkman. He's doing nothing to disturb me, but I can't concentrate.

He's been back from Seattle for almost a month this time. He leaves for the road again tomorrow. On-again, off-again, that's what we've been for the last seven months. It's an oddly comfortable arrangement, one I would have never expected to work for me.

As if he senses me studying him, Neil opens his eyes, pulls off his earphones, and smiles. "Why are you staring at me that way, Chrissie? Are you already sick of having me back in Berkeley?"

I give him a shove with my leg. "I like it when you're home."

His green eyes darken. "If you married me, Chrissie, this would really feel like home."

I try to ignore him and look down at my book. I turn a page and can feel him watching. I look up and say, "You ask me every month. The joke is getting old. Maybe you should give it a rest."

He grins. "I ask you every month hoping that will be the month you say yes."

I arch a brow. "Aren't you afraid someday I might say yes?"

He shakes his head in that lazy way he has, his brown waves doing a gentle float against his pillow. "Try saying yes, Chrissie, and see where it gets you."

I crinkle my nose. "The last time I made a rash decision I ended up as a storage locker for your stuff."

He grabs my book and holds it out of my reach. "I'm not giving you back the book until you fuck me."

I reach for it. He pulls it away. "You're impossible today."

He nods. "Probably."

I laugh. He's so cute when he's being stupid and irritating.

"Are you going home to Santa Barbara after your midterms?" Neil asks.

"I'm not sure. Rene wants to go to Palm Springs for spring break."

Neil makes a face. "She couldn't be any shallower if she tried."

I nudge him with my foot. "Be nice. She's been really nice to you lately. Don't stir things up again. It was awful when she stomped around here, pissed at me all the time."

"She asked me this morning when I was going to get my shit out of here. Does that count as her being nice?"

"For Rene? Yes."

Neil laughs.

"Instead of Palm Springs, why don't you travel with me during your break? You haven't done that before, Chrissie, gone out on the road with me. It could be fun."

I make a *gag me* face.

"Fun, huh? Traveling in a van with you and four guys? Staying in those lovely places you tell me about that Ernie Levine has you staying in? No thanks."

"Not even to be with me?" he says, moving his way across the bed.

"Nope."

"You're such a princess."

I resist as he tries to claim my mouth for a kiss. "You guys should fire Ernie. He's a crummy manager. He books you in crappy venues. He doesn't even try to get you radio play. And he should definitely be pushing you to record something more commercial."

"I'll fire him when you say yes and marry me."

I shove Neil away, laughing. "Go away. You're so irritating at times."

He kisses my neck. "Why do you think I'm joking when I ask you to marry me?"

"Ah—because you are."

Neil surrounds me with his arms. "Maybe I'm not joking when I ask." Then his eyes widen. A teasing glint appears. "Maybe I'm joking." He plants a kiss on my stomach. "Or maybe it means I just want to get laid."

His hands close on my hips, tugging me under him, and then he covers me with his body.

I make an aggravated groan. "I need to study, Neil."

He gives me a kiss, and his hand moves under my

dress, then his fingers are beneath my panties and he starts to lightly stir me *there.* No fair, he knows exactly where to touch me to win.

He pushes his lower body into me, deepening the kiss and teasing me with the erection straining inside his boxers.

I push into him, answering his kiss. We feel really good together lately. There's been a subtle change between us, a strange aftermath of me fucking Alan. Neil pulls my panties off me and then he is working his way into me. I groan as his body fills me, curling my legs around his hips, holding me to him.

"God, I miss you when I'm on the road, Chrissie," he whispers in veneration. "You don't…" A gentle glide deep. "…have any idea…" A teasing slow swirl and pull out. "…how much I think of this…"

His words fade with the sudden thrusting of his body, and I close my eyes, feeling the build up inside him. I kiss his neck. I run my nails across his back and meet the thrusts of his body with my hips.

I cry out, my nails digging into his back, and arch up. The shudders roll down my limbs; rippling wave, wave, and then gone. His breathing is ragged as he tries to keep himself from coming. Then he lets loose inside me.

I open my eyes to find Neil staring down at me. He smiles, kisses me, and pulls out. He lies beside me on the bed, settling me against him. "Do you want to go out tonight? Listen to some music somewhere?"

"I can't. I have to study."

He rakes back his hair with his hand. "Do you mind if I go out?"

I shake my head, amused. "Why do you always ask me that? You can do whatever you want to do. You don't need my permission."

Something flashes in his eyes, and I flush and quickly say, "Neil, don't get pissed. I didn't mean it the way it sounded."

His eyes sharpen on my face. "Then what way did you mean it, Chrissie? How else am I supposed to take that one?"

I sit up beside him. "I was just saying, you don't have to worry that you have a girlfriend who's going to go ballistic every time you're out for an hour."

I can feel him studying my face. "You never get jealous? Not even a little? Not even when I'm on the road?"

"No point in either of us being jealous when we're not together. It's a stupid emotion."

"Is it really that simple for you?"

I pretend to think it over. "Today it's that simple for me. Tomorrow I might be a crazy-ass bitch, so you should probably enjoy it while you can."

Neil laughs, shaking his head. "God, you are crazy. Do you want me to run out and get you some dinner first? There's nothing in the kitchen to eat."

"It was my turn to do the shopping. I forgot. Rene's pissed."

"What do you want?" he asks.

"I don't care. Anything."

I follow him with my eyes as he dresses and moves toward the door.

"Hey, Neil, let me study for two hours. Then I'll call it quits. We can go out and kick around for a while."

"Are you sure? I was just giving you a hard time, Chrissie. I like to give you shit, in case you haven't noticed."

"Nope, it's your last night here. I want to go out tonight."

He smiles. "I'll be back with your dinner in about thirty minutes."

~~~

As we walk down the street toward the club, I notice there's a line. I shove my hands into my pockets to keep them warm and wait as Neil speaks with the bouncer to get us in.

I haven't been in this part of Berkeley before. Not exactly my kind of neighborhood. But the club looks popular. Neil takes me by the hand and guides me into the bar. It's a dim, smoky tomb, pulsing and loud. A lot less trendy than the clubs in San Francisco. The room is packed with counter-culture types. No college preppies here. Hardcore rockers, floor to ceiling. This is Neil's kind of haunt, not mine.

As we walk, making our way past bodies and tables, Neil stops to slap a hand here and there, or to talk when his name is called. More than a few girls check him out and I stay close to his back, laying my cheek there when we stop in a *this guy is mine* kind of way.

Neil stops at the edge of the dance floor, scanning the room as if he's looking for something. I see Josh Moss several feet away sitting at a table.
~~~

"Isn't that Josh?" I ask, rising up on my tiptoes to speak into Neil's ear.

He looks in the direction of my stare. He smiles. "Yep. Josh flew up this afternoon. He's driving to Portland with me. I told him he could stay with us tonight if he didn't have something else going on."

My eyes widen in alarm. "You didn't? That one is going to go over great with Rene."

Neil grimaces. "Shit, I didn't think of that when I said he could crash on the couch."

I do groan internally. "Terrific, Neil. She's finally not pissed at me 24/7 and you invite Josh Moss to stay on the couch."

We're both laughing as we near the table.

Josh frowns. "What's the joke?"

"You are, man," Neil says, giving his friend a quick, hard hug.

"Hey, Chrissie," Josh says.

"Hi, Josh. Heard you're staying the night with us."

Neil pinches me in a place Josh can't see.

"If it's not too much trouble," Josh says.

Neil pinches me again. "No trouble, man. It's cool."

I sink onto my chair and Neil calls out for a waitress. After ordering a round of drinks, it takes only a few minutes before I'm completely forgotten by Neil and he's laser-focused in a discussion with Josh.

They start arguing across the table over *About a Girl* and whether Nirvana is a commercial sellout or not. Crap, not this again. Josh doesn't want to bastardize their music by doing something commercial.

"It's not a commercial sellout," I say to Josh. "It's a popular hit. That doesn't make it a commercial sellout."

Josh sits back in his chair, giving me the *what the fuck do you know about anything* look. "Stay out of this, Chrissie. When we get to talking about the cello and symphony, we'll ask for your opinion."

For a guy determined not to be like the mainstream music industry, Josh is an elitist in his own way.

Neil leans across the table toward Josh. "Don't fucking talk to her that way. She's a brilliant musician."

Josh backs off. "I'm just saying."

Tempers are flaring too quickly tonight. God, what's up with these guys? Road fatigue? Road disillusionment?

"It's OK. I won't say another word."

Neil looks at me, shaking his head. "No, Chrissie. You say anything you want to say. Josh is a prick. Don't let him shut you up."

"I'm not. I just don't want to be in the middle of a fight tonight."

Josh laughs. "You think this is a fight? Christ, it's a good thing you never go on the road with us."

"No chance of that ever, Josh," I say in a deliberate, heavily exaggerated way.

Neil stares at me and my cheeks flush. Crap, why did that one piss him off?

Before their quickly escalating argument can turn into what I fear is about to become a quickly escalating argument between Neil and me, the band breaks. In a matter of minutes, they're making their way toward Neil and the guys sink down at our table, flooding it with beer bottles.

I'm given only a brief introduction as "Chrissie" before the laughter and talk swirls. In the fast-moving conversation, I catch that the band is from Seattle and they've been crossing paths with Arctic Hole for nearly six months at West Coast cities' independent tour venues.

Their lead singer stands up, clutching his beer bottle and pointing at Neil. "You've got to sing one song with us, man."

Neil shakes his head. "No, I'm with my girlfriend."

The guy looks at me and I shrug. Why do I always end up an issue when I'm out in guy world?

The singer points at Neil. "She said it was OK, man. Don't hide behind your girlfriend."

Neil laughs. "Do you mind, Chrissie?"

"Why should I mind? I haven't heard you perform in a while. Go sing something for me."

Neil stands. He winks at me. "One song, but only if I can do something commercial sellout-worthy," he says, staring at Josh.

Everyone laughs, I choke on my drink, but Josh glares.

I watch Neil go on stage with the band. He takes a guitar and launches into a conversation with the guys. Good, he's going to play tonight.

Neil goes to the microphone, adjusts the stand and says quietly, "This is for my girlfriend, Chrissie. None of you fuckers boo."

I watch more attentively after that and then he starts to play. It takes me a minute to recognize the song. It's Elton John. It's *Tiny Dancer*, and it's fucking brilliant. The arrangement, down to the lyric changes, makes it completely relevant and current. The music is just edgy enough, with Neil's rasp and touch of dark wistfulness. A haunting song now, instead of a sweet one. It brings to my mind shades of what Judas Priest did with Joan Baez's *Diamonds and Rust.*

Only this is better. It's pure Neil. And Neil is definitely doing this song for me. *Blue jean baby. SB Lady. Lover of this man…* I listen with over-claimed senses, my emotions running sweetly through my veins since it's such a non-Neil-like thing to do to sing a song for me.

Then I look at the room. The way the girls are staring at Neil. He may be doing this as a goof because Josh pissed him off, but crap, he should record this cover.

The music finishes and Neil unplugs and is off stage, seeming oblivious that his joke was a performance he knocked out of the park.

He sinks down in his chair. He points at Josh. "That was for you, fucker."

Josh gives him the finger.

He turns to me, a smile in his eyes. "Or was that for you?" He kisses me. "Did you like your song?"

When he pulls back, I stare up at him wide-eyed. "Neil, that's a hit. You should record it. Put it on the new album."

"Are you fucking crazy, Chrissie?" Josh exclaims.

Neil frowns, running a hand through his hair. "I'm not recording *Tiny Dancer.* That's your song."

"When did it become my song?"

He kisses me again.

"About five minutes ago."

"Then record it for me, Neil."

Neil studies me, shaking his head like he can't believe I mean it.

"You ready to hit it?" he asks Josh.

Josh and I argue about whether the band should record *Tiny Dancer* all the way back to the condo. Neil ignores us both. We enter the condo and he pops a CD in the player, grabs a blanket from the cabinet, and tosses it on the couch.

"We're out of here, Josh." He takes my hand and leads me to my bedroom. "Come on, Chrissie."

Neil is on me the minute the door closes. I try to talk to him, but he's unrelenting in kissing, undressing, and moving me toward the bed.

Later, quiet and spent, we lie holding each other.

He kisses my nose. "I'm going to miss you, Chrissie."

"I'm going to miss you, too, Neil."

"Did you like your song?"

"No. I loved it. You should listen to me. Record it."

Neil laughs.

"I'd need to get the rights to do a cover, and the band would think it's fucked."

I kiss his sex-damp chest. "I don't care. Do it for me."

I tuck myself into Neil's body and tonight we feel wonderful together.

~~~

I walk the guys downstairs to the van early in the morning.

Josh climbs into the passenger seat as Neil opens the cargo bay, tosses his bag in, and then slams the door.
~~~

He folds me in his arms against his chest. "I wish I didn't I have to leave."

"I wish you could stay longer, too."

"I'll be back before summer," he whispers, trailing light kisses across my face.

I give him a long kiss and go with him as he climbs into the driver's seat. I smile up at him through the open window.

"See ya, Chrissie. I'll call you tonight when we reach Portland."

"See ya, Neil."

I step back, and the old van makes a loud sound as the engine turns over, and then Neil drives away. I stare at the road long after he's out of view. I feel really quiet inside standing in the empty parking lot; none of that chaotic feeling. Maybe it's not such a bad thing that I am with Neil.

CHAPTER FOURTEEN

Rene sits on her knees on my bed. She hops and then shakes me.

"Chrissie! Get up. Get dressed. Pack. Let's get out of here."

I grab the pillow beside me and cover my face with it. "I don't want to go to Palm Springs. It's got to be a ten-hour drive each way. We've only got a week off. I just want to stay in Berkeley. Or maybe go to Santa Barbara. I can't decide which."

"Chrissie." That's spoken as a growl. I lift the pillow and Rene stares down at me. "What's wrong?"

"Nothing. I don't want to go to Palm Springs for spring break."

Rene is studying me in that hyper-analytical way she has as if she's trying to diagnose my mood.

"I'm not letting you stay alone in this condo for a week and have another spring break meltdown. Get over it already. You act like you're the only girl ever to be dumped by a guy. Are you going to be a mess every spring break over Alan forever? Let's go have fun."

I ignore the insult because I never told her about Alan's detour to Berkeley.

"I'm not mourning anything. I don't want to go to

Palm Springs and get wasted."

"Then we won't get wasted," Rene says reasonably.

"We always get wasted when we go out together."

Rene arches her brow. "I always get wasted. You're always no fun."

I throw a pillow at her, hoping she'll go away.

She glares at me.

"If I'm no fun then why do you want me along?"

Rene pretends to think about it. "Because you're fun when you're no fun." She collapses beside me on the pillow. "Chrissie, come with me. Is it Neil? Is he being a jerk? Does he not want you to go?"

"Neil is never a jerk. I wish you'd figure that out and stop being so shitty to him."

Rene's eyes widen and her expression shifts into disgust. "Oh, and thanks a lot, belatedly, for the heads-up last week that Josh Moss would be sleeping on our couch when I got home."

"Was it awful?"

Rene's brows pucker. "Not awful. Sort of a weird. But weird in a good way. We talked for hours. It was kind of nice."

I stare at her. Rene does not like intimacy with guys, and talking for hours definitely falls into the intimacy cubby.

"Talked? Are you saying you spent all night with Josh when he was here and you just talked?"

Betraying color creeps across Rene's cheeks.

"I didn't say I didn't fuck him later. It was really good."

"Slut." I only say it because it's a joke.

"Prude," she says fiercely back at me.

I lie back down on the bed, she copies my posture, and I turn toward her. "Are you still going to Palm Springs?"

Rene looks startled by the question. "Of course. Everyone is going to be there. I want you to come."

"Nope. Not doing it."

Rene gives me a hard stare. "I'm going with or without you."

"Then go. You'll have more fun without me."

Rene springs from the bed. She stops at the door and stares back at me. "You can still pack and join me if you want to."

I nod. "OK."

She closes my bedroom door loudly behind her. Message received, Rene. You're pissed and you want me to know it. I roll over in bed and tug the blankets tightly around me.

Rene pops back into my room two hours later. I'm still in bed.

"I'm heading out now. Sure you don't want to join me?" she asks.

"No. I'm pretty sure I'm going to go to Santa Barbara. I'm kind of homesick."

"Can I still take the car or do you want me to leave it? I can hitch a ride down with friends."

"It's OK. Take the car."

"You sure?"

She crosses the room and gives me a hug.

"I'll see you in a week," she says, rushing from the room.

Five minutes later I hear the front door slam. I feel completed deflated and I don't know why. My emotions cascade over me in relentless waves. I roll over in bed, agitated in my flesh.

It's been seven months since Alan was here. Not one call. I didn't expect that, though I probably should have. *Stupid, Chrissie.* Almost as stupid as thinking spending two days with Alan would change anything in either of our lives.

I close my eyes and begin to drift. Yes, sleep will be good. Very, very good.

~~~

I'm lying in bed where I pretty much haven't moved from all day. I reach for the bottle on my nightstand, pour a glass of wine, and then stare at the tin containing Alan's letters.

I lift the lid. I pull out the most recent one. *Please call me, Chrissie*…I stare at the number printed so precisely beneath his name. Jeez, it's over a year old. Just because Alan isn't touring again until May doesn't mean I can find him. The phone number is probably not even good anymore.

I reach for the phone. Lame, Chrissie, so lame to call him. But Alan deserves to know I got his letters…finally. Shouldn't I at least tell him that I got them?

I punch in the numbers and wait. Ring. Ring. Ring.

"Hello, may I help you?"

I can tell by the voice it's not a residence of Alan's, but an answering service.
~~~

"I'd like to speak with Alan, please."

"Whom may I say is calling?"

Crap. I don't want to give my name. Not to a service. And what if I'm not on the call list? There has to be an approved caller list, and that would be an emotional blow, too much with all I'm feeling today, to call Alan and not even be on the list.

"Miss, can I help you?"

I scrunch up my face. "Tell Alan it's Chrissie Parker."

Click. Static. Click. Did she disconnect me? Oh, this is wrong. Stupid. Pathetic. Why am I doing this?

I'm about to hang up the phone when I hear, "Chrissie?" in a low, raspy voice.

I put the receiver back up against my ear and close my eyes tightly. "Hello, Alan."

Silence.

"I didn't expect you to call," he says.

Weird, blunt Alan honesty. I don't know how I'm supposed to take that one. Happy I called or irritated? I can't tell. Every muscle in my body tenses even more.

More silence. Longer this time.

"I didn't expect *to* call. But I did," I say.

Alan laughs.

"Yes, you called. A good thing. Otherwise I would be standing here talking to no one, looking ridiculous."

I force a laugh that I can hear is a little rough and nervous.

"Are you OK, Chrissie?"

I hug my legs with my arms, pressing my cheeks against my knees. "I'm good actually. It's just…"

"Just?"

I take in a deep breath. "I wanted to let you know I finally got your letters."

Another pause.

"I meant every word I wrote," he says softly. He gives a small laugh. "Except for the mean ones. I was angry some days."

I laugh. He says that with just the right amount of elegant inanity.

"I liked the mean letters. Those are the ones that say you still cared."

It takes a moment for my brain to catch up with my words. *Oh crap!* Why did I say that?

"Are you really OK, Chrissie?"

His voice is different this time. I feel my heart accelerate. I feel my limbs go weak, and I just want to bury myself under the covers and cry.

"I've already told you. I'm good."

"What are you doing?"

"Sitting home, alone, during spring break with your letters." *Oh God, what made me say that?* I force a laugh, praying he takes this as a joke. "Pretty pathetic, huh?"

He doesn't laugh. Damn. More silence.

"I should let you go, Alan."

I start to hang up the phone when I hear his voice in the receiver. I quickly put it back against my ear.

"...don't hang up, Chrissie," he says.

I wait.

Nothing.

"Alan, I think this was a mistake for us both that I

called. Do you want me not to call again? I just thought…"

I can't finish. The even breathing growing louder with each word I speak through the receiver makes it impossible to finish.

"I should go," I say.

"No," Alan says firmly. "I'm in Southern California, Chrissie."

"You're not in New York? You're not on the road?"

"No. I'm in Malibu. Working." He inhales deeply. A long pause. "I'm alone. I told myself I wouldn't do this unless you called. I'm alone, Chrissie. Spend the week with me."

~~~

I pause at the drop-off loop curb at LAX, not exactly sure what to do next.

A car pulls up in front of me. A very sleek, black, foreign sports car. I move toward it and the passenger window rolls down.

"Chrissie. Toss your bag in the back. I'm not getting out of the car. It's better that I don't."

I open the door, drop my bag on the floorboard, and then sink into the passenger seat beside him. Alan starts to speed out of the airport.

We sit in silence as our drive takes us through clogged, slow-moving Southern California freeways toward the beach. After what feels like a never-ending vacuum of quiet, Alan's voice pulls me from my thoughts. "Was your flight good?"

I turn my face from the window and my eyes fully settle on him for the first time since I climbed into the car.
~~~

"It was OK." I struggle for something funny to say to break the tension suffocating me. "For proletarian travel."

Alan laughs, downshifting the car for the slowing traffic ahead. "I should have sent the plane," he jokes quietly. "I know how you hate proletarian travel, Chrissie."

A small measure of nervousness leaves me and I smile. "Nope. I'm a commercial travel kind of girl these days."

"Probably all the traveling between Berkeley and Seattle," he says matter-of-factly.

I can feel his eyes studying me even though his gaze looks locked on the road, and I tense. He just brought Neil into the car with us, and I'm not sure why he did that.

"How long are you on the West Coast?" I ask, changing the subject.

"Four weeks. Then on the road again for another year."

"You said on the phone you were here working. What are you working on?"

"A new album." Alan gives me a small smile. "What did you think I was working on?"

I shake my head. "OK, stupid question."

I stare out the window, focusing on the ocean, as we whiz down the Pacific Coast Highway, away from the town and the hotels.

"Where are you taking me?" I ask.

"I have a house here."

"Since when? I thought you hated California."

"I used to," he says. "I've spent quite a bit of time here in the last two years. Now it's where I prefer to be."

I chance another look at him and I wonder what he's thinking and what he thinks about me being here. No part of this has flowed in a predictable way, but then nothing with Alan ever does.

"I thought you would never live anywhere but New York," I say.

"And I thought you would call me sooner after Berkeley. I never expected to wait seven months to hear from you."

The sharpness of his tone makes anxiety flood my stomach, and then Alan's eyes fix on me. He looks a touch irritated and a touch angry, and I don't know why he should be either since I'm the one who called him.

I turn my head and stare out the window.

We pull into a narrow driveway hugging a stunning multi-level concrete and glass structure rising above the beach in Malibu. I climb from the car before he reaches my door and wait as he walks to me. He doesn't look at me, and I realize that he hasn't touched me, not even in a casual way, since I got here. He's deliberately maintaining space between us.

"Let's go inside," Alan says as he reaches in for my bag. "The press doesn't seem to know about this place yet, but we shouldn't stand out here all afternoon."

He gives me a benign sort of nothing smile. My scalp prickles as every nerve in my body is suddenly blasted by a chill. The press. I don't know how I failed to put *that* worry on my mental list of reasons not to do this. As awful as it was after New York, it is going to be doubly so if anyone finds out we've been together again.

I step back from him quickly and hurry ahead down the walk to the house. I wait as he unlocks the door, and rush into the house before him.

It's warm inside, dimly lit, with a giant wall of glass overlooking the Pacific Ocean. There's a wide patio, one flight of stairs below, just beyond the living room, surrounded by a tiled, concrete privacy wall. The area is artfully decorated with enormous greenery, potted trees and ferns, tables positioned near fire pits, and chaise lounges encircling a blue-bottomed pool.

I drag my gaze from the exterior and take in the interior of the house. It's stunningly turned out in white and black shabby-chic furnishings with natural wood tables and giant floor-to-ceiling canvases encased in glass of boldly colored European Impressionist art. The walls are white, and the floors a darkly painted surface that looks almost like the concrete of the foundation. There are instruments everywhere, personal possessions only lightly sprinkled here and there. The house does not have the feel of having ever been lived in.

I turn to find Alan standing just inside the entry hall. I watch as he moves to the bar to pour himself a tall scotch, and my nervousness prompts me to wander around the room. I pretend to examine a Native American bowl of some kind resting on the coffee table as Alan sits on the arm of an overstuffed chair. I can feel the heavy pressure of his eyes on me. Why is he just sitting there, staring at me and saying nothing?

I search for something to say. "How often do you come here?"

"I spend most of my time here when I'm in the States. This is where I come when I want to be alone."

"Inviting me sort of ruins that, doesn't it?"

"That depends on why you are here, Chrissie."

Startled, I turn to look at him, and instinctive fear rises through my center. Oh no, I've seen that expression before, and how I've imagined this night might play out just radically changed.

It seems like Alan doesn't talk or move, forever.

Then he sets down his drink. "I'm not sure I should want you here. I haven't decided yet. I'm trying to figure out why you called me."

I fight to maintain my composure, but it is not easy with the way he is looking at me. His stare warns that this could go any direction depending on how I answer him. His mouth is slightly open, his breathing is harsh, and I can tell he is struggling to stay calm.

"I don't know why I called. Does it matter?"

His eyes flash, and then he's across the room. He keeps his eyes on me, unblinking, and while nothing is showing on the surface, the anger is jolting through him.

"What the fuck do you want from me, Chrissie?"

I take a step back from him and his features tighten with unconcealed anger.

"I don't want anything," I whisper anxiously.

Alan grabs my chin, forcing me to meet his smoldering eyes. His expression is disconcerted, angry, and even sad. "Then I will take you back to the airport and dump you there. Why are you here?"

Panicked and terrified, I manage to hold it together, even as a weird feeling of déjà vu surrounds me. My mind fills with disjointed scenes of the night in New York when

I was afraid he would dump me in the hallway wrapped in a sheet.

His gaze, burning and angry, never lifts from me, and I am quaking like a leaf. His eyes and posture warn me this is not a dose of Alan theatrics, but a dangerously serious moment and if I answer it wrong we will be over forever this time.

I stare up at him. "I'm here because I love you."

We stand together, staring at each other, and very gradually he relaxes. Now, on top of everything, I feel like I'm going to cry. Alan closes his eyes and exhales, and then he is lifting me from the floor.

CHAPTER FIFTEEN

I open my eyes to a room glowing with moonlight and Alan warm against my back, still holding on to me.

I turn on my other side to look at him. As badly as we started this, the week has been wonderful. I recall his weird manner when we arrived first at the house, his anger and how he stared at me. It didn't occur to me until that moment that I hadn't said *I love you* to Alan. Not in Berkeley. Not on the phone. And not in my first minutes here. It was in my heart. It was in my head. Somehow I never said it.

Slipping from the bed, I spot the shirt Alan was wearing yesterday lying on the floor and I shrug into it. I go into the bathroom, quietly close the door, and I sink onto the icy travertine floor, staring at myself in the full wall mirror. I leave tomorrow for Berkeley. It hurts so much every time I think of returning to my life there.

A light trickle of tears spills down my cheeks since I don't know what happens after tomorrow. I'm still not sure what we are and what *this* is. Logic tells me when I walk out that door we are over, but my heart doesn't want to believe it.

I hear the door open and I lift my face to find Alan staring down at me. He crosses the space between us and sinks beside me on the travertine. "Chrissie, why are you crying?"

"I don't know."

He leans his back against the tub, copying my posture, legs bent in front of him, and lets out a slow, even breath. His eyes lock with mine in the reflection. "If you're crying in here over us being together, then you should stop it now," he murmurs, a trace of irritation in his voice. "It's probably the first sane thing either of us have done in over two years. It's definitely the first sane thing I've done since you left New York."

A soggy laugh pushes its way out of my emotion-tight throat. I lay my cheek on my knees and stare at the scar on my wrist. How ugly the scar looks in all moments of my life except when I'm with Alan.

"I don't think I would qualify as a sane thing for anyone to do, not even you," I mutter, deliberately silly to hide that I feel completely overwhelmed.

He doesn't smile, but shakes his head and eases back from me. He reaches into the tub and turns on the taps. "Why is it you still can't talk to me?"

"It's not just you, Alan."

"I know. But with me it shouldn't be that way."

I watch him as he focuses on filling the tub, feeling my heart clench tighter. He's right. I should be able, after all we've been through, to say anything to Alan. I don't know why I can't and I don't know why I always seem to be my worst *me* with him.

He turns off the knobs, undresses me and sets me in the tub. He climbs in behind me and eases me back against him. His hands move up and down my arms with the soap. "Tell me what's going on inside that head of yours, Chrissie."

"I don't want to leave tomorrow."

"Then don't. Stay."

"I can't stay, Alan. My classes start next week. I can't not show up, especially since I don't even know what this is."

"This?" The way he repeats that makes me tense. "I love you. You love me. That's what this is. It's that simple."

I can feel him studying me, trying to assessing my reaction to this, but it's not simple and I don't know what to say so I say nothing.

"Are you going back to Santa Barbara or Berkeley tomorrow?" he asks.

"Berkeley."

"I won't call you unless you tell me you want me to. Do you want me to call after you leave here, Chrissie?"

I can feel him watching me, waiting. "I want you to call."

He continues to wash me, and I can feel his body relax and quiet behind me. In spite of my internal distress, I feel my emotions start to calm. His long fingers wash me gently, up and down, very slowly everywhere, changing me from disjointed parts into a single vessel, aroused and wanting him.

My hair is lifted from my shoulders and his lips touch my neck. He turns me in his arms, but he doesn't lower me to straddle him. Instead, I'm gently lifted and he lays me on the wide tiled surface beneath the window. My damp flesh chills even as I heat with anticipation. He slides my hips to the edge and I lean back on my elbows atop the stacks of towels there. My legs are brought to rest and dangle over his shoulders, and he's devouring me with his mouth *there,* the strokes of his tongue, torturously light and slow, potent anyway.

His mouth roams my thighs, my hips, my scars, and my sex. My legs start to quake and his hands clasp my thighs, his mouth never breaking contact with me. I start to move against him, impatient in a feral way. I don't know how he does this to me, from emotional disarray to sexually urgent from the first second he touches me.

He goes deeper with his tongue and I'm raging. My fingers curl in his hair and my back arches. I begin to shake more violently, and I come against his mouth in shuddering waves, but only now because he wants it so.

Panting and limp, I lie back on the towels, his mouth still there moving lightly against me. He scoops me up in his arms and carries me back to bed. He lies us both atop it, our bodies damp, and starts kissing and touching me. He sinks his body into me deeply, but stays carefully balanced above me on his arms, surrounding me, and I'm unable to see anything but his face.

I'm breathing hard and I'm pulsing again. He pounds hard into me in a frantic rhythm, faster and faster, less gentle each thrust. He doesn't hold back. He pumps his body in me and lets go.

His body moves from mine in an uncharacteristically quick departure and a ripple of pain moves along my nerves from his rapid retreat from my flesh. My eyes flutter wide to find Alan sitting on his knees staring down at me.

"This is what I'll think of when you're not with me…" he roughly breathes into my capering senses. "How you look at this moment loving me."

~~~

The next morning, I open my eyes to find Alan sitting on the edge of the bed, dressed. Our last night together was intense and I'm emotionally drained.

I stare at him and say nothing. His posture tells me he's struggling with something. Perhaps with what he wants to say. Or maybe with what he doesn't want to say. I can't tell which. Everything feels strange, off-kilter, between us.

Alan looks at me. "This can be anything you want it to be, Chrissie."

He eases forward and sets something on the table beside the bed. I can't look because I'm afraid of what I will see. I watch him walk from the room, and then shift my gaze to the table next to me. Everything inside me collapses in slow, agonizing waves as I pick up the key. The metal in my hand is cold and has a jagged edge. In elegant simplicity Alan has clarified exactly what we *are* in a brutal, single shot-glass-like dose of reality.
~~~

CHAPTER SIXTEEN

December 1992

I curl on the couch, sipping a cup of tea, watching as Neil and Rene battle over video games. Now that Neil is hardly ever here and his music is getting some radio play, Rene seems not willing to break the détente that started when Neil moved to Seattle in 1990.

Rene throws her controller, only just missing the TV. She points at Neil. "Asshole."

He leans back into the couch cushions, laughing in exasperation. "You're not only the most shallow girl I've ever met, you're a poor sport and you suck at video games."

Rene springs to her feet. "I'm going to grab another beer. Do you want one?"

Neil nods. "Yep, bring me one."

He laughs as he watches her walk away and then turns until he's facing me on the couch. "Are you OK? You've seemed really quiet, kind of off for the last week."

I force a smile that does nothing to calm my inner distress. "I'm OK. Just worn out from finals and I'm not looking forward to that seven-hour drive home tomorrow."

He pulls my feet onto his lap and starts to rub them. "Then don't go back to Santa Barbara. Stay with me."

"I've got to go home, Neil. I don't want to piss off Jack by ditching him for the holidays."

"I'd go with you, but I need to get back to Seattle."

I take a sip of my tea. "I know." I smile. "But it's nice having you here now, though."

"I'm not sure I've ever told you this before," Neil says quietly. "You're not just my girlfriend. You're my best friend."

There is a sweet kind of smile on his face now, shy and affectionate, and it makes my heart twist.

"You're my best friend, too," I say.

He shakes his head and looks up at me. "I wouldn't be where I am without you."

I give him a nudge with my leg and make a face. "Neil, don't get all sappy on me tonight. I like it better when you're a conceited jerk."

He laughs, shaking his head. "I'm not a jerk. I just like to mess with you. And don't tell Rene I'm your best friend. She'll start hating me again."

We're both laughing when Rene bounces back into the room, drops a beer onto Neil's lap and then retrieves the controller.

Rene settles on the couch. "Ready for a rematch, jerk?"

Neil sets my feet back on the cushion. "Wasn't sure you were coming back for a rematch. It took you so long to grab a beer I thought maybe you had a guy in the kitchen."

Rene makes a *fuck you* face and Neil winks at me. I feel a smile that doesn't rise to my lips. It's nice they're friends.

They start to play and I watch and sip my tea. I'm pulled from my troubling thoughts by the sound of my mobile phone ringing in the bedroom and I set down my cup.

Rene rolls her eyes. "Her majesty's private line."

I climb over and pause as I pass Rene. "I wouldn't have a private line if you weren't on the phone all night every night."

I go into the bedroom, shut the door, grab my mobile phone from the drawer and flip it open. "Hello?"

"Chrissie."

I lie down on the bed.

"You sound like you were sleeping," Alan says. "I'm sorry. Did I wake you?"

"You didn't wake me. Just feeling lazy today. It's only four in the afternoon here, Alan. Where are you?"

"I'm not sure where I am…" Alan says, laughing. "It's nighttime, though. I'm thinking of you. So I called."

I can hear lots of noise and voices in the background. It sounds like a party, and his voice is raspier, more gravelly like it is when he's just been on stage.

"So what are you doing?" I ask, rolling over to lie on my side.

"Sitting on a rooftop terrace. Drinking. Thinking of you," he says in a sweet way.

"Nasty thoughts or nice thoughts?"

"A little of both."

I start to laugh. "Me, too. You have definitely been

away too long this time."

"For me too, Chrissie," he says. "With the travel from Europe I can only manage two days, but I can be in Malibu in January, the tenth and the eleventh, if you want me there."

"Stupid question. What do you think?"

"I want to hear you tell me you want me there."

I feel tears gathering in my eyes and a sob build in my throat, and I don't want them. Not today. "I told you it was a stupid question, isn't that good enough?"

"Not nearly," he whispers.

"I want you there. Very much."

I sniff back the drips from my nose that came with my tears, covering the mouthpiece so he can't hear. "Why are you going through so much hassle to be with me for two days, Alan?"

"I told you. Missing you. Thinking of you. Nasty thoughts."

He says it succinctly like he's reading a grocery list and I smile.

"And I lied," he says, low and raspy. "There are no nice thoughts. They're pretty much always nasty these days."

"Me, too."

"I'm sorry I can't be with you for Christmas. With the travel time and the short hops, it's not possible."

"Don't worry about it. It's OK."

"I would be there if I could, Chrissie."

"I know." I take a moment to rein in my emotions and then say, "I'm going home for Christmas, so you'd be pretty much out of luck if you were here."

Alan laughs. "I would even eat Mexican food on the patio with Jack if it got me back to you." Silence, and then I can hear his breaths followed by a long exhale. "I'm tired of the road, baby. I'm tired of missing you."

Everything starts to run loose and frantic through me. I need to hang up the phone quickly. I don't want to get upset with Alan since it makes the long hours between the calls miserable for me.

"I've got to run, Alan."

"Are you OK, Chrissie?"

I hold the tips of my fingers to my nose, pressing in almost until it hurts, to keep the emotion from surfacing.

"I'm more than OK. I can't wait for January. I want you here. Now."

I click off the phone before he can answer me. As anxiously as I wait for each call from Alan, sometimes hearing his voice is too hard for me.

~~~

Neil comes into the bedroom three hours later and flips on the lights.

I look up. "You guys done playing with each other?"

He gives me a revolted, pained expression. "Very funny. A disgusting thought, playing with Rene, but funny."

I smile and he sinks down on the floor beside me.

"So why are you sitting here in the dark alone?" Neil asks.

"Just thinking."

He brushes the hair back from my face and says, "You
~~~

thinking in the dark. That's never good. What's wrong, Chrissie?"

I take a moment to collect my thoughts and try to figure out the best way to do *this*.

"You're back on the road again next week for another four months, aren't you?" I ask.

His gaze fixes on my face and there's just enough hint of alarm in his eyes that I tense. I wonder what slipped into my voice just then.

His eyes are now searching my face, more alert and less smiling. "Yes. I told you that already. Four months this time. Ernie has actually booked some pretty good venues."

I can't bear to look at him so I stare off into a vacant space in the room.

"I think we should give us a rest for a while. Take some time off. I graduate in a few months. I'm leaving Berkeley. You live in Seattle when you're not on the road. I thought we might want to take a break."

Silence, and it pushes in on me until I look at him. Then Neil's posture changes from loose limbs into a tense, alarmed sort of arrangement.

"A break?" Neil says. "I thought after graduation you might go on the road with me for a while. We can spend more time together. Make this better for you. I know it hasn't been everything you want it to be, but I thought with you out of school, we could try to make it work better for the both of us."

"I don't think that would be good for either of us."

"Fuck, Chrissie. What are you saying?"

I don't answer him.

"Are you saying we're over? You want to end us?"

That's the door I've been fumbling to get to and for some reason the fact that Neil said it makes it something I'm afraid to walk through. I stare at my hands and say nothing. *Crap, what's wrong with me?* We're here, finally in a moment together where we can let go of each other, and I can't will myself to be the one to bring us through it.

I run a hand through my hair. "We're practically never together. You must have something else going on. Have you ever…" The look in his eyes traps the words in my throat.

Neil stares. "Have I what?"

"It's not like we're a couple or anything. Full time. Exclusive," I say.

Those warm green eyes grow opaque in a way I've never seen before.

"You're out on the road a lot of the time," I continue. "You're a hot guy. There must girls all over you. You must be sleeping with someone else."

In a flash, he turns into angry Neil. I've never seen him get angry this fast.

"You think I'm screwing around on the road? Is that what this is about? Fuck, Chrissie. I love you. Why don't you get that?"

"I just want to know, Neil," I somehow manage to whisper. "It doesn't have anything to do with anything. Not my decision, anyway. I've always sort of wondered so I'm asking. We've always had an agreement. When we're not together, we're not together. Whatever you've done, it doesn't matter. I've never asked. I want to know. And I won't get pissed."

"Well, you've fucking pissed me off, Chrissie."

"Most musicians would be happy if their girlfriend said it was OK to do what they want when they're on the road," I murmur, trying to get this to cool down.

It doesn't work. His face swivels toward me. His eyes are cutting as they lock on me. "So is that what you are? My girlfriend? You've finally figured out you're my fucking girlfriend?"

He stands up.

"What is that supposed to mean?" I ask.

He stops beside the bed and stares down at me. "We have been together for three years, Chrissie. What the fuck do you think we're doing here? I haven't been with anyone else. I know you haven't been with anyone else. That makes us pretty fucking exclusive, everywhere in the world except in your head."

My entire body is covered in a burn by the time he's finished. I stare up at him. "You haven't been with anyone else?" I whisper.

God, I wish he'd stop looking at me that way.

"No." He says it firmly. Emotionally. His eyes widen, heavy with meaning. There's a long pause where he does nothing but stare at me. A ragged breath leaves his chest. "I don't want to be with anyone but you."

The look on his face rends my heart.

"I'm sorry, Neil. I just think we should take a break."

~~~

What a miserable night. I stare at my ceiling wondering how I am going to make it through the morning.
~~~

The long hours awake in my bed felt just like they did Neil's first night at the condo, with him on the couch and me in here. Uncomfortable and weird. It shouldn't make me feel so badly, it's the right thing for us both, but knowing he's out there, no longer a part of my life, is a wretched thing anyway.

I climb from the bed and pad to the door. Opening it a crack, I peek out into the living room. I can hear Neil breathing from the couch. He's still asleep. It would have been better if he'd packed up and left early. It doesn't matter. In a few more hours we'll both be out of here; Neil back to Seattle, and me, a few weeks in Santa Barbara and then Alan again.

I push Alan from my mind. Making it through the next few hours with Neil is enough for one day.

I quietly make my way to the kitchen. Rene is sitting at the table with a bowl of cereal.

"What happened last night?" she exclaimed, her eyes fixed in a probing stare. They move with me as I grab a bowl before settling in the chair across from her. She sits back. "You and Neil have a fight?"

I fill my bowl. "Not really a fight. Not much of one."

Rene studies me then frowns. "I heard you arguing, but it sounded like it ended quickly. I thought it was all good. Then this morning I find Neil sleeping in the living room. It's weird."

She waits for me to explain and I don't look at her. Last night was definitely weird. Neil didn't stay angry very long. He just sort of slipped back into sweet Neil, and the rest of the night wasn't terrible. That's another strange thing I'm struggling with this morning. It hurt how easily Neil was himself again. I don't feel even close to normal today.

"What's going on, Chrissie?"

"Rene, I don't want to talk about it. Not now. Can't we just wait? We'll talk about it in the car on the way to Santa Barbara, OK?"

Rene's eyes widen, and I move from the table to grab a cup of coffee. My hands are shaking as I try to add the creamer.

"Did you guys break up?" she asks.

I whirl from the counter and glare at her. "What part of 'I don't want to talk about this' do you not get?"

I slam down the creamer and hurry back to my bedroom. I should have just stayed in here. I sink on my bed and stare at the closed door. An hour later I hear Neil moving around. I can tell it's him—slower, easy ambling steps, more quiet than Rene's rapid-motion thumping.

I sit in my room, listening to the movements beyond the door. I can hear Rene talking with Neil, but their voices are too soft for me to make out their words. Thirty minutes later I hear the slam of Rene's bedroom door.

Cautiously, I go back into the living room. Neil is already dressed, sitting on the floor, sorting things as he occasionally shoves something into the pack he takes everywhere.

I curl on the couch and watch him.

"You doing OK, Chrissie?"

He doesn't look at me.

"I'm OK. How are you?"

He shrugs, but his jaw tightens. "I'm almost packed up. Is it OK if I don't take everything today? When I'm off the road at the end of April, I'll come back, pack up the rest and send it to Santa Barbara." He looks at me then. "If that's OK with you, Chrissie."

I swallow the lump in my throat. "Sure, Neil. It's fine."

He stares at me. "Hey, Chrissie, don't forget we're friends. You need anything, you call and I'll be here. OK?"

I look away and I can tell by his voice it isn't bullshit and he means it. God, why does Neil have to be such a great guy, in all moments, even this?

After I sit here for what feels like forever saying nothing, because I really don't know what to say after that, he springs to his feet and starts stacking things atop a box. Once his pack is set there, he picks it up.

I stand up and cross the room to him.

"I'll call when I get back to Seattle if that's cool with you," he says.

Tears sting behind my lids. "You can call anytime you want, Neil. I don't want to lose you as a friend."

I stay standing close to him, expecting him to kiss me on the cheek or something, but neither of us move. Then he walks to the door.

I follow him with my gaze, frozen. Everything is less certain and harder.

Neil looks at me and laughs. "Are you going to get the door for me, Chrissie?"

I sink my teeth into my lower lip to hold back the tears. "Sorry, that was stupid of me, wasn't it?"

I cross the room and open the door for him.

"See ya, Chrissie."

"See ya, Neil."

I stare into the hallway as Neil lugs his things toward the elevator. Ending it was right for the both of us, but it still feels like I've done the wrong thing anyway.

CHAPTER SEVENTEEN

I sit on the top step of the stairs built into the cliffs and stare at the ocean.

Even with the sea breeze, I am warm and uncomfortable today. Crap, it's January. Why is it seventy-four degrees? Why is it always seventy-four degrees? Nothing ever changes in Santa Barbara. Life plods along in a slow pace, familiar, and even the good and bad are always the same.

Is that why Jack loves it here? Jeez, there are times it drives me crazy. How everything is always constant and never new and unexpected. The city, the people. Fuck, even the weather. Unchanging, always the same, like me.

Nearly four years at Cal and I'm exactly where I always end up; Chrissie alone on the cliffs, not even close to figuring out me. Ending it with Neil didn't change a thing. I don't feel any better inside, just different, and I still don't know where I'm going to be in the spring after Berkeley.

This Christmas was definitely far from a Hallmark moment. Sure, I got my roses, but no call from Alan. I didn't expect one since I was stupid enough to leave my mobile phone in Berkeley. And I definitely didn't expect that Rene wouldn't call because she's pissed at me for dumping Neil. She hopped a plane to Bermuda with Patty without even giving me a ring. Neil called, though. It was awful, really strained at first, and then it started to gel and smooth. We hung up in a good place.

I stare at the water, shaking my head. I've had a miserable winter break, it felt melancholy not to be with Neil this year, and to top it off, there was *last night*, the night Jack didn't come home for the first time in my life.

God, that was awful in every way. Me sitting with Maria this morning, the two of us having a normal breakfast, and seeing her turn red and get all flustered when I asked where my dad went. Then the rapid stream of English and Spanish, always instantly nerve-jolting because it only happens when she's in a panic about something she doesn't want to discuss with me, the words too fast to translate clearly.

Jeez, I must have sat there ten minutes staring at her trying to figure out that one until I picked out enough words to get *lady friend* and *long-term thing.* At least I think that's what she said, and I'm definitely going to leave it at that—coming face-to-face with the reality that Jack does go out to get laid. It's not like I *didn't* think so, but it's unsettling to have it pushed in your face over a bowl of Cheerios. It hurts that Jack has had a long-term thing and never mentioned it me.

Why would Jack not tell me this? What is it about me that the people in my life can't always be direct with me, not even my own father? And why am I never direct with them?

The sound of a door closing makes me turn and I spot Jack crossing the lawn toward me. Jack is smiling, his blue eyes twinkling, and he looks exactly the same as he always does with me, but for some reason my stomach knots.

Jack sinks down beside me on the step and sets a Diet Coke next to me. Sodas on the cliffs. *Not good, Chrissie, not good. He wants to talk to me.*

I force a smile to my face.

"What you doing out here, sitting all alone, baby girl?"

"Just thinking."

Jack smiles, but I suddenly feel extremely awkward. It's obvious we both know he wasn't here last night. Is it weirder to ask or weirder not to?

I say, "I take off tomorrow."

Jack pops open his can, frowning. "You do? I thought you were staying until the semester starts. That's another week."

"Nope. Heading out of here."

"Going to Seattle?"

"Nope."

Jack's brow crinkles quizzically. "Was kind of a quiet Christmas this year, wasn't it?" he asks.

"It was fine for me."

Jack stares at the ocean. "Feels strange not having Neil here."

I look at him, trying to figure out where he's going with this since I really don't want to have a heart-to-heart with my dad about Neil.

"Neil's always on the road. Nonstop. He's practically never here during the holidays."

Jack laughs. "He's always here. If he's not somewhere in this house with you, you're on the phone with him. Just sort of noticed that the phone didn't ring very much the last couple of weeks. What's going on?"

I shrug and don't say anything.

"I kind of like Neil," Jacks says after a moment of my silence. "He doesn't seem like a dump-and-run kind of guy. He seems pretty hung up over you. You've been kind off since you got here. Preoccupied and quiet. Is it because you broke up with Neil?"

Oh fuck. Direct hit. Vulnerable spot in under five minutes. Maybe I should ask Jack how his fuck went? That would change this up a bit from our normal, completely not normal, father-daughter chats.

I lift my gaze to find Jack studying me and realize Neil was right. There are times when Jack stares at you and it is unnerving, and my cheeks have the bad manners to color profusely.

"We're just taking a break. It's no big deal, Daddy."

Jack shakes his head in that *I'm not buying it* way he has when he's trying to figure out something that's worrying him about me.

"Are you pregnant?"

He says it so quietly I almost miss it and then everything shoots through my body at once. I can't feel my arms, I can't feel my legs, and I can't believe Jack just asked me that.

"How could you ask me that, Daddy? Is that what you think?"

His blues meet mine directly. "Well, you're upset, he's gone. What should I think?"

"Well, you shouldn't think that," I exclaim, full

irritation in my voice. "I broke up with him. Simple. End of story. Jesus Christ, I'm not pregnant. We're both just trying to figure out shit. We've both got our own shit to work through. School ends soon. I don't have a fucking clue what I do then…"

I clamp my mouth shut. Why is he staring at me that way? Oh crap. Any hope this conversation would end in nothing just flew out the window.

Jack nods. "Just wanted to make sure you were OK."

"There's nothing wrong," I say firmly. "I'm just quiet. I've got a lot on my mind. God, can't you just cut me some slack and not overreact to every little thing?"

Jack turns until he's facing me squarely. "I don't feel like I've overreacted to anything. You're my daughter. I have a right to worry. I have a right to ask when I feel something is wrong."

I spring to my feet. "There's nothing wrong."

Jack stares up to me. "Why don't you just sit back down? I know something is going on with you, Chrissie. We can talk it through together."

"Nothing is going on. I dumped my boyfriend. He's on the road all the time. I graduate in the spring. It was time. It was the right thing."

"Who are you trying to convince, Chrissie? Me or yourself?"

Direct hit. Again. No matter how you try to fix your life, I'm learning you can still have doubts and regrets, and at times I regret breaking it off with Neil.

I look down at Jack. "No one. I'm not trying to convince anyone of anything. I'm just pissed off because

Neil is not a dump-and-run guy. And it really pisses me off that you thought he could treat me that way."

"I didn't believe it. I worried it. There's a difference."

"Not to me."

~~~

I go into my bedroom and pack my bag, determined to get the hell out of here quickly.

Last night was tense and awful. Breakfast this morning was even worse, and I just want to get out of here before one more thing comes my way to make me feel badly about the decisions I'm making in my life.

I lug my duffel to the front door, but before I can open it, Jack's there quickly. He takes the bag from my hand.

"I wish you were staying longer," he says.

"I'll call you when I get back to Berkeley."

"When will that be?"

"Three days."

Jack nods, his lips scrunched together, his chin moving out just a touch in that way he has when he wants to ask more and won't do it. I can tell by his expression that it's in his thoughts that I still haven't told him where I'm going. And it's suddenly not unnoticed by me that I'm lying to my father again.

I follow my dad into the driveway and wait by the open car door as he tosses my duffel into the back.

He kisses me on the forehead. "Drive carefully, Chrissie."

I smile. "I will. I'll call you Wednesday."

I climb into the car, Jack closes my door, and I put my
~~~

key in the ignition. I drive away and it hurts, really hurts, to see my dad still in the driveway watching me.

I'm not a little girl anymore. I shouldn't feel badly about not telling Jack about Alan and me. I have a right to my own life and privacy. Jack certainly keeps a thing or two private from me. But I do feel badly, like I did as a little girl. All the things I hid from my father, and all the worry and pain I gave him because of it.

As I drive beneath the high black metal Hope Ranch arch of our neighborhood, I give it the finger. There's no hope for me here. I will always be the same; trapped in a void and never certain of anything.

CHAPTER EIGHTEEN

When I get to the Malibu house, I pull into the driveway and am surprised to see a car there. I'm a day early. Why is Alan already here?

I hurry up the walk, not bothering to grab my bag, and use my key to let myself in. I find Alan in the living room sitting in a chair at the far side of the room before the wall of glass, and it looks like he's been doing nothing for a while but sitting in that chair staring off into space. He doesn't even have a drink in his hand.

I hang back at the edge of the foyer and just gaze at him. He's bathed in bright light, only mildly tempered by the shading on the glass, and the sight of him takes my breath away. I slowly start picking out other details of the room. He hasn't been here long. His bag is sitting there where he dumped it and Alan is a creature of perfect order. It would normally be put away. And he's wearing the type of clothes he travels in—soft jeans, loafers, and a loose, dark silk shirt.

There's something on his face that puts me instantly on edge. "You're a day early. Is everything OK? Are you OK?"

Alan runs his fingers through his hair. "Exhausted." He laughs softly. "But I'm good. Very good."

My brows hitch up since I don't know what to think

of that. He sounds almost pleased—or is it relieved?—about something. I can't tell for sure because he does look exhausted, and more, a strange kind of look of almost tired serenity.

"You look really tired, Alan. It makes me feel awful that you did the extra travel to see me."

He shrugs. "Don't feel awful. I want to be here. It's just road fatigue."

"You look more like roadkill," I tease and he smiles. "Are you sure you're OK?"

"I traveled back early to take care of something and I think it's finally OK. That's why I'm in Malibu and that's why I'm just sitting here. I'm savoring not having anything left to fuck up my life. And I'm definitely better than OK now that you're here."

I smile even though I haven't a clue what he's talking about, but he does seem happy.

"I hate missing you, Chrissie." He crosses the room to me, his eyes unwavering on mine. "I hate leaving you. And I hate not being here with you."

I should probably ask him what's stirring this up inside him tonight, this uncharacteristic happiness, but it doesn't matter. Not now. Maybe never.

"Then take me to bed," I say. "I've missed you, too."

Suddenly, I'm in his arms and he's kissing me, all over my face, sloppily, unlike Alan, overly exuberant, confusing and wonderfully so.

"I love you," I whisper against his lips.

"Let's be good to each other," Alan whispers as I am carried from the room.

~~~

I lie on the bed naked. I hear the sound of the Polaroid. I watch the picture drop to the floor.

I stare up at Alan, trying not to let him see how difficult this is for me. "I hate having pictures taken of me. Why are you doing it?"

"I want to preserve how you look today," he whispers, and his voice is so damn seductive, and the feel of him is all around me, so I don't even flinch when he takes another one.

Alan slept fifteen hours straight after we made love the first time, and has been Playful Alan ever since. We haven't eaten and he hardly lets me get out of bed.

I run my fingers through my hair and he smiles wickedly, taking another shot of me.

"Why do you want those?"

He drops the camera and moves up the bed toward me on hands and knees. He kisses my stomach. "I've got two more months on the road." His mouth moves lower to my pelvis. "I don't want to go. I don't want to do it." His tongue runs up to my navel. "I want a picture"—he's above me, his mouth close to my ear—"so when I'm alone thinking of you, I can look at you exactly how you are, as I finish thinking of you."

It takes me a moment to figure out what he just said. Then I flush, embarrassed, as I push him away. "God, Alan, you're obnoxious today. Why are you always your most obnoxious when you're happy? Give me those pictures."

He laughs, holding my struggling body against the bed
~~~

as I try to take back from him the little picture squares. "Do you ever think of me in private intimate moments?"

My cheeks go scarlet even though he phrased that well. "I'm not answering."

"No?"

His eyes are gleaming now and he's reclined on a hip beside me. "I've gotten very good at imagining you and doing this," he whispers.

My eyes stray and I inhale sharply. I'm more than a little shocked and definitely uncomfortable now. He's fully erect and stroking it with his hand and enjoying my astounded expression. Alan is passionate and unpredictable in bed…but this? It's so far beyond his level of nasty with me that I don't know what to do.

I realize I'm watching and I swallow and look away.

"No, Chrissie, watch me," he whispers into my ear as his thumb brushes my lip. "I want to imagine you watching me do this when we're not together."

My lips part to accommodate my breathing and my gaze moves back to him without my command. His eyes are serious and dark, and they widen as his strokes move quicker. His fingers start to play in my hair as his own breathing changes.

"You don't know how hard it is for me when we're not together," he whispers, and as he moves his hand up and down, I'm getting incredibly hot and shouldn't. My muscles are pulsing and I'm moistening *there.*

His tongue swirls around my nipple and my breath hitches in my throat. His mouth drops open as his breathing increases with the slow building movement of his fingers. My teeth sink into my lower lip, every inch of skin scorching and wanting him as I watch him release into his own hand.

A sound snaps me out of the stupor of my unexpectedly vivid arousal. The Polaroid and another square floating to the bed.

"That's the picture I want. Me watching you want me while I do this."

And before I can say anything, his hands are gripping my hair, dragging my lips back to his. Frustrated, I murmur into his kiss, "Don't ever do that again. It's nasty and unfair."

Against my mouth, I feel the vibration of his laughter. Then his kisses roam from my neck to my breast, as his hands deftly massage my sex before his mouth replaces his fingers there. I dig my nails into the flesh of his shoulders and moan. My head starts to move on the pillow as Alan, with his tongue and fingers, in record time releases the want in my body he put there.

When my shakes subside and my breathing calms, he lifts his face, staring up at me. "I'm never unfair," he says on a low seductive whisper.

He covers me with his body, then swirls his tongue in my mouth.

When he pulls back, I groan. "That was all out of order. I always want to boff after you do that."

Alan laughs, amused. "Boff? How come you can say British slang words for sex and not American?"

I make a face and laugh. "Probably because my first was a Brit."

Alan grins. "Was he any good?"

"I don't know. He's the only Brit I've ever done."

He kisses my shoulder. "He better be the only Brit you ever do," he says, and then the smile leaves his eyes. "It's getting harder to leave you. Not that it's ever been easy. But it is getting harder."

I stare up at him. "It's getting harder for me, too."

He pulls me against his body and surrounds me with his arms. "You could go out on the road with me. It's only two months. It's not like girls don't do that."

I drop my gaze from his and pull away, taking the sheet with me. "I can't believe you just said that to me."

I'm almost out of the bed and his hand stops me. "Christ, that's not what I meant. I was referring to taking time off from school. I don't have girls travel with me on the road and there's no reason you can't travel with me."

I stare at him, shaking my head, trying to steady my anger. "I can think of a lot of reasons."

He rakes a hand through his hair, frustrated with me, and then I'm hauled up back against him, back in his arms, back in the bed. "I don't care what anyone knows or thinks about us. Why do you care so much?"

I don't want to argue, and I definitely don't want to ruin the day with *this* conversation, since it forces me to think of all that will happen and not happen after I graduate. Probably nothing will change with us and that's the hardest part of knowing my life is changing again; that we will be the same, existing only here, and all other parts of us separate.

"I can't travel with you and don't ask me again."

He makes a strange sound, half exhale and half growl. "God, you're frustrating. We can both have so much more, but you won't even talk about it. You haven't even told me what you plan to do after you graduate. What happens, Chrissie, once you're done with school?"

I let out a shuddering breath. "I don't know. How's that for an answer?"

He lifts my chin, forcing me to look at him, but his eyes are no longer angry. They are rapidly searching my face as if he's looking for something and not finding it.

"I don't know," I repeat, not knowing why.

He takes me with him as he sinks into the sheets, his body molding into me and his arms holding me close.

~~~

I wake to the sound of glass hitting glass.

I ease away from Alan and gaze up at him. It's barely morning, he's wide awake, when Alan hardly ever wakes before noon. His posture tells me he's been sitting there quite a while, drinking and watching me.

"You are not returning to Berkeley," he snaps.

All drowsiness leaves my flesh in a nerve-popping jolt. I scoot away from Alan, dragging the sheets to cover me, rapidly searching his face. My heart drops to my knees because his eyes are hooded as they burn into me.

He says, "You still talk in your sleep. Do you know that?"

No, no, no! Why did he ask me that?

"I didn't know that," I whisper, sounding surprisingly calm even though every part of me is frantic and afraid.

He takes a long swallow of his drink. "Neil hasn't
~~~

mentioned it?"

Oh God! "I stopped seeing Neil."

Those black eyes fix on me, unblinking. "When did you end it with him?"

My body chills and then heat rises on my cheeks. I try to stutter out a safe response and somehow manage to say nothing. His eyes lock on me again.

"When did you end it with Neil? Don't lie to me, Chrissie."

I sit up in the bed, struggling to meet his gaze directly, though the way he is staring at me makes it an unbearably painful thing.

"I would never lie to you. I ended it with Neil because I love you."

He sets down his drink, running a hand through his hair. "God damn you. I ask you not to do it and you rip out my heart anyway," he says through gritted teeth. "You won't be straight with me even when I ask you to and yet you just answered me, Chrissie."

The phone rings and it makes me jump and kicks up Alan's temper. He reaches out and grabs the receiver.

"What?" he snaps into the phone. "I'm in Malibu. I'm taking a couple days downtime at the beach. No, I'm not discussing that."

My stomach turns. I can hear Nia's voice through the phone. I can't make out the words, but everything inside me grows cold. I don't know which is worse: how Nia sounds talking to Alan, or that he let me hear them talk because he is angry with me and wants to get in a blow during our fight without even being focused on me.

"OK," Alan says. "That's fine. Tell them I've agreed to that."

He hangs up the phone and I stare at him, shaking. "You're such an asshole. Why do you have to be so mean when you're angry?"

I scramble from the bed, go for my bag and rapidly start packing up my things.

"That's it, Chrissie. Run. Give you an excuse to run, not to have to face anything in your life directly, and you take it. That is what you do, isn't it, love?"

"What the hell is that supposed to mean?" I hiss.

Every line in his face tightens in extreme anger. "You ran off in New York, and you fucked up everything for both of us. You fucked up my life, too. You don't have a right to get angry today."

"It didn't sound fucked up to me on the phone."

"I haven't lived with Nia since six months before I came to see you in Berkeley," he says, almost inflectionless. "I have told you that, Chrissie. We've reached a settlement. I gave Nia everything she wanted so I can finally get out. That call was her bleeding me one last time before we sign the papers. When was the last time you fucked Neil?"

He holds me in an unrelenting stare and his gaze is brutally intense, shards of fury and despondency and hurt. It's too much, from everything uncertain and dangling, to possible and disintegrating in a horrible, unimaginable way; slamming together, brutally, all at once.

I continue to pack, my body shaking so fiercely I can barely grab hold of my clothes and shove them in. "I'm not going to answer that. I think it's better I don't. I think I should leave before we both say things we'll regret."

His eyes harden and some still functioning part of my brain warns that I've just fucked up big time, as Alan calmly grabs his pants and pulls them into place.

"That's how you want to deal with this?" He shakes his head, not bothering to even look at me. "You can leave if you want to, but if you do we're over, Chrissie. Or you can come to the patio, and if you are honest with me I will listen and we'll see where we go from there."

With that, Alan walks away. I stare at the door and sink down on the bed. He's angrier than I have ever seen him, so angry he's quiet. I shouldn't even try to talk to him. The way he is now, this could spin out of control in any direction.

Alan wants honesty. My inner voice reminds me of all the reasons why this is so important to Alan, of all the times people he has loved have lied to him, and warns me of how dangerous it will be for us both if I tell him everything about Neil.

The distraught look on his face as he left the bedroom shames me. I was so unkind to him in how I behaved in this…will he forgive me…will the truth be enough? I don't know, and that scares the hell out of me and I am more afraid than I have been at any other moment in my life.

Somehow I manage to go to my duffel, pull out some sweats, and dress. I open the door. The house is quiet when I step into the hall, and it surprises me that it is. I don't know what I expected, but not this heavy, waiting silence.

I go toward the wall of glass and find Alan on the patio just as he said he would be. I slide open the door and step out.

After a minute or two, Alan pushes off the wall and stomps out his cigarette on the concrete. His jaw is clenching. His gaze shifts and his eyes lock on me.

"Even after this I'm not sure I want us over," he says, sounding frustrated with himself, but he is pulsing with anger even more strongly than he was in the bedroom. "You didn't answer me when I asked before. When was the last time you fucked Neil?"

I stare at him, the tightly held arrangement of his long body parts, and with aching despair I know I shouldn't have come out here to try to talk him. We will both end up bloody, hating each other before this is through.

"We should wait to talk until you're calmer."

Alan's eyes flash and widen. "Not today, Chrissie. That is the worst thing you could do for either of us. Walk out that door without answering every single question I have and we are over. That is the only thing I am positive of today."

I stand frozen in place, searching his face. I can't tell for certain if he means it, but I do know if I stay he will rip us to shreds. We don't have a chance if I stay here.

"No, Alan. If we try to talk this out now, that's when we will end up over. You are just too angry to see it."

~~~

By the time I reach Berkeley, I am something beyond numb. I don't even have the sensation of having driven here. The scenery passed in a blur, unreal, as disjointed moments of my life rose in my memory, now connected, unkind and too real.
~~~

All through the drive, my senses were only claimed by the flashing images of all the mistakes I've made. The mistakes I've made in how I love Alan. The mistakes I've made with everyone in my life.

I pull into the carport, grab my bag, and somehow manage to get into the elevator. I look at myself in the mirrored squares, and it's a strange thing that I should look normal, exactly as I always do, and yet there is nothing comfortable or familiar left inside me.

I hurt the man I love. I hurt my best friend, and yes, Neil is my best friend. I didn't realize it when we broke up, but it is painfully present inside me today.

Inside the condo, I drop my bag, and without turning on the lights I go to my bedroom. I rummage through my drawer for my mobile phone, flip it open, stare at it and start to shake.

It fully sinks in at this moment. It didn't completely have the feel of realness before now, though it probably should have and I don't know why it didn't.

My legs are no longer able to hold me, and I sink onto the bed and stare at the phone. Ten hours and not one message from Alan. Nothing. Not a single call. This time, I should have stayed and fought for him. Even if it bloodied us. Even if it hurt too much. And even if it ended this way.

~~The End~~

For all my current and future releases visit my website: http://susanwardbooks.com
Or like me on Facebook:
https://www.facebook.com/susanwardbooks?ref=hl
Or Follow me on Twitter: @susaninlaguna

Continue the Half Shell Series with the final book, The Girl of Diamonds and Rust (April 2015), and read more of the Parker Saga with the first book of the Sand and Fog Series, Broken Crown (June 2015).

Enjoy my current contemporary romance releases:

The Girl on the Half Shell

The Girl of Tokens and Tears

The Girl of Diamonds and Rust (Releasing April 2015)

The Signature

Rewind

One Last Kiss

One More Kiss

One Long Kiss (Releasing March 2015)

Or you might enjoy one of my historical romance releases:

When the Perfect Comes

Face to Face

Love's Patient Fury

Love me Forever: Releasing Summer of 2015

PREVIW THE GIRL OF DIAMONDS AND RUST

I can't breathe. I can't feel my legs, I can't feel my arms, but somehow my body rises from the chair and moves toward the door.

"It doesn't matter, Alan. If you had called me I wouldn't have changed my decision," I whisper with more injury in my voice than I want to show. "I don't want to talk about this with you. Not now. It's too late."

I'm almost to the door when he stops me. He whirls me around to face him. Those potent black eyes lock on mine directly and the lockbox breaks open. It all tumbles out. My hurt. My regrets. My love for him. In leveling waves, real and present and consuming me.

He takes my face in the palms of his hands. "Please, stop hurting yourself because you hate me. I can't bear knowing that all this has happened because you hate me."

I say it before I can stop myself. "I don't hate you, Alan. I love you."

"Then don't marry Neil. It's in all the trades. It's why I came here today. Don't marry Neil because you hate me. Don't hurt yourself again because you hate me. I couldn't live with that. I swallowed my pride to come here. I couldn't let *you* hurt *you* again."

He pulls me against him, surrounding me with his flesh, and he is trembling with his emotions, as frantic and despondent and in pain as I am.

I don't know why I do it. Maybe it's because this is

goodbye. Maybe it's because I want to stop this. Maybe it's because Alan is crying.

I lean into him and join my mouth with his. His mouth moves on mine tentatively at first, only gentle contact. Then it deepens on its own, and I can feel it changing, that we are both changing what this is.

I pour all my hurt and heartbreak of the last year into our kiss, and it happens as it always did—the second I touch him, I am lost in him and we are lost in each other.

I shouldn't do this… And then the words in my head are silenced as Alan puts me on the bed.

PREVIW BROKEN CROWN

I shut off the shower, deciding not to call Chrissie. I dress for an excursion on my bike. Traveling the rural splendor of the United States on a Harley is one of the few things left in my life I still enjoy. The decision this time has nothing to do with savoring the scenery. The days it will take to travel from New York to California will give me a chance to back out if sanity decides to return. The call ahead of time will do neither of us any good if I decide not to see her.

I sink down onto my bed to make two phone calls. I tell my assistant to clear my calendar for the next month, and hang up as she bellows every reason why that isn't possible. Then I call the garage to get my bike ready.

I tuck into a backpack only what I need for the journey to Los Angeles. I almost leave the bedroom when I recall the lump in my sheets. Tucking the bracelet into my pocket, I reach out a hand and shake the body in my bed.

"You need to get dressed and get the hell out of here, love. I'm going to California. If you're a whore, I'd like to pay you first. If you're a nice girl, leave me your number."

The brown-eyed beauty sits up, pulling with her the blankets to cover her naked flesh. Morning-after modesty, another farce since my memory isn't so dim that I forgot what we did last night. Those pouting red lips smile.

Ah, Boston bred. The girl isn't ruffled by any of it.

Smoothly charming, she says, "I'll bill you. Though it's often considered a blurry difference, I'm not a whore. I'm your attorney. One of your divorce attorneys. I brought the finalized settlement contracts, and though you missed our meeting, I waited ten hours in this apartment for you to return to sign them since your ex-wife has an irritating proclivity to change her mind. I thought it best we jump on the offer and settle it fast since you didn't have a pre-nuptial agreement.

"When I tried to explain, you jumped on me. I thought what the hell, it's been a slow day and I'm earning five hundred bucks an hour for this. Why shouldn't my job have an occasional perk? You have been interesting. I've never been laid by a man who holds an infinity band while he fucks me. I think it's better I don't tell you the things you mumbled. I'll only warn you that you should be relieved it's covered under attorney/client privilege since my meter ticks until you sign those documents.

"The contracts are on the dresser. Please sign them so I can shower, dress and go. It's Saturday, in case you don't know what day it is, and I play racquetball at six. *That* I didn't expect you to know. It was a subtle attempt to speed you up in the signing."

I laugh softly. My attorney is charming. I go to the dresser and do a quick study of the contracts. "Thank you for not boring me with whatever I mumbled and thank you for promising to bill me so it's privileged. You can, however, bore me by letting me know how much this is costing me."

Panties and bra in place, my attorney scrambles from my bed gathering her clothes, then snatches the signed contracts from my hand.

"Me, I cost you seventy-two hundred for this meeting. Your ex-wife cost you one-hundred-sixteen million two hundred-twenty-seven thousand, a combination of cash, future cash, and an interesting assortment of personal property. You did, however, manage to retain the Malibu house that, against my advice, you battled her over, the bill from me five-hundred thousand over the value of it."

I clutch her chin a little roughly and give her a hard kiss. "You, love, were a bargain."

I leave her, half dressed, staring at me from my bathroom doorway. It sounded theatrical even to me. Chrissie would have given me such shit for those theatrics, but the girl seemed to be expecting something like that so I played along.

Thank you for reading. You might enjoy a sneak peek into Chrissie and Alan's future, with Rewind **A Perfect Forever Novella.**

He doesn't laugh. Instead, his gaze sharpens on my face. "I am being nice, Kaley. I came to you. I got tired of waiting."

What? Did I just hear what I think I heard?

Before I can respond, he says, "How's your afternoon looking? Do you have time to take off and come see something with me?"

My afternoon? There is something. I'm sure of that, but I suddenly can't remember a single thing.

"What do you have in mind?"

"I want to show you where I've been living. What I've been doing. I think you'll find it interesting."

Interesting? Why would I find it interesting?

"So do you think you can cut out for a few hours?" he asks, watching me expectantly.

I focus my gaze on the table, wondering if I should go, wondering why I debate this, and what the heck I have on the calendar that I can't remember. God, this is weird, familiar and distant at once, and I haven't a clue what I should do here.

I stare at his hand, so close to mine, on the table. Whoever thought it would be so uncomfortable *not* to touch a guy? It doesn't feel natural, this space we hold between us, spiced with the kind of talk people have who know each other intimately. What would he do if I touched him?

His fingers cover mine and he gives me a friendly squeeze. The feel of him runs through my body with remembered sweetness.

Suddenly, nothing in my life is as important as spending the afternoon with Bobby, and for the first time in a very long time, I don't feel like a disjointed collection of uncomfortably fitting parts. I feel at ease inside myself being with Bobby.

I stop trying to access my mental calendar, and smile up at Bobby. "I've got as much time as you need."

Bobby chuckles and his hand slips back from me. He rises and tosses some bills on the table. "Just a few hours, Kaley. I'll have you back before the end of the day."

I rise from my chair and think *not if I figure out fast how not to blow this.*

Or enjoy the first novel in the Perfect Forever

Collection: The Signature. **Available Now. Please enjoy the following excerpt from The Signature:**

She became aware all at once how utterly delightful it felt to be here with him, alone on the quay, with the erotic nearness of his body.

She closed her eyes. "Listen to the quiet. There are times when I lie here and it feels like there is no one else in the world."

"No one else in the world? Would that be a good thing?" he asked thoughtfully.

"No. But the illusion is grand, don't you think?" she whispered.

Krystal turned her head to the side, lifting her lids to find Devon's gaze sparkling as he studied her. He shook his head lazily. "No. The illusion wouldn't be grand at all. It would mean I wasn't here with you."

It all changed at once, yet again, and so quickly that Krystal couldn't stop it. The ticklish feeling stirred in her limbs. Devon's words, as well as the closeness of their bodies, should have sent her into active retreat, and instead she felt herself wanting to curl into him. *What would it feel like if kissed me? Would I still feel this delicious inside? Or would that old panic and fear return?*

Laughing softly, Devon said, "I'm not used to relaxing. Can you tell?"

"I wasn't used to it before Coos Bay either. There is a different pace of life here. At first I thought there was no sound. That's how quiet it seemed to me. Then I realized that there is music, beautiful music in this quiet."

After a long pause, he murmured, "You'll have to bring me here every Saturday until I learn to hear music in the quiet."

Krystal smiled. "Once you hear the music it's perfect."

"It's perfect now to me." His voice was a husky, sensual whisper.

He was on his side facing her. *When had that happened?* An inadvertent thrill ran through her flesh, and she could see it in his eyes—the supplication, the want, and an unexplainable reluctance to indulge either.

Devon was no longer smiling, his eyes had become brighter and more diffuse. His fingertips started to trace her face with such exquisite lightness that her insides shook. For the first time in a very long time, she felt completely a woman, and wanting.

Was it possible? Had she finally healed internally as her flesh had done so long ago? Was she finally past the legacy of Nick? Was what she was now feeling real? Should she seek the answer with Devon? Or was it better to leave it unexplored?

"You are a very beautiful woman," he whispered.

She watched with sleepy movements as his mouth lowered to her. It came first as a touch on her cheek, feather soft between the play of his fingers. Her breath caught, followed by a pleasant quickening of her pulse. She was unprepared for the sweetness of his lips and the rushing sensations that ran through her body. His thumb traced the lines of her mouth as his kiss moved sweetly, gently there.

His breath became rapid in a way that matched her own, and his mouth grew fuller and more searching. The fingertips curving her chin were like a gentle embrace, but their mouths were eager and demanding. Flashes of desire rocketed through her powerfully. Urgency sang through her flesh, a forgotten melody, now in vibrant notes. She found herself wanting to twist into him. Reality begged her to twist back.

ABOUT THE AUTHOR

Susan Ward is a native of Santa Barbara, California, where she currently lives in a house on the side of a mountain, overlooking the Pacific Ocean. She doesn't believe she makes sense anywhere except near the sea. She attended the University of California Santa Barbara and earned a degree in Business Administration from California State University Sacramento. She works as a Government Relations Consultant, focusing on issues of air quality and global warming. The mother of grown daughters, she lives a quiet life with her husband and her dog, Emma. She can be found most often walking at Hendry's Beach, where she writes most of her storylines in her head while watching Emma play in the surf.

Spare a tree. Be good to the earth. Donate or share my books with a friend.

Printed in Great Britain
by Amazon